Acknowledgements

I want to thank all the people in my life who made this possible, including those who directly worked on the project. This is a second edition of the Holy Grail War: The Hedgehog. I'm thankful for the editors, the many beta and alpha readers who had their eyes on this project, and gave me wonderful feedback and support.

The Flames of War

~The monsters and demons aren't hiding in my closet or underneath my bed: I'd be fortunate if they were that far away. No, they are all running amok inside my head, and they're relentless!

I T WAS SUPPOSED TO be a training exercise—nothing more—but on that day, a war hero walked into his own execution. Guns roared, and engines revved. Bullets fired from all directions, striking the metallic debris of crashed helicopters and planes. Blood painted the desert sand of Nevada crimson, and limbs were sprawled over the sand mounds. Military vehicles were blown to pieces. Many of those still had bodies in them; the rotting carcasses were wreathed in flames as their arms hung out the windows, blood dripping down into the sand like oil.

Ghost, in his black fatigues, smelled the putrid rotting of flesh, and he heard the buzzing of flies as they roamed above the corpses littering the desert. His limbs were heavy, and his body hot with the oppressive heat of the wind and pelting sand.

Ghost ducked behind the bags of sand, his heart pounding. He knew his brain was searing these images into his mind, never to be forgotten—should he miraculously make it out alive today. Did he even want to? He covered his mouth with his hand as Slithers, Ticker, and Butcher crouched to the side, hiding behind the sandbags. The gunfire finally subsided. Slithers' bloody hand covered her mouth as she stifled a cry, knowing that even the slightest sound would give away their position to the Americans. The Americans they had sworn to protect and fight for! But had they?

Ghost took several measured breaths. His heart pounded, trying to free itself from its fleshy prison, doomed to die. He cursed to himself, swearing under his breath. His right hand trembled, his finger coming dangerously close to the trigger, ready to fire into the scorching hot sand. One word rattled inside his mind like an echo chamber.

Treason.

He felt the ground around him suddenly tremble, just like his hand did. He stifled a gasp. He jerked his head upwards, still covered by the sandstorm. Military vehicles rolled over the dirt of the desert, driving along the road and kicking up the sand along their path. The convoy drove past, and he was allowed a moment's rest, just a moment. No telling when the helicopters would soar overhead and ping his location. *What is happening? I don't understand any of this!* he thought to himself.

"Time to go," he said, his eyes scanning the horizon as he carefully peered over the sandbags.

"Ghost." Butcher's face was grave, her hands trembling at her side, her teeth gritted. "Why did we do nothing? They are dead because we did nothing. What did you do?" She turned her head to him, her blood-stained hair swinging in the air as she snarled at him.

"I did nothing. You did nothing. They did nothing," he replied, knowing full well, and bearing the guilt of their four dead team members. That was *his* fault. *I let them die!*

As always, whenever lives were lost, his heart felt weaker, being restrained by those imaginary lines that occasionally, if by accident, rose up to the surface of his skin. The guilt swept over his chest and his heart felt like it was bleeding inside him.

"You and I both know, none of us were making it out alive tonight. These last few moments are going to be the most defining moments in our time. We were born to live and die in obscurity. But we need to go. We—we'll see them again before the night is over, on the other side." A tear escaped his eye and he choked on it. "But damn it all, we are blowing up Area 51, and taking every last one of those sons of bitches with us. That will be our legacy, and perhaps they'll learn their lesson to not repeat this mistake ever again."

We were just unlucky. That's all. We were just thirty-two monsters who got the unfortunate short stick.

"Ghost! That is not enough. We need to do more than just—"
Bang!

Ghost saw a flash in the distance. The bullet howled, whistling in the air. He immediately turned to face Butcher. Knowing the trajectory of the bullet, he was filled with a sense of dread. He opened his mouth to scream, but nothing came out. Butcher was next, and then there would be three. He winced as the flashing bullet grazed his cheek. His heart raced as the shot missed him, and his pupil watched the bullet in front of him, spinning as it soared through the air. He was in a daze, not knowing how the sniper had known that they were here. Or had he been watching all along?

The bullet penetrated Butcher's eye. Ghost's brown eyes opened wide as he gasped. Blood sprayed all over the place as Butcher was knocked down, bullet shards exiting out the back of her head. Fortunately for her, though blind in one eye and in excruciating pain, all the shards had miraculously missed the brain. Ghost blinked as the blood sprayed.

Ticker ducked down immediately, pulling out his Barrett M82 and relaxing his grip. His eyes aimed down the barrel of his rifle. His rifle swiftly swayed as he surveilled the sandy horizon for the sniper. He found the sniper; the bright reflection off of a scope got his attention as the sniper was taking aim again. His trigger finger curled around the trigger. The trigger clicked back, the rifle shot immediately, the end of his barrel flashing. The round hit the sniper's cover, forcing the sniper to pick up his rifle and hide at a different location.

The gunfire was so loud that it nearly deafened Slithers' ears. She covered them with both of her hands, her face pulling into a grimace as tears streamed down it. Her limbs trembled, and her eyes were gaping open. Her brown hair drippled blood on the ground. Ghost heard the ringing in his ears; just like everything else, they'd been issued hand-me-downs for earplugs.

Butcher cackled a raspy laugh, her voice cracking. "Pain. It hurts. Ghost, it fucking hurts! Isn't it great?! I can feel it." Her tone became soft. Her arms and fingers trembled; her other eye was wide open. She set one hand over her wounded eye, and blood seeped through the cracks of her fingers. She took several deep breaths. "Did they—did they feel it too?" She sat up and ripped off a piece of her sleeve and wrapped it around her eye. "I bet I look fucking dashing. Damn it all. We can't sneak back there, then." Butcher struggled to get to her feet and drew her MK-16. "You said it. We are not getting out of this alive. Not one of us. I'll buy you time. After tonight, we're gonna make sure they know never to mess with Task Force 7 again! After all, there won't be a Task Force 7."

Butcher jumped out from behind the sandbags, latching onto a flash grenade. Tossing the black cylinder, she closed her eyes. The grenade made a deafening explosion of bright white light, dazzling the soldiers nearby. The noise deafened more ears as she aimed her rifle, firing at the temporarily blinded soldiers staggering over their own feet, some stumbling for cover behind sand mounds. Soldiers further away started firing upon her; bullets pelted her limbs. As if on instinct, she pulled out a smoke grenade and dropped it at her feet. "RUN, DAMNIT!"

Ghost, Ticker, and Slithers immediately turned around and sprinted away from the execution zone. Ghost could hear the rapid gunfire behind them. He could hear the whirring of helicopter blades in the distance with his overly sensitive ears. He had to stay focused on the mission, ignore the fact that this was the last time he would see Butcher again.

The remnants of Task Force Seven rushed at their inhuman pace, kicking up sand with their strides, leaving a shroud behind them. The sand got into their boots, heating their feet. Area 51 was not far from them. The base which kept so many people away successfully would be penetrated and devoured from within with the rage that filled what remained of Task Force 7.

As he got closer to his objective, Ghost pictured Butcher lying dead, face down on the scorching sand, blood streaming out of her body after being pelted with bullets aplenty. He pictured her having died with a defiant smile—a fake one, but perhaps this one in his mind was genuine. He again heard the whirring of the helicopters and felt the rumble of the ground as tanks and armored vehicles with heavy machine guns mounted on them drove in their direction. What remained of Task Force Seven fled with such haste that they couldn't hide their tracks.

It's okay. It's okay. Nothing is going to change tonight. We are all going to die, and I have accepted it. Butcher, I'll see you soon. Ghost blinked his eyes as tears streamed down, and his face cringed as he stifled another childish cry.

"Ghost," Ticker said from the front. "Do we have a plan, or am I just blowing a hole in the front?"

"This was supposed to be a training exercise. I don't have time for briefing. Just get in, kill everyone, blow the hull and we go down into the facility to the blow it!" Ghost snapped. "Nothing about any of this is normal! Maybe with this distraction, we can make it."

Slithers never took her eyes off the horizon in front of them. "Don't hide it, Ghost. Don't give us hope where there is none. There never was. That promise was bullshit."

"We can't blow it up if we're dead, now, can we?" Ghost answered angrily. "Ticker, Slithers, switch. Ticker, while you're running, I need you to prep that bomb. We won't have time to do it when we get there."

Ticker let out a deep sigh as he shook his head, crusted blood flaking from his blond hair. He slowed down to let Slithers pass him. "If I screw up, we're going to be dead before we started."

"You're the best at it. I trust you." Ghost frowned. "We're dead anyway, what difference does it make?"

Ticker sneered. "Those might be the last words you ever say."

Ghost saw Ticker swing his rifle over his shoulder and pull up his satchel, then pull out a large black device which was just marginally larger than a claymore. The device had blue, green, and red wires of various thickness, attached to numerous knobs. Underneath the device was a metal magnet. Ticker moved some of the knobs and turned them. He shifted the wires around, moving them around the knobs and into various tubes inside the device. Ticker was meticulous; no one knew bombs better than he.

Ghost saw the chain linked fences with guards stationed around them, walking back and forth as they patrolled the perimeter. The searching lights of a sentry tower swayed in the distance. The soldiers patrolled in their camouflage gear, their American flag patches on their shoulders—something Task Force Seven was forbidden from ever wearing. After all, they were never considered soldiers. The guards' sidearms were holstered with singular shot rifles aiming down at the ground. There were some unarmored Military vehicles resting about with drivers inside, and other soldiers were moving heavily reinforced crates onto trucks. Their eyes seemed to scan the perimeter and the horizon.

Ghost knew Area 51. He knew of all the experiments and weapons development, but one thing they never invested in was security. *I guess Task Force Seven was all they ever needed!* Rumors and all that kept the common person out, and quite frankly, the absurd rumors of harboring aliens kept enemy interest in the classified Air Force base low, surprisingly. There would be no more wars for a while anyway; Ghost had made sure of that.

I can't afford mistakes; however, I can't afford the time necessary to prevent them. But nothing about this damn training exercise would be considered normal. We are all that's left, Ghost thought to himself as he considered his options.

"Slithers. Kill 'em," he ordered from behind, raising his rifle, his eyes gazing down the barrel's iron sights.

Ghost noticed, before he looked onward to something else, Slithers sighing heavily and shaking her head. She was exhausted, he knew that. They all were. Fighting these wars for years was finally taking tolls on them, but this battle—or training, if they wanted to call it that—this was taking an entire toll on them mentally, killing soldiers with faces they recognized. Ghost heard the sound of her rifle firing several controlled shots. They found their targets' heads, blood spraying out of the victims' bodies as they collapsed onto the ground. The ruckus of gun fire soon followed in front of them as loud alarms went off.

Ghost lobbed a grenade swiftly out to the fence. It shattered the foundations hidden underneath the gates, forcing them open. Soldiers swarmed out the buildings, their eyes already aimed down their holographic sights, training their aim on Task Force Seven. Slithers slipped through and made a beeline to the left, dodging behind a building. Ghost moved in front of Ticker as he laid down suppressing fire. His heart jumped as bullets came for him. The temperature dropped, red veins covered his eyes; as the bullets fired, they appeared to slow. He could track their trajectories, moving his body to avoid being hit in anything vital. The bullets pelted his arms and legs, but none were of a high enough caliber to sever them. Ghost knew these soldiers had never seen *real* war, and their weapons were inadequate against the likes of him, *a monster.*

Ghost felt the wounds, the warm blood trickling down his legs. He felt the lead penetrate his body like needles and tear through the other side, spilling more of his own blood behind him. He felt the temperature drop around him as Ticker finished his calibration behind him, but what he could not feel was pain. Yes, they'd even taken that away from them. From all of them. *Butcher, what does it feel like?*

Slithers rushed behind another building, shooting other soldiers who were distracted with Ghost and Ticker on the entrance. She tossed a flashbang in front of her as she dodged behind the cover of some wooden crates. The crates were not ideal; the bullets shredded through them, sending debris, splinters and ballistic fragments flying as sparks emitted from the crates upon impact.

Bright white light emitted from the black cylinder as it exploded, blinding the soldiers nearby, some of whom ducked, attempting to find some cover. Slithers breathed out, jumping over the crate with her eyes aimed down the barrel of her rifle, swiftly pulling her trigger and gunning down the disoriented soldiers, bullets penetrating their chests as they fell. Reloading, she jumped behind a crate where another soldier was crouching. He swiftly moved to get up, and fortunately for Slithers, he was in perfect melee range. He swung his rifle at her. She blocked the stock with her arm, hastily pulling out a knife. The blade impaled his throat; she twisted the knife, rending his neck. She ran behind the last line of defense and up towards the sentry towers, aiming up high and unloading into the sentries as they sounded the alarm for more soldiers to come up from down below.

Slithers fired upon the last line of defense from behind. The remaining soldiers were killed immediately as bullets penetrated their bodies from numerous directions.

Ghost raised his hand and dropped it, motioning to Ticker to follow him as he ran to Slithers. "Slithers, turn that damn alarm off!" Slithers went to a sentry tower, climbed up the ladder, and shortly after, the alarm stopped. "Ticker, plant it right here!" Ghost pointed to the ground where an almost unnoticeable crack indicated a hidden door for larger vehicles to come in and out of the base.

This would be the best point of entry; after all, every unfortunate soul down there already knew trouble was coming. He glanced over to Ticker and pointed at the crack. Ticker took out the device and attached heavy duty magnets on the bottom, planting it upright over the door. Ticker flicked a switch, and a red light turned on. Ghost exhaled deeply, taking just a moment to reflect on the magnitude of what he was doing, and taking a moment to realize this was going to be the closest thing to a funeral they would ever get.

"We'll wait," Ghost said with panted breath. "We'll wait until they get here."

The remnants of Task Force Seven pulled corpses together behind a building about fifteen meters from the explosive. Ghost took an arm from one of the corpses and cut it open, pouring the blood over his face. The three of them pulled together some smaller crates in front of the pile of corpses. Ticker and Slithers followed his example as they hid underneath the bodies, their eyes open, watching.

They all took measured breaths, allowing their heart rates to finally slow down as they hid underneath the mass of bodies. They had been racing ever since the first shot was fired, and none of them remembered how long ago that was. *Three days? A month?* None of them had any sense of time anymore. They hadn't slept since it had started.

Time passed. Ghost couldn't tell how much time. He knew it had been long enough for the enemy to regroup from Butcher's efforts, but they were taking far longer than necessary. Ghost assumed security below was waiting for further orders before coming up from their little foxhole. Perhaps General Snells assumed that the modest force at Area 51 would hold them off long enough for an appropriate response. One thing was for certain: General Snells was coming for them, and he never left a stone unturned. Ghost knew this from working with him for the last decade and a half.

They certainly took their time getting here. Ghost saw the soldiers walking onto the premises. He saw their gazes and their heads turning, looking over the carnage. He saw their eyes aiming down the barrels of their rifles. Their faces were grimacing and cringing with the stench, but there was one thing different about these soldiers than the rest of them: they had clean faces, as if they hadn't been out today, or had been on leave and were coming back to see all of their friends dead. And who else to blame for that than them, Task Force Seven? These soldiers had black eagle patches on their shoulders.

Ghost's eyes scanned from underneath the arm resting over his head, trying to get a count of these black eagle soldiers. Many of them were hiding behind parked armored vehicles, their sights trained on the corners of the buildings—places where Ghost would normally hide for cover, but not against this foe. He heard the whirring of the helicopter blades coming closer, dusting the sand off the ground and into Ghost's face. He closed his eyes and continued to listen to heavy boots clamor on the metal plates covering the ground. There was one thing that truly concerned him. *Where is that damned sniper?!*

Ghost had no choice but to carefully listen to the number of footsteps taken, counting with each pace as the rapidly approaching steps were now faster than their beating hearts. It was impossible to discern where *precisely* they were. But they likely marched down the middle, as he suspected they would, right to the device. He knew too well. He counted their footsteps. Right when he thought them to have passed over the device, he whispered: "Ticker."

Ticker needed no more words. He pulled out the remote in his side pocket and pressed the black button.

The device started whirring. The light blinked red repeatedly. The soldiers who were right in front of the device saw the lights, glancing down swiftly and stepping backwards. "It's a trap!" one called.

Boom!

The explosion was like a small hurricane, blowing flames and debris in all directions. The soldiers immediately caught in the blast were now black, unrecognizable husks. Others were flailed into the nearby buildings and other objects, snapping their bodies as limbs were strewn over the vicinity. Ghost could hear the bones cracking and crushing underneath the tremendous velocity and sudden halting of their respective trajectories. Outside by the armored vehicles, the soldier's eyes gaped open in a daze. Immediately, they retrained their aim at the vicinity, looking for movement from whoever remained of Task Force Seven.

"NOW!" Ghost cried out.

The remnants of Task Force Seven jumped from underneath the bodies, sprinting towards the explosion where the door into the bowels of Area 51 lay. They were more refreshed and confident, firing at the armored vehicles. They were right there by the hole.

Slithers jumped down, throwing a dazed soldier off the internal catwalk into a burning heap as molten metal seeped from the opening, melting through to the bottom of Area 51. Ghost was a few steps in front the hole, and Ticker followed behind him.

Bang!

His heart raced again. His eyes shifted behind the armored vehicles to the flash. *Sniper. You, again.* He could see the bullet flying right towards him. The bullet was too close for him to dodge it, being already midair. *Good-bye.* He closed his eyes, welcoming the precisely aimed bullet.

Thwick!

Ghost eyes opened. Blood sprayed across his face. In front of him was an arm, severed by the shot. He swiftly looked to his right, and Ticker was in front of him. The ballistic fragments scattered as they struck Ghost's arms. He now knew the round of the sniper: a

.50 caliber Barrett, if he had to guess. Ghost saw Ticker pulling out a satchel with his other arm.

"Take this. Quick."

Ghost looked at Ticker's arm, pouring blood out like a faucet, his other arm trembling as his body began to feel the effects of rapid blood loss. Ticker breathed deeply, shaking his head. "I can't get you much time. But damnit! I'll try." Ticker kicked Ghost into the hole, and he charged toward the armored vehicles. It was not long before the roar of gunfire continued, drowning out the screams.

Ghost landed on his feet, following Slithers down the steel grated walkways. His calculations were correct; the damage done here had been more than enough to send the soldiers on the upper levels to their untimely demise and cause significant disarray for everyone else.

The guards down here were disheveled, looking in every direction, not going to their battle stations, not knowing where everything was. Many kept their hands on top their heads, limping to their next location, while others were laying on the ground, covering their wounds with their hands, trying to keep themselves from bleeding out. *Perhaps if they hadn't relied on us too much, they might have had a chance down here. We carried your burdens, you little shits.* Ghost and Slithers descended to the second level.

Ghost sucked in the air through his teeth, stifling a whimpered cry. *And then there was only two left.* He knew it was time, but that didn't make this any easier. He raised his rifle, firing with Slithers at the disorganized men below. Their corpses littered the ground, and their blood painted the walls. They made it down three more levels. The stench of gunpowder filled the air.

Red lights from the alarms flashed, the buzzing from said alarms piercing their ears. This level was more open, and the soldiers were more organized, preparing barricades and riot shields. There was reinforced steel for cover; even Ghost and Slithers's rounds would not pierce them. Soldiers held their ground behind cover. "Slithers, take right!" He pointed right. She went to the right, firing at the shield walls, keeping the soldiers behind cover as Ghost strode to the left.

Ghost inhaled *essence* from the metal and blood in the ground. This essence passed through his body, and he suddenly felt refreshed as black veins protruded across his skin. He felt the temperature drop, his hair sticking on ends as he passed through the barricade, behind their iron defense. The soldiers' eyes stretched open, and their trigger fingers trembled as he opened fire behind them. These soldiers immediately turned around and shot through Ghost. Slithers slipped through the other side, crossing her fire with Ghost's line of sight. The soldiers were in a disorganized mess as they started shooting in random directions. Their fire was immediately suppressed, their bodies strewn behind the reinforced steel cover. Their blood made a large pool at Ghost and Slithers' feet. Ghost's black veins receded back into his body.

"One more level." Ghost said. "One more level, and we're done." *Bang!*

A shot came from above. Ghost's eyes opened wide before he hastily spun around, aiming his rifle at the top of the catwalk, upon which stood a single marksman. Ghost pulled the trigger of his rifle, and he felt uncontrolled kickback into his shoulder as the bullet ripped through the marksman. The walls were painted with blood. Suddenly, Ghost realized that the shot had not been aimed for him. Turning around, he looked at the worse thing he could imagine, and suddenly, he knew pain.

Slithers smiled as tears streamed down her face; she covered the wound with her hand. Black blood spilled through the cracks of her hand like the inside of a sinking ship. Ghost had enough medical training to assume the bullet had struck the liver. She leaned against a wall, breathing heavily. He bolted over to her, pulling out a med-kit, hoping against hope to save her.

"No. There isn't time," she said, grabbing onto his hand with hers. "They're coming down. I don't have long. You know it's not worth it. You don't have time to waste. With what is left, I will stay behind and *will* myself to get you the time you require."

Ghost didn't want to be alone. He inhaled and exhaled deeply, trying to mask his frustration. He didn't want to cry, but couldn't stop a singular tear from rolling down his face. She was the last person he ever wanted to say good-bye to, and now he couldn't even muster the right words. "I understand," was all he managed to say. He turned and sprinted to the set of stairs heading down to the last level.

"Ghost!" she shouted.

She shouldn't be wasting energy talking. "Be quick about it," he snapped at her, hearing the echoes of military boots descending from above. *If only there was more time.*

"I'm glad I got to spend my last moments with you," she said. "I don't know how to say this, so I'll be blunt: I love you."

He nodded. "I love you, too."

"Ghost, if you make it through this, promise me that you will live. And hold no hatred in your heart for the hell we've been through. Promise me that you will find another light. Even a small, fading one should suffice. Now, go. There isn't time."

Another tear escaped his eye. He could find no words. He nodded to her and turned. *This isn't fair. What did we do to deserve this?* He sprinted down the stairs, down into the next level.

Ghost inhaled the *essence* from the air, and red veins protruded from underneath his skin as he came to a brightly-lit white reactor room. Th were polished metal rods, some rising with sudden changes in the water levels. There were four large bronze tubes connecting these rods to more volatile parts of the reactor. His eyes scanned the top of the room to locate the command center, his eyes scanned downward again for a doorway, red around the hinges.

He moved around the first bronze tube and strapped the bomb to it. He placed the strap close to the bottom. If anyone was looking for it, then they would find it, but Ghost knew too well that they would not be looking for it. They'd be too busy trying to kill him.

Not more than five minutes passed and the room behind him was roaring with gunfire. It would not be long before he was completely, utterly alone, and they would be on him shortly like flies to a pile of feces. He could not be certain if he had enough time to prime the bomb for explosion. And he still didn't know why any of this was happening. He finished priming the bomb, and he inhaled some of the *essence* from the air. The veins crawled from his skin, emerging from him and surrounding the bomb.

One of the silver rods ruptured, and steam filled the room. Ghost felt the radiation and tremendous heat fill the air. He felt the heat open up patches of his skin, and lightheadedness followed as he ran toward the exit, tripping over his feet. This continued as the radiation seeped into his body at such a high degree that he vomited on the door. Swinging it open, he jumped inside and slammed the door shut behind him, panting and breathing in more *essence*. There was an explosion in the reactor, followed by several rapid strikes against the door from chunks of radioactive debris.

The bomb was unnecessary. I literally came down here in the middle of a fucking meltdown! Are you serious?! Well, that was part of the problem anyway, but that didn't mean they couldn't have stopped the reactor from blowing. One more thing left.

Glancing up the stairs, he saw the last door leading upwards to the command center. That reactor explosion had bought him enough time. He inhaled the *essence* from the air, and the red veins on his skin faded into his body. The veins returned to his body a light cerulean. His strides sent him up the stairs, tackling through the door to an empty command center.

He swiftly looked to the monitors and saw the soldiers move away from the reactor toward where he was going. The soldiers placed iron blockades to the reactor before shifting down other corridors, congregating elsewhere. Ghost shook his head and sighed as he grabbed a chair and logged into the mainframe of the computer, disabling the failsafe procedures.

He locked the console. He took a breath. *Goodbye, Slithers. I love you. And Ticker. And Butcher. And all of you. You're my only friends. I'll see you soon.*

Ghost was fatigued. Pushing the chair out from under himself, he narrowed his eyes towards the door heading out the other end of the corridor, where he assumed the command center evacuated to. He took a deep breath of relief; this last-minute mission was to be a success, but now, he had to pretend to want to make it out, to keep them away from the command center and prevent them from resetting the protocols.

I'll see you soon.

He breathed in the *essence* from the steel and iron in the room and the blue veins turned grey and opened the door. The corridor was empty except for the clatter and clamor of heavy boots stamping down the halls. Ghost aimed down his sights as he ran down the hall.

He made a turn down the hall, sprinted down some stairs, and rushed out the door. Bullets immediately shot past his head. He returned fire against soldiers stationed up in the catwalks. His eyes glanced to the side, where his best friend lay in a pool of her own black blood.

Slithers' body was riddled with bullet holes, and all her limbs were so penetrated by bullets that they had all severed and been scattered across the room. Blood overflowed from her mouth. As if that wasn't enough, for good measure, someone left a KA-BAR knife protruding from her heart, impaled blade deep.

One month ago, Slithers and Ghost were laying down in the fields of Paulding Forest, staring at the break in the trees. The moon and stars shone bright that night. Ghost's hands held Slithers', their fingers interwoven. They were alone, together. They were not off fighting, not with the rest of Task Force Seven, and far away from the U.S. military. They were alone, except for a few crickets singing their songs.

Ghost felt her fingers tightly grip his, and she pulled him to his side. They locked eyes. Slithers smiled that smile, but bags filled her eyes with exhaustion, the same bags he always wore upon his face. "We'll be free soon," she told him that night.

But she still held that smile, curled upon her lips.

The ground sparked as bullets continued flying towards him. He laid down suppressing fire. He lobbed a smoke grenade on his position and lobbed numerous grenades down the hall and through the catwalks. The halls echoed with gunfire as the smoke obscured his visibility. Taking off his equipment vest, he ripped another vest off of a corpse. Several more bullets came closer, penetrating him in the limbs and chest. Coughing, he donned the enemy's armor.

He sprinted through the smoke, firing at soldiers hiding behind the cover of the other rooms. *Three levels to get to the surface. Just three.* Ghost grimaced, grinding his teeth as the fire from the guns lit up the faces around him. His watery eyes glimmered with the bright lights of bullets emitting from their respective rifles. Bullets which struck him in the silver veins, sparking around him. He never blinked as he rushed to the stairs.

Clunk! Clunk! Clunk!

A dropped grenade *clinked* against the stairs as it fell. To Ghost, the echo was louder than the constant gunfire. His attention shifted as he was in midstride. The grenade started flashing fire from behind its pineapple-shaped shell, sending shards everywhere. Instinctively, his veins breathed in more *essence,* and he felt refreshed as if water coursed through them. He knew this was unnatural. The grey light in the veins over his body thickened.

Find the light. Whichever light flickers. Find it! Ghost thought.

The explosion sent the shards piercing through his body, ripping out the out through his back. Blood sprayed out. He felt cold as the blood spilled from his body. The explosion propelled him backwards. He landed on the ground, rolling onto his side. He immediately stood up and sprinted back to the stairs. He aimed down his iron sights as he deftly reloaded his rifle.

He charged up the stairs, screaming as the grey veins persisted on his body, shooting everyone in his path. His aim was never faulty despite the lack of spirit he had. His spirit felt like it was a man hanging from a noose over the Grand Canyon. His heart was empty. He stopped caring as the bullets penetrated these monsters' bodies, letting them plop to the ground like empty husks being prepared for their tombs. He stopped caring about the lives he was taking. He stopped caring about the country he'd fought tooth and nail to protect, but more importantly, he stopped caring about his life.

He ran, leaving a trail of blood behind him as he made it to the next level, which had little more cover than before. He simply jumped over fallen filing cabinets. Bullets sprayed from above as the roaring continued with heavy machine-gun fire. More of that *essence* filled his body and the veins on his body swelled—*clunk*—emitting more grey light in the room. Bullets hit Ghost, but they struck the veins, the bullets halting and shattering as fragments deflected off of him. He still felt the impacts push vibrations through his body.

So much, so much blood. I fought for this? I never would have if I knew this was going to be the futile result!

"Peace, is this your idea of some cruel joke? Because this isn't funny and I'm not laughing!" he cried out loud, his voice screaming down the halls, fading into the roar of the flames.

He made it through another doorway.

Boom!

A great ball of fire was hurtling at him from the other side of the level. He swiftly turned before being hit by a burning filing cabinet. He felt the warmth of the flames, and the force bruised his arms. His firm grip was nearly ripped away from his rifle. The filing cabinet pinned him against the wall. The fire burned his clothes as he hastily pushed the incendiary filing cabinet off of him. He let the orange air burn as he got up, ignoring its caress on his body. It could only be described as an alien sensation: nothing more. Nothing more.

At last, Ghost made it into the morning on top of Area 51. Sighing heavily, with a pulsating chest, he breathed in more *essence* from the air, and the grey veins receded into his skin, returning to cerulean. He carefully eyed soldiers training their sights on them from behind the rubble no doubt created by Ticker, whose body was nowhere to be seen. Standing upon the rubbled plane, he stared, knowing full well that a gunfight with his exhaustion was suicide. Hell, why did he care anymore?

He took a long look at the soldiers surrounding him like an animal in a cage. *After all, that is all any of us ever were. Just an animal who needs to be put down. This had better have been worth it.*

His fingers trembled. Scampering with heightened pace, he raised up his rifle like a club. His cerulean veins crept from his hand to the rifle. As he swung the rifle down, the rifle and the veins attached to it shattered as it sliced through the soldier's ballistics helmet and the soldier's skull. He pulled the pin out of a grenade hanging from the soldier's vest as he kicked the corpse, rolling him into the rest of his platoon. He turned to another soldier who was running at him, using his own rifle as a club. Ghost ducked and swung his foot into the soldier's windpipe.

The grenade exploded, sending the corpse's limbs flying and metallic debris into the soldiers nearby. Ghost dashed at the group, loosely pulling out his KA-BAR knife, and slit the throat of another soldier. Soldiers screamed out, trying to put down the animal. More pin-less grenades fell from the bodies. Ghost dashed to another group of soldiers. Bullets began to impale him again as an explosion sent more debris his way.

Only one platoon left!

Ghost struck the man in the chest with a knife. The soldier, who had some life in him, ripped out a pin of a grenade as he stabbed

Ghost in the arm, twisting the blade. Ghost felt the blade twisting in his arm, but pain was just as elusive as ever.

Ghost ripped out the knife in his shoulder and stabbed the man's tendon, ripping himself away before the grenade blew. Shards of the grenade penetrated Ghost, ripping apart flesh. His fingers trembled again. He turned to the side and threw a spinning knife, impaling a soldier between the eyes.

He took a deep breath as he strode onto the scorching hot ground, blue veins prominent, moving faster than before. As his body felt like a soulless husk, his face became still, like it was carved in a mountain.

Ghost pulled a grenade from his own pocket. He pulled the pin out and threw the grenade behind him. He pulled out a second grenade. He pulled the pin out and threw it behind him. He started slashing at soldiers' necks with the knife until it dulled.

The grenades behind him blew. The roar of the blast was deafening, and the dying gurgling screams of soldiers behind him continued.

Ghost impaled the last soldier with an iron pipe from a plumbing apparatus. The corpse trembled and leaned on him before collapsing at his feet. He heard groans of soldiers who had not yet passed to the other side. He pulled out his sidearm, pointed it at the nearest one, and pulled the trigger. The man's brains splattered on the ground.

Ghost returned his sidearm to his holster. His eyes were stretched open, and he couldn't bring himself to look at the mound of bodies around him, many of which he had killed. The sands were stained in blood, carcasses were blowing in the wind, and limbs were scattered all over the rubble. His heart sank as he realized again the sanctity of life and how easy it was for him to take it away. Violence: it was all he'd ever known. Even then, it had succeeded, or was he perhaps the epitome of human failure?

Finally having a moment, he felt memories of his comrades sweep over his mind, of their faces and their smiles, as if compelled to remember them not in pain, but happiness. A life filled with nothing but constant war, and this was the result. He gritted his teeth as he knew not what to fight for, not anymore. He was the last of Task Force Seven, the only survivor. *Damn it all. Why is this happening? This was supposed to be a training exercise!* He felt like a dull stake was being ceaselessly, violently hammered into his chest as the guilt swept over him. *I murdered these people. I murdered ... everyone.*

Bang!

He looked up at the flash in the distance. His heart jumped, and then settled back down as he remembered he didn't care anymore. The high-caliber round penetrated his chest and blood sprayed out of his back. The blue veins retreated back underneath his skin, and he resembled a normal human again. The numerous bullet holes in Ghost's standing corpse were now flowing out of him, like he was a strainer. *To live and die in obscurity. A corpse is all I ever was, and all I will be.* He coughed as blood sprayed out of his mouth. He still looked onward at the sniper.

Finish it!

Just as he thought those last words, he heard a loud whistle in the air. His head tilted up as blood drooled from his mouth. Black birds in the morning horizon flew swiftly, their velocity ringing in his ears as they came nearer. More whistling came. He looked right above him as the planes swept overhead and large metallic cylinders dropped out of their bellies. He smiled and let out a chuckle as he grasped onto his elbow with the knife impaled in it. Uncle Sam was sparing no expense on them. Ghost covered his heart with his hand as he took a deep breath, not making a move. "I pledge allegiance to the flag—"

The bombs struck right beside him, clouding everything in sight. The explosions and flames pushed through him in a torrent of fire. The red air caressed his corpse as sharp debris penetrated him, ripping his flesh apart. Nothing would escape as the fighter jets turned back around and lit the field up with their guns. This continued until nothing remained.

Area 51 became a crater filled with rubble, limbs, burnt faces and melted dog tags. The smoke was filled with radioactive particles, and the ground became a hazardous wasteland. The buildings were brought to ruin, the remains scattering in the wind. Blood watered the ground. Every. Single. Inch.

CHAPTER 1

Peace in the Gardens

~Not of my own choice, I became a hero for peace, and I did whatever I was ordered to do. I killed, and I killed, and I killed. I killed without halting. I killed until at last my heart stopped beating. Every life I removed meant I was one step closer to brokering world peace. And then, at last, I achieved it. With such an impossible task, you'd think that would make me happy. But that wasn't the reward I acquired 'cause I became unnecessary, and I was framed for treasonous activity not of my own doing, and I was executed. Again, and again, and again!

SAMANTHA AND JENNIFER SAT upon their checkered picnic blanket, their cooler off to the side. They were sitting at the Boston Common across the street from Park Street Church. The church overlooked them, spanning the entirety of the corner of Park Street and Tremont street, hovering over the opposite side of the common. The red bricks of the church were dotted with two rows of contrastingly white windows, square on the bottom row and grandly arched on the top. There were clocks on all four sides of the brick church leading up to the belfry, and the belfry above pointed upwards like a white castle tower, reflecting the light of the bright sun.

Samantha and Jennifer took great care in getting the creases out of the blanket. Samantha was laying face up, letting the sun beat down on her face, which was shielded by large sunglasses. She was resting in her t-shirt and gym shorts with her arms at her sides. Jennifer was laying right next to her, her face away from the sun as she lay on her belly, her legs bent in the air, shoeless, and her face buried in *Pride and Prejudice*. Samantha heard the birds chirping as they fluttered to the treetops, and the dogs barking at squirrels scampering up the trees. She could hear the annoying sound of some pop music being played by some obnoxious college kid with a boom box. *I thought those were out of style. Those shouldn't even be a thing anymore.* Out of the corner of her eye, she could see Jennifer twirling her brown hair with her finger.

Samantha glanced at her silver-chained watch wrapped around her right wrist. Her ponytail sprawled to either side of her golden head. "3:27," she read aloud, closing her hand to a hard fist. Samantha didn't like being kept waiting. "When are they going to get here? The sandwiches are going to get soggy! They really know how to ruin a good picnic."

"Patience is a virtue." Jennifer snickered, bowing her head deeper into her book before putting a plain bookmark in between the pages and closing it. She turned a playful smile to Samantha. "You know Michael. And Tim is usually only along for the ride. Michael likes to take his time, never in a rush to do anything."

"You'd think he'd be able to keep time better." Sam was being sarcastic, reflecting on the work Michael did: business consultations. "Maybe he's working."

"On a Saturday? Fat chance." Jennifer cackled out loud, turning on her back and covering her face with her arms. "More likely he is just lounging around waiting to come until the last minute. Michael does as Michael does." Jennifer twirled her left wrist in her air.

"Not like me." Samantha spoke plainly, clicking her tongue. "Consulting and logistics are two completely different things."

"No. But who comes thirty minutes early for everything except you? You are unnecessarily early for everything." Jennifer chuckled, removing her arms from her face and squinting at the afternoon sun. "I swear, you wouldn't be yourself if you didn't get to your own funeral thirty minutes early."

Samantha shot a sharp glare at her. Jennifer wasn't looking; her eyes were closed as her face was focused on the sky. Samantha closed her eyes again and turned her face towards the sun. She looked up into the clouds and started to look at the shapes in the sky. Samantha reflected on this; yes, she was early for everything, with anxiety if she wasn't running at least fifteen minutes early, but was it really all that necessary? Perhaps she could pray about her anxiety for such a trivial matter.

"I'm not that bad, am I?" Samantha didn't think she was that bad, just punctual. Though, she found more often than not that her version of punctual was typically fifteen minutes early. She was never late.

"Well, yah," Jennifer told her, rather sarcastically. "I invited you over to my house *after* dinner, which was at five. I invited you at 6:00PM. You showed up in the middle of my dinner. You really are funny with time."

"Wait!" Samantha pointed to the sky. "Look right there, it's a cloud. It looks like—"

"What?" Jennifer interrupted, opening her eyes as she shielded them with her hand. "Don't tell me? No. Don't. Sam. Sam. No. Bad. That's bad! Sam! Don't say it!"

"It's a curtain van!" she exclaimed.

"You really need to stop taking work home with you." Jennifer sighed as she looked at the cloud that Samantha was pointing at. She saw something different. "I see a cloud, an image of condensed gaseous water. Only you would be excited to see some logistical import solution in the sky." She looked closely at it and rubbed her chin and smiled. "That might be something, now, wouldn't it? A very entertaining idea to have freight stuck in the sky somewhere! No wonder my lab supplies never show up on time."

"I'm not sure if that's what clouds are made from. But it's a curtain van!"

"I'm not a meteorologist. I'm a biologist. Something like that is a little out of my realm of expertise." Jennifer shook her head.

"Cloud gazing?" came a voice from above them.

"Late as usual, Michael." Samantha scowled at him; his short light brown hair waved as the wind passed through it.

"Hostility is not appreciated on a Saturday, Samantha," Michael said rather nonchalantly, smiling. "Besides, I brought a Tim with me."

"Cloud gazing," Tim repeated and pushed his glasses closer to his face as he looked at the cooler. "I see you brought the sandwiches. Did you get drinks too?"

"Really?" Jennifer put her hand defensively on her chest. "Really? You think we would forget such things? Do I hear a sense of distrust from you, Tim?" She stood up with Samantha as they went over to the cooler to open it. Inside the cooler were sandwiches, bottles of water, granola bars, and cans of soda.

"I never knew you to be reliable." Tim directed his joke to Jennifer, wiping some sweat from his forehead.

"Wow!" Samantha exclaimed to Tim. "Rude." She turned her attention to Michael. "So, anyway, why were you so late?"

"Well," Michael sucked his teeth as he scratched his back over his shoulder, "I was with another friend. He needed someone to talk to today." He exhaled deeply. "You see, his mother died eight years ago in an accident, I think. Today was the anniversary. She died in Nevada. There was some training accident with the U.S Army that apparently went horribly wrong, killed over two-hundred thousand people. So, he needed a shoulder."

Samantha sucked a breath through her teeth her eyes wide and her chest puffing. "You could have invited him to hang out with us. Jennifer and I wouldn't have cared."

"I did, but he declined." Michael's smile faded. "He certainly needed a friend. I was there until he was over it, just to make sure he was going to be okay before I left him."

"Well, let's put these grim talks aside for now," Jennifer said, clapping her hands together. "I'm hungry. We've waited long enough!"

Jennifer pulled out the wrapped sandwiches, tossed one each to Samantha, Michael, and Tim, then tossed each of them a bottle of water. They unwrapped their sandwiches and ate.

"What is this?" Tim spat it out. His face cringed as his mouth made obnoxiously loud chewing noises.

"Oh, that's just peanut butter and jelly." Jennifer shot a smile over to him with her eyelid drooped down halfway.

"What! You know this! I am allehgic to freaking peanut buttah!" he cried out.

"Well, well, well," she snickered as she covered her smile with her mouth. "I hope you didn't fehget yeh epi pen."

"Tim, shut up and eat. We all know that's a lie. You just hate peanuts." Michael had some of his sandwich dangling from his mouth.

Samantha said nothing. Samantha was a little distracted thinking of Michael's friend and those many people who had died. *That's a lot of people. Radioactive waste leveled what formerly was a large metropolis.*

"Michael?" she asked.

"Hmm?" He took a bite and was chewing on his sandwich.

"That incident you mentioned," she began.

"Not this again." Jennifer shook her head as she took a drink of water.

"Did you ever hear anything about that incident? I can't imagine something like that happening here," Sam asked.

"I have not. But then again, it was eight years ago. We were all likely still in middle school, except maybe Jennifer here." Michael snapped his fingers to point to her. "Where were you eight years ago? Jennifer, you must have heard something. I mean, that's a lot of people. I find it very hard to believe there wouldn't be a lot of media attention. Maybe Uncle Sam covered it up well. After all, a mistake at that kind of scale would only tell our enemies we're weak."

"The only problem with that theory is that there weren't wars we were involved in back then," Tim argued. He rose his chin up. "However, there always was the possibility they were hiding something they didn't want the general public to know. You know about the rumors on Area 51: aliens, spacecrafts, and so on. Maybe they got sick and tired of it, and boom, nuclear meltdown solves that problem."

Jennifer took a drink of her water. "Not much. I think I was over in Texas with some family. I did hear something about it, but the news came in very briefly and in spurts. Like the news could have been censored; kudos for you, Tim." She snickered at him. "News censorship happens, doesn't it? We've had the most recent election to tell us that. Besides, with a wealth of information, any number of them can be falsified facts, and if someone reports on fake facts, they could get their butts sued! For the first few days, all I remember was that Nevada was a like war zone for over eight weeks. That was the only thing consistent regardless if you watched left-wing or right-wing news. U.S government officials finally came out and said it was a training accident. I didn't believe it; still don't."

"A *training* accident killed twenty percent of a million people?" Michael nearly spat out his water. "I don't know if I believe that."

"Well, I don't think many people believed it. But it did happen around Area 51. So, it is believable it could have been an accident, I guess. I mean, they hide things pretty well there, and most people who believe in aliens would believe that an alien laser just went off!" Jennifer waved both her hands excitedly with the last statement.

"Well, it was eight years ago. Most people probably forgot about it by now. Well, except those who lost someone close to them, but it was in Nevada, so we probably don't know too many people who would have been affected by it. That's not exactly something someone likes sharing. Hey, my parents died in Area 51!" She attempted to sound gleeful. "When would that ever come up in conversation?"

"Almost never," Samantha commented. She loved Jennifer, but sometimes she could feel cold. She knew Jennifer wasn't a cold person, but with her bubbly and spontaneous personality, the things she said could come off as callous. "But they had children who they left behind. It's sad, really."

"It is in the past. For some, it's best left there. For others, they'll never forget. And the memory will only die when they do," Jennifer replied more calmly.

"Well, it serves no purpose focusing on something like this right now. It is in the past, and apart from Michael, none of us really know anyone directly affected by that, unless they are exceptionally good at hiding it. The only thing we can do is pray for their peace of mind," said Tim. "Hey, I have an idea. Let's throw the pigskin around."

"That's a great idea! I haven't done that since high school!" Samantha jumped up at the suggestion. *I guess it was my fault.* Sam was especially thankful for Tim providing an out from that conversation.

"That wasn't that long ago, it's only been six years." Michael chuckled. "You say that like it's some kind of throwback."

"It is," she replied.

"You were on the football team?" Tim seemed surprised.

"Yes. I was. A little-known fact, I was once a tomboy," she answered.

Samantha proactively packed up the picnic blanket and cooler and carried them to her car, which was parked nearby. She opened her trunk and put the picnic in, slamming the trunk shut.

A lone man by the crosswalk caught her attention. His hand was in his shorts' pocket and he stared blankly at the trees over by the common. He seemed happy, with a smile written across his lips, but his eyes told a different story, sunken with lack of sleep and outlined with puffy eyelids.

She returned over to her friends, who were already tossing the football. She sprinted in and intercepted a pass intended for Michael.

"Uhm. That's my ball, Sam." Michael turned his palms to the sky.

She lobbed the ball to him. Tim seemed very focused on it. Jennifer seemed to be swaying back and forth as the wind blew. Samantha was happy to have the football back into her hands again. It had been too long since she'd held a ball, too long since she's tossed the ball and had the feeling of her own enjoyment without the extreme pressure of winning a game.

The first signs of a city at dusk appeared as the streetlights flickered to life, illuminating the sidewalks, which were now more hushed and empty. The light over Park Street's MBTS station lit up the faces of people standing in the limbo of the station. Droves of people briskly walked through the station's steel-frame doors to try to catch the train. Some individuals still lounged by fountains, sitting on benches and chairs; others relaxed on the grass, laying down and looking up at the empty sky with no sense of time or place to be.

"Michael?" Samantha asked as she threw the ball to him.

"Yeah?" He let the ball strike his chest as he caught it.

"It's getting late. I want to walk through the Garden before the sun completely sets." She pointed at the shining streetlights. "Can we?"

"Honestly, that sounds nice." Jennifer exclaimed, letting out a yawn. "We should all go. Isn't that right, Tim?"

"Tim didn't say no." Samantha answered for him.

"Wait, I didn't—" Tim opened his mouth to protest.

"Then it's decided. Come on, Tim, I know you don't want to, but it's not far. It's not a big garden, man," Michael said. "It's literally on the other side of the street."

Tim sighed. "Fine." He put the ball back into the little traveling bag he kept with him everywhere. "Let's go see this Boston Public Gahden."

The four of them walked through the other side of the Common, leading them across the street and into the Boston Public Garden through a set of black gates. They were underneath the cover of trees. Some swans were floating down the body of water to the right side, and on the water was a coat of leaves, hiding something underneath.

Samantha found something peaceful about it. It was quiet, soft, like the good Lord's creation. Everything seemed to be in perfect harmony here, nestled away from the city but protected from the loud, busy noises of the car horns and alarms. The natural noises of the miscellaneous birds, insects, and squirrels drowned out what few cars drove by. It was a little utopia inside the hustle and bustle of the city, right in the center of Boston! It reminded her of the woods in Vermont, a place she rarely visited anymore now that she'd left.

Tim and Jennifer were talking amongst each other. Samantha chuckled behind them as Jennifer, the bubbly biologist, had a way of annoying Tim, the introverted events coordinator. One might have thought that Jennifer should be the events coordinator and Tim the biologist. It was this irony of their personality traits and respective careers that made Sam chuckle. Of course, one might have thought they were dating with the way they talked, but Sam knew better.

It was good to just slow down a little. Samantha appreciated, given the busyness of her and Michael's respective work weeks, being able to just simply settle and get drawn back in with the majestic pull of the natural world. They usually had no time to just sit back and relax.

Samantha noticed that the air suddenly felt wrong and thin. Exhaling the frost from her breath, she stopped in her tracks with gaping eyes. She felt the cold air fill up her lungs. The hairs on her head stood on end. The chilling air felt like a cold day of winter to her. She rubbed her shoulders to warm herself up. *It shouldn't be this cold. This is spring!* She turned her head to see the man from earlier. His hand was still in his pocket; his smile was still wide—too wide. Again, just like before, he wasn't looking at anything specific. His stare was just blank, his eyes sunken in and overbearingly tired. This man was to the world as his smile was to his face: out of place, like he didn't belong there.

She moved her feet again, catching up to Michael before the man would notice her looking at him. There was something off about the man, but she couldn't place her finger on it; the fact remained, the sudden temperature drop was unnatural. Shortly after she returned to Michael's side, the warmth returned to the air, or perhaps she'd just entered an area where the air was warmer. Perhaps she was feeling things that weren't there.

"That's much better." She felt a little at ease, returning to a sense of equilibrium. The air felt natural, unlike the little pocket of superstitious air she'd walked through. *Did anyone else notice?*

"What?" Michael asked, turning his head to her but continuing to walk toward the end of the Gardens.

"Didn't you notice the temperature drastically dropped?" Samantha's eyes narrowed. "The temperature just dropped back there. I hope I'm not experiencing hot flashes."

"I wouldn't worry about it. I mean, I didn't notice," Michael said. "It's New England. We experience four seasons in less than a week."

"That may be, but it shouldn't have dropped that much!"

"I told you, Sam, I'm not a meteorologist," Jennifer called back to her, turning her head.

"I wasn't asking you!" Samantha snapped.

"Well, that was rude," Tim commented, looking back at them over his shoulder as he kept walking. "What's got you all worked up?"

"I just—I just saw a man."

"This is Boston. There's always someone around." Michael chuckled, finding Samantha's little episode humorous.

"Not with a blank stare. Not with a smile as wide as his," she replied. "And the temperature."

Jennifer looked around behind them. "I don't see anyone."

"You're just imagining things," Michael asked.

She shook her head, clenching her fists at her sides. "I know what I saw; I know what I felt." She turned to try to catch a glimpse of the man again, only this time, he wasn't there.

"You didn't have a load to pick up, did you?" Michael asked. "You know, one of those Saturday loads that needs to be picked up, but you have no way to confirm if it did or not until Monday, and by that time it's much too late."

"God no! I took care of that one already," Samantha said as they finally exited the garden.

"Aww. Where did the sun go? I still want to be out." Jennifer yawned. "Kong's is not far off from here."

"Cheap beer," Tim commented.

"Not me." Samantha didn't want to go out anyway. The presence and disappearance of this peculiar man made her want to curl up in bed with a book. She also didn't want to spend more time with Jennifer or Tim; they especially didn't seem to believe her. She was a tough girl, but she couldn't help but feel hurt that none of them, especially Michael, believed her. "It's too late for me right now. I'm still recovering from that nightmare those two drivers put me through yesterday."

"What did they do?" Michael asked. Her trucking nightmares were never boring.

"The driver just dropped their trailer in the doors and unhooked their trucks from their trailer and drove off to get breakfast without telling anyone. Back-to-back. Then my customer got frantic because as far as he was concerned, he'd lost a truck but inherited two trailers he didn't want anything to do with!" she said, letting out a deep sigh. "Oh well, at least he pays well for every other load he gives me. Alright, I'm tired. I'm going home, going to bed. I'll start fresh in the morning. Tuesday?"

"Yes," Michael said. "As long as I don't get caught in one of those overseas conference calls. Those are a pain."

"I hear you. Michael, are you coming?" Tim asked.

"Nah. Next time," he replied.

"Party pooper," Jennifer frowned.

CHAPTER 2

Terri Nation

~I've been cursed with isolation, you see.

BRIGHT HEADLIGHTS BEAMING ONTO the bricks and concrete of the sidewalks on Park Street. The trees' leafy branches swayed in the wind like ballet dancers. Droves of people were scampering into the Park Street MBTA station, entering the metal and glass doors and hastily marching down the stairs. The other buildings on Park Street had closed their windows, but some had the lights on to light the sidewalk for other travelers. There was a fancy restaurant on the upper end of Park Street, nearly below the street level, with no clear way to get inside. Samantha wondered where the entrance was.

A car drove by, speeding through the red light, honking its horn. The tires squealed as it turned the corner, and Sam covered her ears as the noise scratched her inner lobes.

"I take it you didn't get an overseas conference call." Samantha knew Michael couldn't make it every Tuesday, because his clients operated in numerous time zones, and sometimes he was forced to stay late.

"No. I got an email that that's not going to be happening for a while, I think. Tensions are rising quickly overseas, with Poland and Ukraine." Michael covered a yawn with his hand.

"What do you mean?" Tim's head immediately jerked, turning to Michael with alarm. The lights from inside the church flashed out as the receptionist flicked the switch off and on.

"Well," Michael began, his eyes darting back and forth, making sure no one else was listening. "Look, you didn't hear it from me, and I'm not sure the validity of this, but it has a lot of clients overseas concerned. We won't be trading anything overseas for a while, or that's what I heard. And this is just a rumor, but apparently NATO is disbanding."

Sam turned her gaze to the ground, kicking some pebbles to the side. She reflected on what that might mean. If NATO disbanded, would the U.S.A be protecting anyone anymore? And if not, who were the allies? Would it turn into a world where every country was independent, just waiting for a large superpower to come in and swallow them up? What would keep those superpowers in check? What would that do to diesel fuel prices? Ukraine and Poland, what cause did they have to be tense with one another? All these questions floated in her head. She suspected the rate of fuel might skyrocket, but even that was a guess.

"Wait. What?" Jennifer jerked her head immediately toward him, and her jaw dropped. "Why? That's a big development for that to just be a rumor. Michael, you realize it would take fifty liars to even think of spreading a rumor that big!"

"Again, rumor. That's all I know, and you didn't hear it from me," he explained.

"Dang it. I think I might be fine. I don't know how much my customer takes in imports. I think it's all local though," Samantha said, interlacing her fingers between her hands. The only thing that would really affect her in the brokerage would be the gas prices. It would make it difficult to find trucks cheaply to deliver truckloads of groceries.

Michael sucked air through his teeth. "Yeah, and I'll likely take a pay cut, as many of my associates are over there. But the effects of that are going to change the market considerably. Sam, I think it's only a matter of time before the effects catch up to you, even if this is a rumor."

"If it's only a rumor, what's the harm?" Tim asked.

"The market changes drastically, constantly. There's no way to accurately predict what it will do. Besides, even these rumors will affect the market eventually, creating a great rift in the economic sphere. These rumors, even if they aren't true, will cause an economic collapse eventually, or just a severe recession," Jennifer explained. The doors opened and the rest of the congregation walked outside. Samantha stared at Jennifer, shocked that she'd put so many coherent business sentences together in a row. She didn't give Jennifer enough credit, apparently. "I'm not an economist. My brother is in stocks. Options, specifically. He told me about all of this. The market is impossible to predict, but we can get close; behavioral finance and all that."

"There's your answer. Even if it's false, it's bad." Michael shook his head and patted his pants with one of his hands.

"Well, there goes my 401K flying right out the window," Tim exclaimed, putting a hand through his hair. "Oh well, I suppose I could opt out of it now; I'll just get taxed heavily on it. Thanks for the heads up."

The noise of the rest of the emerging studiers came to a dull roar. Brian came up to them. He had a thinly shaved beard and mustache and lively eyes. He was scrawny for his height, built much like a basketball player, only significantly shorter. "Hey, you guys coming to Terri Nation?" He wrapped his arm around Michael like an old friend, an overbearingly enthusiastic smile on his face.

Samantha rolled her eyes at the mention of Terri Nation, the local pub right around the corner where they often all went out for some dinner and drinks to continue fellowshipping together after the study. After all, why waste a perfectly good night to play catch up?

"You know it." Michael shook his hand. "Wouldn't miss it."

"Great! I'm going to head back over here now. I need to recruit some of the newbies." Brian disappeared into the small crowd, talking to a few new faces Samantha didn't recognize.

"Well, I suppose it's time," Michael said. "You all coming? We should start leading the cattle."

"Such a specific metaphor," Samantha said.

"Not really."

Michael and Tim started walking backwards up Park street towards Beacon street, waving their hands towards the others, ushering everyone to follow. "Last stop, Terri Nation. Who's coming?"

Michael and Tim started chatting to each other as they briskly walked up the sidewalk towards the City Hall.

Many of the other people around them continued to talk. Others started following in small groups. Jennifer linked arms with Samantha. A girl called Erin ran towards them from her group. Her giddiness gave her a child-like aura that was only complemented by the freckles across her cheeks. Samantha braced herself for what she expected to be ten times the amount of Erin's normal bubbliness.

"So, what are you smiling about?" Samantha asked as they walked onwards.

"Well, our office just hired another broker out of nowhere last week. He seems to have already settled in." Erin smiled. "Though he often refers to me as the press."

"The press?" Samantha's eyes widened.

"My last name. Gutenberg. The Gutenberg Press," Erin explained.

"Okay, but what does that have to do with you smiling already? Do you like him or something?" Samantha teased.

"Erin's got a crush again." Jennifer chuckled, elbowing Samantha in the side. "Seriously, if it is not one man, then it is an equally terrifying different man, sometimes a stranger."

"I do not!" Erin scolded. Samantha assumed Erin was blushing in the dark. "Jennifer, you always find a way to make something innocent sound so inappropriate. Anyway, he's very smart, apparently. He is an excellent resource to go to for help. My job would finally be secure if I went to him for advice."

"How do you know that? He just started the job last week," Jennifer said. "No one learns the job that fast."

"He already closed a few hundred-thousand-dollar-deals last week," Erin said. "Either he knows what he's doing or is extremely lucky."

"What?" Samantha couldn't believe it. She herself was working a deal with another customer, but she was not making nearly that much in gross revenue, although it was a different business altogether. "How?"

"I'm going to ask him tomorrow. I'll let you know. Although, I don't know how that will help you. You're in logistics, not in stocks." Erin snapped her fingers.

"Maybe I'll just invest in a mutual fund." Samantha sneered. She had little interest in stocks to begin with.

"You two go ahead and talk finance if you want. I'm sticking to my germs. Much more interesting," Jennifer said as they turned onto Beacon street.

"So, what's his name?" Samantha leaned into Erin, bumping against her.

"He goes by Ted," Erin answered. "He said he's from Ohio. Not a very social person though, doesn't talk much."

"So, enough about this individual that neither Sam nor I are going to meet. July Fourth. Erin, are you still coming? I need to order the canoes, and I need to have an idea of how many I need to reserve. We plan on meeting at Kendall Square at 6PM."

"Yes, I'll go," Erin exclaimed. "I'd love to go. I might be late; I need to skip lunch to leave work early."

"Don't worry about food, there will be plenty. I'll be packing sandwiches again," Jennifer said. They were approaching Terri Nation, which was on the corner heading back down towards Tremont Street. The City Hall was staring down at them with the lights from behind the gates and the statue of Joseph Hooker riding on a horse.

"That's probably not the best thing. You might want to think of something else. Sandwiches don't taste good out in the open sea," Samantha suggested. "Maybe we can get Michael to cook something with his smoker. Or perhaps just bring some vegetables or something."

"But poor dear Erin will be hungry. She's skipping her lunch after all." Jennifer chuckled as she opened the door into Terri Nation. "I mean to be fair, most of us, except me, will not have time to actually eat something after work. I mean, you get out late enough as it is."

"It'll take a few hours; it's fine," Samantha replied.

They walked through the restaurant section of the bar, through the wide hallway, then took a left at a statue of a little girl flying a kite at the side. Michael and Tim were already sat in the back of the upstairs bar, talking to one another about something while sipping on their drinks. Michael was always trying the weird concoctions that the bartender, Scott, mixed. He was like Scott's guinea pig.

Samantha walked up to the bar to talk to Scott.

"What's goin' on, Sam? What can I get ya?" Scott wore a black vest over a white button-up shirt and black slacks. Everyone on the wait staff wore the same uniform.

"House Cab is fine," she answered, pulling out her card. "I'll close out."

Scott took the card and went to pour her a quick glass of red cabernet wine. He always had a heavy pour.

"Scott, I'll take your specialty. Whatever that is at this moment," Jennifer said. Like Michael, she was also an adventurous drinker.

"I'll also take a cider. Bottle please," Erin called out, one hand raised as her other hand reached for her pocketbook.

"Together or separate?" Scott called as he reached behind the bar and undid the cap of a frosted bottle of hard cider.

"Together. I'll buy it," Erin said, nudging Jennifer in the side. "The least I can do if I'm trusting you with my food on the fourth of July."

Erin winked at Jennifer and squeezed her shoulder.

Scott mixed up a concoction of Bourbon, triple sec, Coke, muddle mint and cucumbers. Jennifer frowned curiously as the drink was handed to her. Her eyes skimmed over the physical ingredients, noting that the beverage, whatever it might be, should taste refreshing; however, such a taste would likely contrast unwelcomely with the bourbon. "Well, it is different." She took a sip, then made a puckered face. It did contrast, the way Jennifer had expected it to. "Did Michael like this?"

"He liked it." Scott started chuckling. "Do you?"

"It's certainly different. I'll give you ten points for originality." Her face cringed. "I haven't decided if I'm going to like this or not yet. Give me a few minutes."

"Gotcha," he answered with a chuckle, quickly moving back to address the rest of his guests.

Brian came in with a crowd of nearly fifteen different guests. *Looks like he succeeded in inviting the new people here. Well, this certainly is great for the community. They are all new to Boston, or many of them, anyways. This isn't a bad spot to be,* Sam thought. Brian's friendliness and his great charisma were what kept Samantha interested in these little late-night gatherings, and surprisingly, kept her going to Park Street Church instead of some local church.

Samantha knew that Scott was going to have a good night. She sipped her wine as she gazed up at the TV screen. Scott generally kept the news on in the back unless they requested the sports channel. He was always very friendly, though when she'd first come there, he'd seemed like a tired and disgruntled man. He couldn't have been more than thirty. He hid a smile underneath that thick beard of his.

Sam looked over at Brian again, noticing he'd taken out a little pen and piece of paper, engaging enthusiastically in conversation with everyone he'd invited. He spent more time with the new faces than the old ones, nodding as they spoke, showing his elite listening skills. Sam guessed that he was offering to buy them a round tonight and jotting orders down on his notepad. Brian leaned over the bar top and slapped his hand on it, then looked intently in Scott's eyes as they engaged in some unrelated conversation which Sam couldn't hear. Brian read off the slip of paper, and Scott immediately punched some buttons on the electronic touch pad and printed out a receipt, handing it to Brian before hastily disappearing behind the bar. Brian immediately returned to the newcomers, turning their hesitant smiles to enthusiastic ones. Samantha thought, *Brian is better at making anyone feel comfortably at home.*

Then she noticed something familiar. The hairs on her head felt like they stood on ends, and the chills came over her, cascading like a powerful wind. Goosebumps rose up from her arms. She looked around, trying not to alarm anyone, hoping it may have been her imagination. Other people around the bar were putting on their sweatshirts or wrapping themselves with their arms. She chose to ignore it. *Someone probably just turned the thermostat down. But damn, it's cold!*

Out of the corner of her eye, she noticed someone. He was sitting by himself at the other end of the bar, perhaps ten paces from her, drinking a glass of red wine like hers. *Merlot? Or Cab?* It was the same man from Saturday, first at the cross walk, then inside the Garden. Now here. And it seemed the last time the temperature dropped so much and so quickly had been with him around. Who was he?

Scott brought this man a plate of mashed potatoes. This man still seemed to be smiling very widely as he thanked Scott for the plate. Scott asked him if he needed anything else, but he declined, and said, "I have more than I require right now. Thank you."

Sam took a closer look as the man took a fork and put it into the mashed potatoes and started eating. She squinted her eyes at the man to see some lined scars on his face. The words he'd spoken had barely made it to her ears with the volume of the bar.

Twice she'd seen the man in a social setting. Twice she'd seen the man isolated in the social setting. Perhaps he was new to Boston, and looking for friends; perhaps he was socially inept. *Well, I'm not Brian, but I'll see what I can do. I at least know something to spin off on,* she thought.

She took a sip from her glass, scanning the bar top for Scott when he got a second. She raised her arm and called him over. Scott walked over, drying a beer glass with a towel. Scott leaned over the bar, setting the glass down and resting both palms firmly on the bar top. "What's up, Sam?"

"That man over there." She leaned in over the table, pointing a finger to the man in the corner before retracting it around her wineglass.

Scott turned his head briefly to look. "That's Ted. He's been coming here lately."

"Do you know what he does?" Sam asked.

"No. He's a polite person, but a man of few words."

"Well, thanks for that. That was it. Thank you!"

She started walking towards him quietly. He ate silently. She was standing behind him as he was engrossed in his food, scarfing it down quickly. He took a sip of his wine again, turning the glass and looking into it as if he was lost in thought.

"Well, well, well, so a rat sneaks behind me, eh?" said the man. He never bothered to look up from his wine. "To what exactly do I owe the pleasure?"

Samantha abruptly halted. Her wineglass trembled in her hand as she looked down at the ripples inside the glass. *Did I make a sound? No. Wait. Could he smell my perfume, or was it the wine?*

"The scent of Cabernet was coming closer and closer. I could smell it approaching me, and then suddenly the scent just lingered. You can't be more than twenty-three inches behind me." He turned in his stool and looked up to her, and his smile was still wide. "How may I help?"

"Startling. Well, I'm not a rat." Sam chuckled nervously.

"And yet you came to me as silent as a rat."

Well, he's not socially inept, that is certain. He's eloquent and very formal. She found him to be unnerving, yet intriguing all the same. "Rats can be silent nuisances, but I couldn't help but notice that I've seen you before," she commented.

"Well, this is the Heart of Boston, as they say. Odds are there are many faces we see again and again, and maybe we recognize a few reoccurring faces here and there, but we never make a point to meet one of them. I know I certainly don't," he replied. His smile never faded. He stood up and raised his glass to hers.

She clinked their glasses together. "Cheers."

Sam found him to be more mysterious. He'd greeted her with a friendly smile, but the words comparing her to a rat were a bit unsettling. He was confident, this was evident, but was there something about her he found to be untrustworthy? She bit her tongue, fearing she'd made some kind of social error. *Brian is better suited for this, but I can't back down now.*

"That is something true you have just said. My name is Samantha Harris," she said. She brought her hand out to meet his other hand to shake it.

He reached out his hand to meet hers and shook. Samantha could hear the bones in her hand crack; he had a very firm and strong grip. "My name is Ted Anderson."

"It's a pleasure to meet you." She didn't want to make it too obvious that she'd asked about him.

"To be sure, Miss Harris, the pleasure is all mine. Now, I ask again: to what do I owe the pleasure of such an introduction?" There was something different about him, though; his brown watery eyes looked right into hers. Ted appeared to her to be in his mid-twenties, but the eyes told a different story, as if they were much older than his body.

"I ran into you twice on Saturday. Right on the corner of Park and Tremont, and then again on the same day at the Garden, towards the end of that night," she admitted. "You seemed to be by yourself, while everyone else was grouped together, or coupled."

"Was that around the time the temperature dropped?" he asked.

Her eyes blinked repeatedly. *So, I'm not crazy.* "Y-you felt that too? I thought I was just imagining things," she stammered as she took another sip from her glass, looking cautiously at Ted. She felt something in her gut, like she should be wary of this man. Numerous people had been with her that night, and only she and Ted had felt it.

And only they acknowledged it. *Why didn't any of them feel anything?*

"Yes, I felt it also," he said. "Well, that's New England for you."

"Yes," she said, lowering her voice a little bit. "Have you been around Boston for very long?"

"A few weeks," he answered.

"What brought you here?" She thought to ask another question, hoping to find something to latch on to. She could hear multiple steps behind her, and the music played from the speakers, and the chatter sounded like white noise.

"Work," he answered.

"Where are you from?" She was dissatisfied with the answer, as simple as it was. Sure, it very well could be true, but there wasn't enough information released from him to pose any meaningful conversation.

"Ohio."

"What part?" *You're like a steel trap.*

"Delaware." He shifted on his stool as he took another bite of his mashed potatoes.

"There's a store I deliver to frequently over there," Sam said excitedly. She'd finally found something.

"Oh, and what is it that you do?" His expression didn't change, but he leaned back against the bar and crossed his hands over his chest.

"I work for a 3PL. I deliver groceries for a major wholesaler. I'm a broker." *Dang it.* She wasn't expecting him to start asking questions. Not that she had anything really to hide from him, but she wasn't done trying to figure out who he was.

"As am I. I deal with stocks," he answered. "And options."

It finally hit her. He might work with Erin. "Do you know Erin Gu—"

"The Gutenberg Press? Yes. I work with her." He laughed.

"Yes!" She laughed. "That is exactly what she said you call her. She said something about you today on our way over here."

"Terrible things, I'm sure," he replied, never lessening that smile.

"No, she said you were very good at your job."

"No. I am just very lucky." He got a buzz from his phone. "Excuse me a moment." He pulled out his phone and opened something up. Samantha assumed it was a work-related email. He read it intently. He shut the screen off from his phone and put it back into his pocket. "Well, on one hand, that was terrible. On the other, I'm glad I sold all of those."

"What?"

"Oh, NATO just disbanded, and Russia just declared war on Ukraine," he said nonchalantly. "I just sold most of my foreign assets. Those values are going to drop overnight. I wonder, how will the rest of the European Union fare? Will they follow suit? Will they get involved? Most likely, as they have always done. It's unfortunate that the world came to this, but we're here in America; unlikely to step in unless one of them starts bombing the harbors again."

"How do you know?" she asked. *Well, I guess that confirms the rumor Michael told us, but how exactly are you this calm about it?* Samantha knew that national allegiances were trembling as of late; the news told them that much. To her, it seemed most everyone was inches away from everyone's throats at any given time, and Russia and Ukraine were now the only confirmed cases of political collapse. How soon would this uncertainty reach America? Sam couldn't help but wonder.

"Like I said, I'm very lucky. However, some of the higher-ups might think I actually know something when I don't." He let out a brief sigh. "Oh well; I'll cross that bridge when I get there."

Sam turned abruptly. "Michael!" she waved at him as he was now talking with Erin. Samantha noticed that Erin frowned at them with her pouty eyes. She noted that Erin seemed to be boy crazy; she didn't expect that kind of behavior from someone going to church weekly. *But we all have our own shortcomings.*

"Ted, this is my boyfriend, Michael," she introduced them.

Michael walked over with a friendly smile on his face and introduced himself. Michael shook Ted's hand, and Samantha could hear the bones in Michael's hand cracking.

"Firm grip. I like it!" Michael released his hand.

"So, Michael, you know that thing you talked about earlier?" Sam asked.

"I said you didn't hear it from me," Michael said defensively, turning to her abruptly and frowning.

"It's on the news already." She frowned, knowing that since these rumors were true, global collapse might not be far behind. She guessed this would immediately affect Michael's line of work drastically.

"Wait. What?" Michael asked. "Already? I just found out about it, but I thought those were rumors."

"Rumors have an unfortunate way of being steeped in truth. Odds are, if something is completely unbelievable, it is probably true," Ted said. "I knew of the rumor, but thought nothing of it until this morning. Thank God I followed my gut. I can sleep peacefully now."

"Well, it is only a matter of time, then. Someone's going to punch someone important," Mike replied.

Ted threw his head back in laughter.

"I think that already happened," Samantha said. "Apparently Russia's on a warpath again."

The phone vibrated in Ted's pocket again. He pulled it out of his inside pocket and looked at his notification. "They're not the only ones on a warpath. Well, I guess it was only inevitable that this would happen."

"What now?" Samantha asked. She was considering how this news was going to affect her. It was clearly going to affect her business. Oil prices were going to rise. Rates for truck drivers were going to rise to reflect that change. Her rates were contracted. Renegotiating her contracted rates was likely to be fruitless. Her individual margins were going to decline. Her profitability was going to plummet. *How soon before this all hits home?*

"Trade deals with China aren't going well, apparently," Ted explained. "That being said, it's only a matter of time before someone declares war. It is like twenty years ago."

"Those were not good times," Michael said. "Every major nation was at everyone's throats."

"Precisely. The global economy was trash then." Ted raised his hand in the air. He dropped it back down. "And just like my hand, we'll probably be freefalling for a while—well, then it starts to decline, and that's when we'll really be freefalling."

"You seem to know a lot about this," Michael said, taking a sip of his exotic, but potentially terrible-tasting drink.

"I was in the Army before I came here. China was never too keen on Americans." He kept his smile, but reluctantly gave that answer. "I know too much already."

Samantha knew this would pique Michael's interest. His brother was in the 75th Ranger Regiment, "What was your—"

"My occupation in the Army is classified, above top secret," Ted said softly. "I can't disclose any information on what I did. I hope you understand."

"I do," Michael said. "My brother is in the Army. He is much the same way. Doesn't give out much information."

Erin finally walked over, her hand resting across her chest. "Ted, did you just get Adam's email?"

"Yes, Gutenberg's Press. I did. I got both of them. Well, if you have any foreign assets, I'd suggest selling them now. The market is still open. You may find a buyer, but if you don't, I'd advise holding onto it and riding it out, or selling it as soon as possible." This was clearly meant for Erin, and he gave her advice to work on, but Samantha picked up on something, noting just how volatile the stock markets were: Sell now, unless you can't, then hold onto it until it rises again. Or just sell later. The window of trading that fast was small.

"Did you already sell yours?" Erin asked. "How did you know this would happen?"

"I didn't. I just guessed. You should listen to those rumors more closely." He chuckled.

"This is going to be a nightmare," Michael said, ruffling his hand through his hair.

Jennifer popped up with her drink in hand. "Michael, you have terrible taste in this stuff. Why do I let you talk me into these things?"

Samantha felt a weight lift off her chest as her attention was immediately turned away from the horrific events happening with the world to something, albeit random, more pleasant. For that, she was exceedingly thankful for Jennifer's interruption.

"First of all, I didn't say anything." Michael laughed, nudging her shoulder with his.

"I mean seriously, this is disgusting, why would you drink this?" she turned her gaze to Ted. "So, who is this who is hogging up the party?"

"I mean, you can barely call this a party," Samantha said as Erin was back onto her phone, monitoring her emails.

"I have to go. I'll see you next Tuesday!" Erin walked over to her green purse.

Samantha waved as Erin walked out of the bar, relieved, as Erin's constant pining after men was growing tiresome.

"This is Ted. You know; that Ted." Sam clicked her tongue as she pointed to Erin on her way out.

"What Ted—oh! *That* Ted! Well, I'll say little to compromise anything. I'm Jennifer, and welcome to our little dysfunctional family," she joked. "Never mind me. I'm the crazy one."

Samantha chuckled. *She's never boring.*

"Speaking of, Ted." Jennifer seemed to take over the conversation. She would have made a great executive. "We are going to rent a few canoes over the Charles on the Fourth of July. I know it's two months away. You should totally come with!"

"Fireworks, over a body of water," Ted said. "I appreciate the sentiment, Miss; however, I'm afraid I must decline."

"Oh, well, that's too bad. Everyone here is going." She turned her head as if looking for someone. "Now, where is Brian?"

"He drove Tim home," Michael answered. "Tim had an early meeting for an event that's scheduled tomorrow. He couldn't be out too late."

"Such a shame. He really is personable. More fun than I am!" She wrapped her arm around Michael as she smiled.

Samantha and Jennifer's minds were thinking alike. No matter how hesitant one could be, Brian could always get someone to bend.

"I doubt that very much," Ted commented, making eye contact with her. Jennifer's hazel eyes gleamed in the dim light of the bar.

"Oh well, I guess you can't come under any circumstances, then, huh? Nothing we can do to persuade you?" Jennifer tried to coax some more amiable answer out of him.

"Unfortunately, no," Ted answered. "But I appreciate the offer, all the same."

"Oh well."

"Well, what about Tuesday next week? Are you doing anything after you get off work?" Samantha pitched in, eager to see more of this mysterious person. She'd barely struck the surface of who he was, and to her he seemed one dimensional. She was eager to get the full picture and get the story of those ragged eyes and that enthusiastic smile. The contrast didn't sit well with her.

"Um?" Ted hesitated. Sam briefly noticed his hand shaking as he hid it in his pocket. "Depends if I decide to leave work or not. I'm a workaholic, and perhaps that depends completely on the rest of the information I know you are inclined to give me."

"We have a Bible Study that we go to on Tuesdays. It starts at seven at Park Street. This next week is Tasty Tuesday, so there are snacks before," Samantha continued, linking arms with Michael.

"I think Sarah is making baklava," Michael said, sipping his who knows-what-it-tastes-like drink.

"Oh, yes, that's a splendid idea." Jennifer butted in again, clapping her hands together. "Seriously, Ted, you must come. It's much less of a commitment than going canoeing with us in July. Especially if you're new to Boston. It might be nice to have some kind of community that doesn't include drowning yourself in work."

"I'm not going to lie; I do like working," Ted explained, sipping more of his wine. "But with everything else that is going on in the world, I likely won't be able to find anything worthy buying in those oversea markets anymore. What's one day going to hurt? Where is it?"

"It's the church on Tremont and Park street. The door is open on the other side of Park Street where the—" Samantha began.

"Freedom Trail?" he asked.

"Yes, that's the one," she answered.

"7:00 PM?"

"Yes. But it's Tasty Tuesday, so you don't have to show up right at seven. You can show up a little after," Samantha answered, suddenly conscientious about how much she'd been speaking. "It is the best time for a newcomer. We'd love to see you there, but no pressure."

"I'll be there." Ted drank the rest of his wine and grabbed his tab. "I'll see you Tuesday."

Samantha smiled as he left, and she felt a weight being lifted off her chest. *I'm still not Brian. Brian could have gotten him to go out for the Fourth for sure.*

"So, how did you meet him?" Michael asked.

"Spill it, Sam, spill it. Details, girl!" Jennifer exclaimed. "I need details."

"I saw him twice on Saturday. First at the corner of the church, and then at the garden," she answered.

"Like when you swore the temperature dropped?" Michael inquired. He seemed a little more curious now.

"Yes. He was there when the temperature dropped, and then again when the temperature dropped again in here. Didn't you feel it?"

"Yes," Michael admitted. "But that could have been anything. I wouldn't worry about something so trivial as the temperature dropping, especially here in New England. The temperature and weather changes daily; besides, if it happened in here, it was probably just the air conditioning." He glanced at his watch. "And look at the time! It is time to be going. It's closin' time."

CHAPTER 3

Tasty Tuesday

~It was said that Saul killed his thousands and David his tens of thousands: I'd be fortunate if my numbers were nearly that low.

TED'S BLANK STARE POINTED into the sky. He ignored the hustle and bustle of men, women and children scurrying past him like rats running away from a legion of cats. His right hand was in his pocket as the wind pushed past him. The cars were halted at the intersection of Park and Tremont, as the cars driving down Park Street took a right turn, avoiding the numerous street signs and jaded traffic cones. He sighed as he looked at the red bricks leading up the stairs into the side of Park Street Church, and the glass doors.

He looked back at his watch. *6:45.* "Well, now is a good as time as ever," he said to himself. "Let's get this over with."

He pulled the first door into the side entrance open. He went to the second opening, scanning the entire room. He noted there was a fire escape to his left, right next to an elevator, but the only other exit was the door he'd walked through. A receptionist read a newspaper, his feet atop his desk. He seemed disinterested in anything but the paper. Beyond the threshold of the second glass door was a table with a banner which read "Park Street Café." There was a tall man behind it, also very cheery. *I wonder.* There were numerous empty tables behind the other man.

The man smiled at him and waved him in with a large hand. "Welcome to Café," he said, reaching out his hand for a shake. Ted returned in kind, never letting that smile go. "My name is Steve. Is this your first time here? I don't recognize you."

"You could say that," he said, firmly gripping the man's hand. "Ted."

"You came on the best day for it then! They're still setting up in there, so not everything is ready to get started just yet. They're still setting up the coffee table. How did you hear about Café?"

I'm from Ohio. I'm a stockbroker. Nothing more. You don't need the truth, just bare essentials. "You could say a little bird told me. So, tell me, what is the general setup of such a night?" His hand retracted from Steve's, retreating back into his pocket.

"Normally we sing, we pray, then we break up into small groups. There are many small groups here, and there is usually the simple connecting group that works perfectly for newcomers. But we do this once a month to foster some sense of community between small groups," Steve answered.

"Trying to make it impossible for someone to be forgotten, I see," Ted smiled, making sure to cheerily bare his teeth, hoping this would pass for genuine enthusiasm. *No one needs to know.* "A very good system in place, I suppose. I guess that is why I received such a warm welcome."

"I'm glad I was able to warm you up to the place." Steve laughed. "Well, that must be them now. I think they're getting the paper plates out."

"I guess I'll head in. It was a pleasure to meet you, Steve."

"You also." Steve immediately turned to the table. "Oops. I forgot." He took out one of those sticker nametags. He wrote 'Ted' on it before handing it to him. "Just so everyone can know who you are."

"Why, thank you so much!" Ted enthusiastically took the nametag and stuck it on the right side of his chest. "Something to identify the body."

Steve stared at him, blinking repeatedly as he jerked his head to the side. "What?"

"Sorry, you'll have to forgive my dry sense of humor." Ted smiled wider. "Oh well, Steve, I'm sure I'll see you again."

Ted turned around and walked into the Fellowship Hall, which was brightly lit. The room was a large square, with numerous chairs set up in a circle for everyone to sit down facing one another, like how friends would sit around at a campfire. Ted pictured a small bonfire in the middle of the room. He noticed that the wall in the back appeared to be a sectional leading to the corner of the main entrance of Park Street Church, likely leading to the sanctuary upstairs.

His hand trembled at his side. He became hyper-focused on the menial task of making a cup of coffee. His eyes focused on an electric coffee maker at the center of the room with small paper cups at the side. He walked over to it and pushed the 'on' button. He took out a cup and put it underneath the nozzle of the machine and picked one of the plastic coffee-filled cups, waiting for the machine to warm up and heat the water to a boil.

The machine clicked. He opened the top and put his plastic coffee-filled cup into the machine, softly pushing the lid down. He pushed another button, and a brown-black liquid filled his cup. He waited patiently for the cup to fill. He opened the top back up. He took out the plastic empty cup and threw it in the nearby trash. He clasped both of his hands around the paper cup and walked over to one of the nearby white pillars. He leaned up against it and sighed. His eyes scanned the room rapidly, watching carefully for anyone who would come in. So far, only the usual blonde-haired girl, who was surprisingly tall for an American, came out to put more plates on the table, which included the honey-scented baklava.

He looked back down to his cup of coffee, the ripple circling around his cup, waiting to be halted, waiting to stop and reach perfect stillness within these paper walls. Peace finally reached the cup, and the ripples were stilled, as his trembling hand was now stilled. He at last brought the cup to his lips and sipped on the hot liquid. He let it settle on his tongue and immediately swallowed the first sip. *It tastes like—*

"Hey, what's up, man? It's great to see you!" came a cheerily familiar voice.

He looked up from his cup. He smiled back at Michael, who had a white button-up shirt that was buttoned just below his neck and khakis. "Hi," Ted said softly. "Just drinking a coffee."

"Yeah, I hear you. With all that's happened lately, I bet you're ripping your hair out," Michael said. "Fortunately, I'll be fine, but my conversations are now being recorded over there. I mean, it's not like I actually have anything to hide. I don't have any national secrets."

"Too bad. I wouldn't mind hearing them." Ted laughed. He couldn't scan the room as well if he was distracted by talking to Michael. "Honestly, it's not that bad. It just greatly affects who I can and can't deal with. I can easily move assets around. It's not that hard. After all, they say that if you look at the nations who rose and fell, you can predict the future. I find the same to be true for wars."

"Yeah. I know you mentioned you were in the Army. That must give you a different perspective on what's going on. Maybe you're seeing what I'm not," Michael went on. "Do you think it's something I should be worried about?"

"Not really," Ted replied. "Economically, it'll be a disaster. However, it wouldn't take too long to change and get things back on track once the dust is settled. At least, most likely. That is just a guess. I just happen to be very good at guessing."

"So I've heard. And you seem to be very lucky." Michael continued to smile that welcoming smile. Michael's hands were at his sides, but not in his pockets.

We were never allowed to have our hands in our pockets, but I don't recognize you. Never mind. You were too young; even if you were, I wouldn't have known you. You are inconsequential.

"Some of my old comrades called me the Amazing Doctor, as it appeared I could tell the future. I was only ever wrong once," he said dryly, his tone dropping. He hoped Michael hadn't noticed.

"You don't sound too thrilled." Michael frowned.

"Yeah, you could say that." Ted never abandoned his smile. "Sometimes luck ain't all it's cracked out to be. Sometimes luck is just a little more than a curse. For example, I wished I'd guessed wrong on one deal, because the profit margin would have been exponentially higher than if I guessed correctly," he explained. *Yeah, that's how I'll explain it.* "But money isn't everything. I have enough of it as it is. I really don't need anymore. I just do it now to keep busy. I really don't have a high cost of living."

"Well then." Michael chuckled.

"Michael, you didn't strike me as the making friends-type." Jennifer snuck up on them. Her hair was combed, and she had it tied with a red scrunchy. She was wearing a green shirt paired with some gym shorts. "Seriously, how long have you been here?"

Now that Ted had a better look at her, she looked oddly familiar. Seeing her in the bright light of the Fellowship Hall was both a blessing and a curse. She looked uncannily like his fiancé, before her passing. The appearance was the same, sure, but Jennifer was a little taller than her. *Let the dead stay dead.*

"Not long, maybe five minutes." Michael smiled back at her as he wrapped his arm around her shoulders.

"Well then, Ted, welcome back to our dysfunctional family!" She sipped her cup of coffee while she was juggling a plate with baklava. She looked at Ted and then down to both of his hands. "No baklava?"

"No, I haven't had the chance to grab it." Ted smiled at her as he took another sip of the coffee. *Now, what is it you want?*

"What? Michael, hold my things!"

She shoved her cup of coffee, plate, and plastic fork into Michael's hands. He still didn't have his own cup of coffee, and this flustered Michael before regaining his balance with the new items in his hands. Unfortunately, some of her coffee spilled over the side of the cup and onto his hands.

"Well, as you can quite imagine, she can be a handful." Michael chuckled. "She can be overbearing at times, but we love her all the same."

"I can see that," Ted said. His pupils scanned the room immediately again as more and more people started pouring into the Fellowship Hall.

"You know, you wouldn't think she would be a social butterfly, or even this vibrant as a scientist, but there's always that one who will be unique among them," Michael said, staring at his coffee-covered hand.

"Yes. I've come across those myself," Ted explained. "There's always exceptions if you know where to look."

Jennifer came back with a plate of baklava and a fork. "Ted, this is for you. This stuff is homemade! You can't come here and *not* have it!" She presented it with a bright smile.

Ted reluctantly released his hand from his cup and grabbed hold of the plate, watching the people in the room carefully, memorizing every face, every verbal exchange he could see, as he studied each facial expression and their changes. He could tell when they were sad, and when they were happy. The faces had stretched smiles, and the light twinkled in their eyes, the dimples in their cheeks shone brightly, and their smiles didn't seem to have much effort behind them, like these smiles were genuine. Ted wondered, why weren't they miserable? How happy could they actually be?

"Come on. Take a bite!" Jennifer smiled enthusiastically at him. "You must tell me how it is."

"Why are you fixated entirely on the baklava? You didn't even make it," Michael said. "Come on, let the guy eat it at his pleasure. Sheesh. You'd think you're some raving chef shoving food they're allergic to down their throats. Like Tim."

"Excuuusse me!" Jennifer raised her voice to Michael. "Well, I was clearly talking to Ted. Now, perhaps I wouldn't have to be over the top if you weren't romanticizing your own bromance."

"What?" Michael's jaw dropped and his head shook in disbelief.

"You've been hogging his attention for five minutes! I want a turn to pry into that little cage trap of a brain he's got."

Ted's heartbeat raced inside his chest. He felt his palms accumulate sweat. *If anyone was going to crack me open, it would be you.*

"I'll let you two have your privacy. I'm sure you'll want to be alone." Michael gave Jennifer her coffee and baklava plate back.

"Thank you." She handled them with care, taking a sip of her coffee.

"Why would I want that?" Ted protested, never losing that tremendous smile of his. He mustn't appear nervous, as nervous as she was making him. *Is she going to trigger me?* He fought his hand's sudden urge to tremble.

"Ah, I'm sure I'll see you around. Come hang out with our group. Like Jennifer said, it's a little dysfunctional." Michael laughed, using this excuse to get away from Jennifer.

"So, I hear you're a scientist?" Ted asked.

"Now, now, eat your baklava first. And tell me how it is. Then we can talk."

He snickered. "You're putting a lot of effort into trying to make me give baklava a chance."

"You know it." She smiled and waved a finger at him. "Now eat up, mister."

He took a small bite of the baklava. The sticky honey dripped on his tongue, a taste he was certain was supposed to be sweet, but alas, it tasted like nothing. He could also feel the enthusiastic piercing stare coming right in front of him. "So, tell me how it is!"

"It's delicious," he lied to her. "I thoroughly enjoyed it. Thank you." He moved his focus to his coffee.

She looked up to the ceiling. "Well, I suppose you *could* call me a scientist, but I am more of a researcher than anything."

He sipped his coffee. "And what's your area of expertise?"

"Biology. I study organisms, viruses, bacteria. An old man once said, 'The more germs I get, the happier I am'! I suppose that sums me up pretty nicely, now that I think about it. Oh well; one can't exactly marry a germ, but they keep me plenty of company."

"I can't tell if you're eccentric, or objectively insane," Ted joked.

"Well, excuuuse me good sir," she said, pressing her forefinger to his lips. "Are you accusing me of being socially ambiguous?"

He retracted his head from her fingers, shaking his head. He paused a moment and smiled back at her. "Absolutely," he retorted, unsure if this little interaction of her touching his mouth was appropriate. He couldn't be certain.

"Well, good," she chuckled, taking a bite out of her own baklava. "That's what I was going for!"

"Alright," came a loud, booming voice. Ted immediately turned his head to the nearby speaker. He saw a man in his thirties who also looked to be a little tired, though not nearly as tired as Ted was. He was holding a microphone and speaking into it. "Alright, welcome to Café. My name is. . ."

Ted tuned out the speaker. He had little patience for long monologues. His eyes started scanning the room again. Some people, like him, were not paying attention to the speaker, like they didn't need to; as if they'd heard the same thing a million times. Over and over and over again. He looked closely at the exit.

He noticed Samantha there, chatting with someone else. She had a cup of coffee, but not the baklava. *Perhaps she's dieting. Or came in too late to make her way to the food. Doesn't matter.* She was leaning against the doorway.

Ted tuned back in.

"If this is your first time, we'd like to welcome you. Of course, you are most welcome to join any of the open small groups here, but if this is your first time, I recommend joining our connecting group, led by our two leaders there. . ."

"Is your *family* part of that group?" Ted asked.

"Oh, yes." Jennifer had a playful smile, as if she remembered the punch line of some unrelated joke, then she giggled, "Shall we, Mr. Ted?"

"Absolutely," he replied. He walked with her, by her side, eyeing carefully for the trash can, drowned out by the large number of people. *So, people still believe in the faith, despite all the lack of faith in it. I wonder why? Is there something here that can quiet my mind?* He was nearly pushed to the side, and missed the last trash can, which was on the side of the door. He threw his cup and plate away with the rest of the baklava.

Eating is such a chore.

As Ted was nearly lost again in the crowd, Jennifer quickly grabbed his hand. He fought the urge to pull it away. Instead, he just let her have it, but he didn't hold her; his hand was limp in her grasp. They walked through the initial doorway back into the main hall, shifting just right past the elevators. He noticed a few people going into the elevators and entered the doorway to the left up some stairs. He followed Jennifer into the back of this part of the church where there were three additional rooms. They moved to the left, although he never took his mind off of each individual face that walked into those separate rooms.

The door to the room he entered was the only exit. The tables were arranged to form a boxy circle, creating the similar feeling of the hall having a bonfire in the middle of it. This was a place for friends. *I don't belong here. Why am I here?*

The ceiling stretched for what Ted could reasonably guess without a ruler was approximately fifteen feet high with a second floor. That floor was set up like an internal balcony. Looking down on him were rails and bookshelves that layered the room.

Tim waved; he was already sitting at the other end in the corner. Jennifer led Ted to the right corner, closer to the door, and close to the leader of the group. Samantha came in shortly with another girl who Ted didn't know. Michael came in and waved, trading a smile as he sat down next to Tim and immediately went into a side conversation.

The man leading the discussion looked at the clock hanging above the white board at the back of the room, and a woman, presumably his wife or other equivalent, wrote something on the board: 'Meaningless.' Both of them were casually dressed.

Well, I knew that already.

"Alright, so I see some new faces here," the man began, greeting new people as they came in. "So, let's get started while we have some stragglers coming in."

"Icebreaker, anyone?" the woman suggested. She looked up to the ceiling, her chin resting on her hand with her index finger resting above her nose.

"Well, I'll start. What's your name? Where are you from? What brings you to Boston? And uh, what do you wish you could see more of?" the man started, addressing the group sitting around the tables. "As you know, my name is Jack. I'm from Houston, Texas. I was brought to Boston through work. I work as a nuclear physicist at your local plant. No, it's not all that local." He chuckled to himself. "So, if there was one thing, I wish I could see more of? Good question, if I do say so myself. I suppose I could stand a little more rain."

Ted listened intently to everyone as they went around the room, telling their names, their wishes, where they were from, and their occupations. With a little more digging, he could find out exactly where and what times they worked. This was dangerous information being given so carelessly. They came from numerous states and numerous countries. He counted that there was at least one from each time zone in America, and nearly every ethnic group.

They, for one reason or another, didn't want to see any more from the world, but they desired to see less of something. They wanted less racism, less strife, less hunger, less war, less death, and less conflict. Without adding anything, by just omitting these things, they could obtain more peace, a perfect peace. *A peace like ten years ago. That bloody peace. If you take one conflict away, you are only enforcing another. It is all meaningless.*

"New guy. Hello? It's your turn. It's not time for bed yet!" Ted heard Jack's whimsical cry as the leader clapped his hands repeatedly.

"My apologies," Ted replied, returning that smile back to his face. *How long was I in that trance? This whatever it is, was taking control again in my mindlessness. I need to be better with it.* "My name is Ted. I'm from Ohio. I came to Boston for a change of pace. If I could see more of something. . ." his voice trailed off. "I can't think of anything."

"Nothing at all?" the woman asked.

Ted felt Samantha staring at him, and pointed his pupils towards her, seeing her frown as she studied him like he was some kind of rat in a maze. Jennifer nudged him with her elbow. A smile returned to her face. Ted blinked quickly with the sudden pressure assaulting his arm, and he felt the nerves in his fingers want to tremble.

"Come on, Ted." Jennifer pulled on his arm. "I know you want to see more. Everyone wants to see more of *something* in the world. What is it?"

"Now, now," he turned to her with his wide child-like smile. "I've seen plenty of the world already. If I saw any more of it, that would be downright selfish of me. I can't take in anymore of the world while the sights can be enjoyed by someone else."

"Well, I guess that's one way to look at the world." Jack chuckled.

"Well, if Ted doesn't want to say anything, he doesn't have to," the woman replied. "We are an open book, but we don't expect that of anyone here. Now, Ecclesiastes."

"Yes, one of my favorites," Tim commented.

"You would say that," Michael joked.

They studied the first chapter, and all Ted gleaned from it, was that everything was meaningless in life. Every dollar one made, every friend he made, relationship maintained, career goals, life goals, and everything in between, whatever they were, was all meaningless. All those things were meaningless. *I already know that.*

Yes, Ted had money, he had a house. It was all pointless, and he knew it. He knew the feeling all too well. And he didn't care for any of it. He didn't work for money, after all; just for something to do, something to keep him busy from his own thoughts. It was all pointless.

His hand started to tremble. *No. Not now! Damnit! You stay still.* He put his trembling hand in his pocket.

"Well, now, we don't like to popcorn it up here. We'll split up into smaller groups of three or four and offer prayer requests," Sarah explained.

The chairs were rapidly moved into numerous smaller circles. Ted felt uneasy as his hand wouldn't stop trembling, however, he kept the trembling to a bare minimum. Even a sniper couldn't have told how slowly his hand trembled, even though it felt to him like a speeding bullet.

Ted was in a circle with Jennifer, and Erin. He looked at them with his bright smile. He was careful; he always was when dealing with circles like this. His ears would be his eyes, and he could sense the room, every movement, every noise. No sound, no matter how little, would escape his ears, just like nothing and no one could escape the defense of his mind's eye. He was as he'd always been, ever watchful, but no longer by his own choice. He'd become so conditioned to it that it just turned on. This was the exact reason he'd failed at his one goal, that same goal he'd given up on, he kept failing. Again, and again, and again!

"So, this is the part where we wear our emotions on our sleeves," Jennifer explained. "Forgive me if I sound like a tour guide." She turned her head to Erin. "Prayer request?"

Erin frowned. "I—I do," she stammered. Her voice was solemn; her head was bowed down low. Her eyes were wide open, staring blankly at the floor, as if what she was looking for was buried below the bowels of the church. Her thighs were closed shut, and her elbows met her stomach, one hand wrapped around her other fist. She kept them close to her, as if holding in some secret desire she longed to keep hidden. Her right heel rose from the ground, and then rested back down. Again, and again, and again. "My mother was di—diagnosed with stage four liver cancer." Tears streamed down her face; she began coughing and tearing up.

Ted tried to look concerned. He noticed something else. He would have thought there would have been others around who would have rushed to console her weeping. But at last, he found that she was not the only one weeping in the room. There was at least one other person in the additional small groups weeping, likely due to some cruel hand fate had given them. *Like the hand I was dealt.* It was also the first time he'd ever noticed Jennifer not enthused. She wrapped her arm around Erin and pulled her close. She said nothing. She just let Erin cry over her shoulder. That was a prayer in and of itself. Words needed not say more.

Should I really be caring about this right now? No.

Ted did his best to show his concern, however. He retained that smile. He moved his chair a little closer and put his hand on Erin's back.

"Ted," Jennifer began, shedding her own tear. "Before I begin, do you have something to pray for?"

"Nothing that cannot wait. This is more important, I think," he answered. *But is she?*

"Okay, then please, but don't feel pressured, bow your head."

Erin's head was already bowed down low, and tears dripped down from those closed eyelids. Jennifer's tears were more controlled as she bowed her head. Ted bowed his head down, but he didn't close his eyes. He kept his eyes focused, his pupils continuing to scan the room. The rest, as if they'd all received the order from the same commanding officer, had their eyes closed and heads bowed. Most were holding hands.

He immediately wiped a tear from his face. *Is this genuine? No. It can't be.*

"Amen," Jennifer finished her prayer. Ted had tuned out the entire prayer, as he'd been focused on his own individual thoughts and the behavior of everyone in the room. One by one these prayerful people raised their heads up, opening their eyes. Many of them were happy, as if a burden had been lifted from their miserable chests. *How?*

The room was filled with chatter again. *Thank God.* The silence irritated him. He found that he could no longer keep tuning everything out, not in the silence, not like this. Silence was much better when lives were on the line. He looked around the room again. Some people were getting up and putting their chairs right back towards the tables to leave. Some of them left in pairs, and others left by themselves after finishing their conversations.

He sought to do the same. He got up before his hand was grabbed by Jennifer. "Hey." She wiped her face clean of tears with her free sleeve. "I told you we wear our feelings on our sleeves here. I hope we didn't scare you off."

"Miss Jennifer, I'm afraid it will take a lot more than that to scare me off," he lied, turning to Erin with a solemn face as she was still weeping and wiping tears from her face with her palms. "I am sorry. Truly, I am."

"I-it's not your fault." She looked to him, "You don't have to be sorry. Buh-but I appreciate it."

"Now," he turned without skipping a beat, returning that smile to his face, "I must really be going."

"You're not coming out with us tonight?" Jennifer frowned.

"Not tonight. Maybe next time," he said. He tried to pull away, but Jennifer wouldn't let go.

"Wait. Let me get your phone number," she said.

"As you wish, milady," he spoke dryly.

"My, my, aren't you the romantic?" She pulled out a pen and piece of paper from her purse and handed it to him. He immediately wrote down a phone number on the piece of paper and handed it back to her. "At least you're honest about it. Unlike some men." She took out a piece of paper and wrote her own phone number on it. "Here, take mine."

"It's a pleasure." He took the phone number and placed it in his wallet.

"Now, now, Tedward." She smiled at him. "I think you know the pleasure is all mine."

"Of course it is." He smiled back. *You have no idea how true that is.* "Maybe I'll see you next week or around. But I must be going."

"Good night, Ted," Jennifer said.

Samantha transitioned from her seat, pushing it in and briskly walking towards them, trying to catch up to Ted. How good of a host could she be, if she didn't at least make the effort to make sure he was comfortable? After all, it was her who'd invited Ted to the study. However, he made a beeline for the door, at a brisk pace she knew she couldn't keep up with. She glanced over at Jennifer, who turned to Erin. For a moment, Samantha thought that perhaps Jennifer had come on too strongly for Ted's comfort, prompting an exit. Or perhaps something else was going on with Ted. Something unseen.

"Are you coming out tonight? If you are, I believe it's my turn to buy you one." Jennifer's hand wrapped around Erin's shoulder.

"I think I need a break," Erin said. "I need some rest, actually. Maybe next week. I just—I just need to get some sleep. Start fresh in the morning."

"What's wrong?" Samantha turned her gaze towards Erin, noticing wiped tears and reddened eyes. She placed her hand on Erin's back, rubbing it.

"My mother has stage four," Erin said abruptly.

Samantha felt a sudden weight fill her chest as she covered her mouth with her hand. "I'm so sorry. I'll pray for that, and healing for her."

"Some rest will do you good. I understand, Erin," Jennifer said. "I'll put your chair away. Don't worry about it. If you need someone to talk to, you can always text or call me."

"Thanks." Erin stood to leave.

Michael followed and put her chair away. He smiled at Jennifer. "So, how did it go?" he asked.

"My dear Michael, whatever do you mean?" Jennifer snickered as she pushed her chair back in.

"You got him alone." Samantha shuddered as Michael mansplained himself to reiterate the obvious. It was one of her pet peeves. *I'll work on that.*

"Well, I certainly couldn't let you hog him. Besides, I don't think he'd care to listen to more of your business monologue." Jennifer gave him a slightly annoyed glare. "I suppose we can finish this up at Terri Nation. Let's be off. I have very important business at Terri's Empire."

"Only you can make it sound that much better than it actually is." Tim chuckled, shaking his head.

Samantha, Jennifer, Michael, and Tim followed the crowd out of the room and back toward the lobby, where there seemed to be an abundance of people talking with each other like old friends.

Samantha always found it interesting that these people felt so close. Even if they were only apart for a single week, to her, every Tuesday seemed like a reunion. They briskly exited the church and recruited a few people to go out. Not that they needed to do that—Brian would take care of it, as he always did—but it was good to show interest to the newcomers.

Samantha and her immediate friends walked to Terri Nation and headed toward the back end of the bar. It was much less crowded than the previous week. Perhaps there was something foul in the air. Samantha did notice four unique individuals by the bar, toward the end of it where she'd met Ted the week before. Two men and two women having strong gin. They were talking to one another in a variety of accents. That was what got her attention. Samantha picked one up as Irish, and the other English, and one she could only guess as Russian. The fourth wasn't quite Russian, but it had a similar sound to that of the eastern European countries. It would seem odd, since Russia had declared war on neighboring countries as of late, and these individuals were speaking to each other as if there was no animosity between their nations. She found it most peculiar.

Scott made their drinks. Samantha was drinking a dark beer this time, and Tim was held off with a white wine sangria. And of course, Michael and Jennifer got whatever the special was. This one he served in bola glasses.

"So, Scott, what have we the pleasure—" Michael began.

"Or displeasure," Jennifer added.

"—of drinking today?" Michael finished. They drank well together. Tim and Samantha were smiling, as it was rare that they could get that close together with the two of them. They paired well together, like a fluffernutter sandwich. Their banter bounced off one another like they had been friends for years, but truth be told, they'd only known one another for a year, and they'd all met there at that bar through Café.

"It was some recipe I found on some website," Scott answered as he printed out separate slips. Jennifer already took a sip. Samantha guessed she enjoyed it with the way Jennifer rubbed her buttocks against the stool. "I don't know much about it, but last time it was made a lot of people died." There was silence. Scott turned around. "I'm kidding. It's vodka, chocolate, and seltzer. Nothing too fancy. I may have put some basil in there."

"Oh my God! I am allehgic to freaking basil!" Jennifer joked. Scott's eyes lit up in surprise, like he was looking at a dead person.

"Isn't that my line?" Tim laughed as he brought up his glass to sip his sangria.

Jennifer placed two fingers on her lips as she looked Scott in the eye mischievously. "Two can play at that game."

"Okay, cool." Scott laughed it off as he walked backwards toward his other guests, giving them two thumbs up.

"Alright, you've kept me in enough suspense. Now that you've had him all to yourself, what was he like?" Michael asked.

"Yes. I am dying to know. Spill the beans, Jenn!" Samantha pushed.

"Whoa, whoa, whoa." Tim put his hands up defensively. "You leave my beans out of this. It wasn't my fault."

"No, Tim, it wasn't your fault. And we're certainly not talking about your beans," Michael jeered. "Besides, that was actually some good chili. Jenn, spill it!"

"Fine." Jennifer took another sip. "Really nothing more than what he shared with the rest of the group during that very questionably boring icebreaker."

Samantha pondered with the fresh liquor to her nose. She remembered something which she'd neglected to mention previously, though perhaps a sensitive question: "Jennifer, did you make note of the scars on his face?"

"I did notice those scars, like lines or streaks across his cheeks. I didn't say anything. That isn't something you want to ask someone who hardly knows you," Jennifer said, trading that playful smile of hers for droopy eyelids. "Your brain is working. What is on that mind?"

"I haven't formulated a complete thought. I'll have to get back to you." Sam's gaze shot back to the other end of the bar.

"Did he have something to do? He seemed in a hurry to leave." Tim's smile faded.

"Yeah, I wondered about that," Samantha commented, turning back to Jennifer.

"Well, he didn't say. I was able to snag his number before his prompt getaway."

"Getaway. Yes, that's the appropriate word for it," Michael poked fun at Jennifer again. "It's hard to escape your clutches."

"I wonder if it had anything to do with the study." Samantha wondered if that had been the most appropriate study for someone in a field fueled by money.

"Could be. Honestly, it isn't the best first book for someone. After all, a wise man once said, 'Meaningless, meaningless, it's all meaningless!'" Jennifer raised her hands in the air as she sat back down on her stool and crossed her fingers.

"Well," Samantha said. "Tell us how you really feel."

They all looked at Jennifer, waiting for her whimsical response.

"My thoughts on the matter are all entirely 'meaningless.'" Jennifer smiled.

Michael, Tim, Jennifer, and Samantha all laughed at the joke. It was ironic, and certainly the lesson could have been very depressing if taken out of context. After all, not everything was meaningless.

Samantha could feel her hair standing on end. Her hands remained in place as the ripples in her cup of beer moved towards the edges of the glass. She looked closely. Tim and Michael didn't seem to notice. Jennifer put on her sweatshirt in response to the chill. *Where is this coming from?*

She looked at the strangers in the bar. She noticed that one of them, the taller man with the Irish accent, appeared to be flicking his fingers back and forth, violently tapping against a piece of paper on the bar top. She looked back down to her cup and drank some more. She fixed her eyes back on the man and the piece of paper was gone. *I'm not that drunk, am I? I hope not. I've barely had a drink.* Was she imagining it? The paper was gone, and the man didn't appear to be tapping anything anymore. The man wore a black suit to match the lengthy black hair tied behind his back.

"You okay there, Sam?" Jennifer glanced at her and tossed her head back.

"No. Yes," she corrected herself. "I just thought I saw something. It's nothing."

"Soooo," Jennifer began.

"Are you okay or not?" Michael asked, putting his hand on his hip disapprovingly. "I'm beginning to worry about you."

Samantha moved her gaze back over to the strangers. "I thought I saw one of them violently tapping a piece of paper. The tall one," she whispered.

Michael shifted his attention toward them, hiding his body and face behind Samantha just enough to avoid looking suspicious. "Are you sure it isn't the air conditioning going down again? You've mentioned this numerous times now. I really don't believe a person could be the cause of it. Besides, tapping a piece of paper isn't exactly unusual."

"I—I'm not sure," she replied.

"Well, only one way to find out," Michael said. He took her hand.

"Michael! Wait! What are you doing?"

He ignored her as he pulled her to the strangers. One of the women there looked at them and smiled; she had a very youthful face with red eyes. Samantha found her eyes to be especially peculiar, unless… was she high? The tall man looked surprised and turned to them. There was an unpleasant scowl on his face.

"Well, well, well, what sort of beast have we ensnared?" he said in his Irish accent.

"Well, we're here every single Tuesday night, and haven't seen you here before. Me and my friend here would like to say hi and introduce ourselves. My name is Michael. This is Samantha. Sam for short." Michael introduced the two of them charmingly.

"Hii!" Samantha introduced herself awkwardly. No matter how hard she tried, she didn't do well in friendly social situations. She was great on the phone, though.

"Okay," the man said. "And to what do we owe the unfortunate circumstance of such a forced introduction?"

"Culain, I do not want another repeat from last week's escapade," said the girl with black hair. She was the one with the Russian accent. "Please, it was a mess. We don't need another one."

"As you wish, Ilya," he replied, before returning a sneering smile toward them. "Now, I don't know what it is you think you saw, but you didn't see anything. I don't know what you think you felt, but it was nothing. You don't know anything. Now, kindly piss off!"

"Wow!" Michael replied nonchalantly. "I was just being friendly. There was no reason to be rude. And what we—"

"What you think you saw was nothing. Now, before I lose my temper, kindly piss off," the man called Culain said. "The less you know, the better."

"Michael, let's go." Samantha pulled on his arm and shrank back behind him. She didn't trust them, nor did they—or at least the man called Culain—seem like people she wanted to be friends with. Culain seemed like a man that would sooner hurt you and then make you apologize for inconveniencing those around you. Michael nodded to her and turned around, pulling her back to their quartet.

He seemed unnecessarily rude and unprovoked. There was so much anger in his voice, despite that smile. There was a raw emotion to his tone, as if we were less than he was. It is wrong for me to judge the man. I don't know who he is or where he comes from, or what he's going through.

"There once was a couple in a bar; in life they hoped to get far. Thought they were destined, their ankles were nailed in. I needed their love to be marred," Culain mocked them as they retreated.

CHAPTER 4

The Empty House

~After all my years of living, I have only one regret: not strangling myself with my own umbilical cord. Now I can't even die right.

TED FORCED A SMILE, his eyelids getting heavy as he sat with his bag resting on his lap on the subway. At 9:00 PM, the redline was fairly crowded riding towards Alewife. Listening intently, he rested his head back as he sat, watching everyone on this subway, hoping not to see any familiar faces. He noted the diverse population on the subway, white, black, Hispanic, Asian, male, female. There was a significant diversity in the socioeconomics of the people on the train; some seemed to be struggling families with old, fading purses, while others seemed to be well off, dressed professionally with pressed clothes and makeup. Some of these people were alone, just monitoring something of no value on their phones as they were glued to their screens. Some were coupled up, talking to one another. Some kids had their faces lit up by their parents' phones while the parents leaned their heads back, hoping to get a moment's rest. He saw many isolated single people curving their lips into smiles. Some of them wore their smiles genuinely, while the smiles of others were blank and lifeless.

He kept his trembling hand in his right pocket. He smiled as he inconspicuously watched everyone. Many people here had no quarrel with one another; however, many buried their wretched faces into their terribly cursed hands. They had no problem with showing their emotions to such strangers. Perhaps they knew that they would never see anyone on this train ever again. The sense of anonymity was appealing, but something Ted dared not risk.

The next stop came. Many people walked off at Harvard Station. Fewer people walked on. These were students and professors. The professors immediately opened their briefcases as they sat down and worked on grading or additional source material for another class they were teaching. The students were busy talking, and he noticed one in particular, a girl who looked like she should still be in high school. She put on her headphones and sat at the end, pulling her knees up to her chest and wrapping her arms around them to keep them close. She stared down the train with an empty expression on her face.

He felt like he was looking at someone familiar. The face, the hair, the stance, and that damn blank stare. There was nothing inside her. No happiness, no sadness, no hope. It was like she was tired of sharing her smile, jaded from putting up with the damn façade called life, but also not particularly open about showing her despair to others; she might not want to inconvenience anyone with her self-erasure. The emptiness he knew all too well. The emptiness was hungry, and it ate happiness and hope like a pig. Why bother, as hope was only a façade: all it was was postponed disappointment. It only ended one way: with despair.

He looked away from her and turned to look out of the window in front of him. The subway started moving again. His forced smile met that of another tired woman, probably in her thirties. Over a decade older than him, he presumed. She also looked tired, brushing away her ragged blonde hair out of her face. Her eyes, like his, were sunken in, but she made an effort to smile back at him.

He tried to navigate his gaze away from her and to an inanimate object. He found a convenient advertisement on the pole. It was an ad to a show on Broadway. The show looked like people would be entertained, with a group of ethnically diverse characters wearing a variety of clothing. Their faces were brightly lit, and smiles painted across their lips, and they even had a twinkle in their eyes, or he imagined they were twinkling at the time that the picture was taken for the advertisement. He only found a handful of people that shared that same twinkle, just a little spark of light in their souls, and yet, with everything moving, he felt trapped in this train. He envied the people in the picture; not their clothes, not their smiles, but that little twinkle of light, that happiness or joy or whatever it was. That was what he was after. He saw the same twinkle in Sam's eyes, in Jennifer's and in Michael's, but he couldn't be around them.

He waited patiently as the subway came to Davis Square. The doors opened and he scanned the train again. Everyone was laughing as they were walking off. From their jerseys and backpacks, some satchels and purses, he assumed these were college kids going to some party or a nearby bar. He followed them out. He walked through the dimly lit concrete corridors to the escalators, then out to the fresh breeze of Davis square. Cars were honking their horns and buses were dropping people off in droves. He walked through the Square onto College Avenue.

He looked up at the sky. Like the girl on the train, it was empty of clouds and stars. Feeling the oppressive moon mock him, he walked on. His trembling hand remained in his pocket, and he kept his smile bright and wide as he blankly stared at the sidewalk on which he walked. His heart raced inside his chest and sweat dripped from his palms.

He walked down five kilometers. He came to a blue house with white trim on the door and windows. He walked up the steps and put his key into the keyhole. The door creaked as he opened it. The lights were out, as they should be. He stepped into the house and closed the door. He locked the knob lock. He turned the mechanism for the bolt lock. It clicked shut. He lifted the chain to lock the door with its third lock.

He turned around and leaned against the door. He dropped his bag to the floor, and it sounded like a rock hitting the ground. He let out a sigh as he leaned back against the door.

His smile began to fade as his lips curved downwards. He gritted his teeth as he stifled a noise from his mouth. His face crinkled as tears streamed down the sides of it. He felt his knees tremble; his feet slid from underneath him. His body struck the ground, and both of his hands were in front of him, trembling uncontrollably. He clamped his eyes shut as he cried out. He put one hand over his heart, clenching his shirt.

He took heavy breaths and choked on his sobs, but the tears never stopped rolling down his face. His weak knees struggled to pull him back up. It was unlike someone from Task Force 7 to allow such an inconvenience to bring him to a halt. He *willed* his knees to be fixated and forced himself to stand up.

He *willed* the first step. He couldn't stop sobbing, his tears dripping from his face to the empty hardwood floor. He felt nerves snapping throughout his body, physically telling his body he was in pain, but he never felt the pain itself. He took regulated-interval breaths as the tears came down.

He *willed* his second step, and he put out his arm to the wall, leaning against it.

He scanned the room hastily, looking for something to use to walk around. He couldn't do it himself with the constant trembling inside his body like earthquakes. He was in his living room. The floor was almost bare. There were no bookcases, no TV, no radio, no coffee table, nor any other furniture on the ground. There were no pictures on the walls There were only two things: a display case, and a noose on the floor, cut up into pieces as it was worthless to him; he couldn't use it effectively. Inside the display case was where he kept certain items of personal value, half of which would have been absolutely useless to everyone else. Otherwise, the room looked like he'd just moved in today without the moving boxes.

Inside the display case was a spear. The spear he could use. It was the same spear Metal had used. He remembered Metal reaching out for hard-to-reach places with his scrawny little arms when he was just a kid. The red handle of the spear was wood and had some faded written markings upon it. The spearhead was rusted, and Ted couldn't find a way to restore it safely, not without being caught. He'd actually been surprised to find the spear shortly after the nuclear meltdown in Area 51 eight years ago.

He *willed* his third step. He cried out as his knees gave out again, as the oppressive mockery of the damned moonlight entered his house, beating down on him. The burden of this was too heavy for his knees to bear, even his iron will was not enough to *will* himself back up as he tumbled forward, hitting his head on the ground.

"Why?" he sobbed. He reached out his right hand and pulled himself towards the display case. "Why? Damnit!" He reached out with his left hand and pulled himself closer across the empty living room. "I did everything you told me to!" He reached out his right hand and pulled himself closer, the tears came down so hard, they were missing his face and merely dripping on the floor. His shirt became wet with his tears as he dragged himself across it. "Damnit! I hate you!" His voice was like that of a child, disappointed in their father or mother for bringing him into this cruel world. "Was that not enough? I didn't have much to take anyway. Why did you take them from me?" He continued to grit his teeth together as he pulled himself closer and closer to the display case.

He finally reached the display case. He pulled himself up, his tears dripping onto the glass. He leaned against the wall and pulled out another key from his pocket. His hand trembled as he tried to get it into the keyhole. The key trembled in his fingers and fell to the ground. It struck the ground with a force; the noise was so heavy he could feel it. He took a heavy breath, and slowly let it out. "Fuck it," He took his free hand and made a fist. He slammed his hand into the display case, cracking the glass. Shards went everywhere. His arm was bleeding, and his knuckles became raw with the impact.

His hand reached for the spear, then froze in place, hovering over it. His tears still streamed down, and his eyes stretched open when he came to the sudden realization, reacting to the shards of glass imbedded in his flesh. He could see the red, warm blood cascading down his arm. "I—I still can't feel it," he said silently to himself. "Iah—I can't feel anything. I can't feel anything anymore." He grabbed the spear, and it trembled in his hands. He pulled it out of the display case and put the haft of it against the hardwood floor, with the rusty spearhead raised up to the ceiling.

The unwanted emotions flooded him again, as if there was nothing in between them. He struggled as his knees became weak again as he made his way to the kitchen. He took deep breaths with every staggering step.

He found the wastebasket by the doorway into the kitchen. The wastebasket was filled with empty plastic cups and plastic silverware and paper plates. He avoided the basket and made it into the kitchen.

The kitchen was just as bare. The cupboards were disheveled. There was no kitchen table nor chairs. The counters were empty apart from a roll of paper towels and napkins. There was nothing like a toaster, toaster oven, or even a coffee maker on his counter. It was bare. The sink was the only thing that had anything else in it. There were dirty pans.

He managed to get himself to the sink. He reluctantly took his hand off his spear and reached into one of the empty cupboards. He took out a sponge and put soap on it and ran the hot water. He scrubbed the dirty pans clean, slowly putting everything into it, doing whatever he could to distract himself from his thoughts. *Anything!*

He was dismayed that nothing would empty his mind. He cried even louder. His tears fell into the sink, splashing on the pans. He cleaned the last frying pan and threw it at the wall. It made a loud noise as it stuck into the wall, just hanging there.

He gasped as he suddenly remembered the noose that he'd made for himself in the living room. He'd hung there last night, but as if some fluke of nature, he'd phased through the noose.

Ted firmly tied the noose, hanging it from his ceiling, giving it a strong tug to ensure it would hold him. The rope was thick and sturdy enough, but one could never be too careful to make sure it was done right. After all, this was going to be the last attempt; either he would succeed, or he would just give up trying. Satisfied, he grabbed one of his kitchen chairs and planted it underneath the noose. Stepping on the chair, he slipped his head through the noose. He used his hands to tighten it around his neck. Exhaling, he kicked the chair out from under himself.

He fell; the rope held him. He felt the air to his lungs restrict, and he felt that unwelcome refreshment of the essence yet again filling his body. His arms jerked at his sides as the grey veins protruded over his skin. Air was completely exiled out of his body, and he felt his consciousness wane. If only it was that simple. Another type of essence entered his body, and the veins darkened from gray to black as he phased through the noose. Another failed attempt. And, as promised, the last one.

That was the last straw. *I can't even die right!* He stared at the frying pan, stuck into the wall like a knife. He sighed as he turned and leaned against the sink. His head was raised up as the streams never stopped coming down. He was a slave to his own thoughts, and his master was relentless!

His trembling hands went back into his pockets. He took out his wallet and opened it. He found a picture and took it out. He opened up the folded photo. His hand trembled as he looked on sixteen faces in military uniforms. All of them were of the same height, half of them male, and the other half female. One of the women was wrapping her arms around the waist of someone else.

That other someone was himself; his own face was scratched out of the picture.

He sucked in some air, clamping his teeth down. The tears rolled down a little faster onto the photo. *This fate is cruel.* He allowed his feet to slowly slip from under him. He looked closely at the photo. Their uniforms all had their number "7" on the patches, right above where the charging American flag would have been—that is, if they hadn't been forbidden from wearing it. He glared up at the ceiling. *You mock me.*

He trembled, pulling himself from the ground. He leaned towards the sink again, glancing at the frying pan stuck in the wall. He took his spear and used it to walk, however shakily, toward another room. It was dark. He turned on the light.

The room was large and square, and just like every other room in the house, it was next to empty. It had only two things in it: a sleeping bag with no pillow and a safe. That was it. Even the paint on the walls was bland and passionless.

He walked over to the safe and laid the spear to the side of his sleeping bag. He turned the knob of the safe to open it. There was no money, and nothing that anyone would find of value to steal. He pulled out a notebook and turned to a blank page. He brought a black inked pen to the page, where it froze in place as his hands trembled again. He gritted his teeth once more, and his face twisted from abstract tormented sadness to nothing short of an ungodlike rage.

At last, he put the quivering pen to the page:

> *My name. My name. My name. Your name? What were they? Were they as generic as Michael or Samantha? Or were the names on your birth certificates more genuine, and more unique? I never knew your names. I don't even know what was written on mine.*
>
> *What were we? For years we lived together, and we never even got a proper serial number. We were insignificant.*

Too insignificant and too much of a burden for the common man to even come up with a name, or even a number. They didn't even care enough about us to assign us a number.

What were we to them? Nothing more than a tool? A valuable all-purpose tool? A tool that only has one use, to strive for that sense of purpose. We obtained that purpose, for even a short while, and now it's being ripped apart! Were we too expensive to keep around? Why even bother with us, then? I had but one wish, that this Hell could be undone. But what good of a world is that without conflict? We had no purpose without conflict. And we got rid of the conflict. We shot ourselves in the foot and watched it bleed!

Eight years it's been. Eight long damn years. I loved you. All of you. And I will never be able to tell that to your faces. I will never be presented with that gift, and now I am cursed to live in Hell. Yes, that is fitting for a wretch like me. Funny, isn't it? I've killed more people than I care to count. It's funny how someone like me can take life so easily. The first one was someone close to me. The first. That was the only one that truly mattered. Every single one after that became nothing but a statistic. Why, then? Why? Why do I still see their faces at night? Every single one of them? Can I not rip out my eyes? Then would I stop seeing them? No. I have no hope in that. Because now each face is seared into my brain.

I have no hope in life. I have no hope now in my living death. And I can't kill myself. I've tried too many times to count. Just the sadness of my heart. My heart, if I could rip it out to show the world, would be filled with scars and bullet holes, but the wretched thing still keeps pumping! It still keeps beating as if it itself is too stubborn to die. Why can't I be like normal people? If they are sick and tired of it, they hang themselves and die. Why must I be cursed with a living death, and cursed to fail every single attempt? Damn it! I can't die right!

This gift I have, I know not how I got it, or why. I don't even know if you had this gift, but I imagine you didn't. Not when I saw you being shot to shreds. Why can I fade through reality when you remain solid? I valued this gift enough when you were around because I needed to be alive to protect you, all of you. Now that you're gone, and I failed, why won't this just shut off and let me die?

What were your names? What was mine? We didn't have any. We didn't have any serial numbers. We weren't given any dog tags. We truly were given no identity, only to assume a fake one for the duration of your short lives, and for the rest of my cursed one. How fortunate you are to be dead right now. You can't feel anything. You have no heart, and I myself am nothing short of a monster filled with ancient regrets. No.

That's not true at all.

After all my years of living, I have only one regret: not strangling myself with my own umbilical cord. Now I can't even die right.

He closed the notebook. He placed it in the safe and locked it up. The notebook was the only thing keeping him grounded in the world. It was the only thing that allowed him to function every day. Those little reminders helped remind him of his own suffering. He got into his sleeping bag and leaned his phone against the safe. He put it on, so the clock was facing him.

There was no need to set an alarm for himself. There never was. Not anymore. His eyes were drifting to sleep, and the clock read: 10:23 PM. *Here we go. Again. And again. And again!* His eyes closed as he drifted to sleep.

CHAPTER 5

Area 51

~We were supposekjd to get married on Saturday, but for her, Saturday never came.

GHOST WAS WATCHING DOWNWIND in the arid heat. The day was still young; however, these past eight weeks had felt like four decades! The heat was dehydrating them all, and he was without sleep. He couldn't afford sleep, and neither could anyone else. Not with the overwhelming rattling of gunfire, the roaring of engines, and the tremors from the earth underneath the massive weight of the tanks.

This was supposed to be a training exercise, but it was something more than just that. This was no exercise; this was a massacre. His ACR rifle was beginning to jam up, and he was running low on ammunition. He wasn't around any useless bodies he could easily loot for more. And only God knew how many more there were out there.

Ghost, Ticker, Butcher, and Slithers were hiding in a crater out in the desert. It was no natural crater, but a crater built by artillery strikes aimed directly at them. The sand was scorching hot, much like what Ghost imagined death would be. His hands held his rifle tight as the noise began to die down.

He could feel the sand pouring down his back from the sides of the crater as numerous trucks drove by. The trucks were mounted with machine guns and bright flashing lights. He caught the sight of a car splattered with blood like someone poured a bucket of red paint on it. The windows were smeared in it, and even the wipers were coated in the flesh of someone who'd blown up nearby; most likely another useless grunt caught in friendly fire. For now, they were safe and out of sight in the crater; for how much longer, he could only guess.

"Ghost," Butcher whispered. She kept her hand on her rifle while pointing at him with three fingers. "What is going on?"

"For once, I don't know," he answered. His mind was rattled, still completely in the dark since the first shot. "And keep it down."

"Is everyone dead?" Slithers asked. Her hands were burying her face. Her face was smeared with blood, but it wasn't hers.

"Ghost." Butcher's voice trembled. "What did you do?" She pointed her rifle at him. "What did you do?"

Keeping low to the ground, he edged towards her, training his rifle on her in response. He was already on high alert; even the smallest form of hostility forced him to react immediately.

Ticker sighed and dropped his rifle to his side. "Look, right now, that doesn't matter," he interrupted their little squabble. "Look, we need to find a way to get away from this all. We were fools."

"What do you fuckin' know, Ticker?" Butcher demanded. She turned abruptly, face cringing as she spat on the ground.

"Don't you see? I pay attention. What are we? Soldiers. All we are is an expendable asset and nothing more. We are only tools to be used and then discarded. We should have seen this coming!" Ticker answered. "There haven't been any wars lately! Hell, we haven't been deployed in two years!"

Butcher drew her knife and was prepared to throw it.

"No," Ghost replied, his finger hovering over the trigger, careful never to touch it until he intended to fire. "Butcher, that is enough.

He's right. We should have—no. I should have seen this coming. I'm sorry."

"Captain," Ticker began. "Think of something get us out of here."

Suddenly, the radio coughed. *"Captain? Are you out there?"* the voice of Venom said. Her sweet innocent voice spoke loudly and trembled through the radio. *"Captain? Captain?"*

Venom was with one of four separate units of Task Force Seven had been split up into for this training exercise.

"Answer that!" Butcher stamped her boot in the hot sand.

"No," Ghost responded. He stood up as he scanned the blackened red horizon. "We can't, if we are going to get out of here."

"Everyone else is dead, damnit!" Butcher snapped again, her hand pointing a trembling finger at him. "How can you leave them to die like this?!"

"They are soldiers, just like we are," Ghost told her. "We have to trust that they'll make it out. Besides, they're listening at least. If we make it known someone else other than her is still alive, we're only asking for more trouble than we already have."

The radio crackled. "Captain? Is anyone out there? Is anyone there?"

"Then do you have a plan?" Ticker asked.

Ghost put his hand over his mouth as he bowed his head down toward the ground, scanning each independent grain of sand like each individual grain represented an idea. These ideas were innumerable and all bad. He sighed. "Well, we are going to need a distraction."

"God, no." Slithers looked up at him with wide, teary eyes. Her hand clenched his tightly. "You can't possibly be considering killing her?"

"What? No. I would never even think about killing her, or any of you for that matter. Something that our dear leader would consider without a second thought. No. We need to get to Area 51.

We'll blow up the pillars holding it in place, which will greatly affect the reactor below it."

"There are civilians nearby. Ghost, you are proposing desecrating the nearby cities. If we do this, we would be no worse than they. We would be murderers." Ticker looked at him with wide eyes. Ghost could tell that despite it all, he was not keen on getting innocent civilians killed, especially recreating Chernobyl.

"Look around you, Ticker. Like it or not, we are murderers. We are the orphan makers!" Ghost snapped at him. "I don't like it, but that is our one chance out of here. All other chances are gone and will lead to one-hundred percent failure. This has a chance of success, no matter how small."

"Yeah, and what is the success ratio?" Ticker asked.

"Half of a percent," Ghost said. "They have us right where they want us. We are out of food and water. We'll be dead before the day is out, whether by being shot or by natural means. We don't have the luxury of waiting for the perfect moment to strike. This is our only chance, and we need to take it, even if the odds were infinitely worse."

"A lot more people are going to die tonight," Ticker said, bowing his head with a graven face. "Is this what we've become?"

"The monsters and demons aren't hiding in our closets or under our beds. We'd be fortunate if they were that far away. How do you run from them when they're hiding in our heads?" Slithers asked. "We weren't born for this world. We were born with the sole purpose to live and fight for peace, and we've obtained it. Now there's no need for NATO anymore. There's no need for the military or hostile occupations. We've taken that need away. And now, we're meaningless. We were born with the sole purpose to live and die in obscurity." She wept softly. "Even if we did make it out, what would we even do? We have our lives ahead of us, and—and—and then what? We have no identity to stand on. We have no hope. We have no families; they're all gone. It will be impossible for us to integrate into society. We don't even know how they behave! Maybe it would be better if we all just lied down and died."

"Don't say that!" Butcher snarled, but even her harsh tone couldn't keep the tears out of her voice. "Don't you fucking say that again!"

"No." Ticker wept, wiping the tears with his sleeve. "She's right. Can't you see it now? We were damned from the start. We have no friends. We have no family. We have no name and no identity. We lived and trained together for sixteen years, and this is our end. This is a fucking tragedy if ever there was one. Can't you see it, how much better off the world would have been without us in it?"

Ghost caught a glimpse of Slithers as she bowed her head and folded her hands together, touching her forehead as if saying one final prayer. She said something so inaudible, he had to pull in the air towards his ears to hear. The soundwaves from her soft voice traveled swiftly into his ears. "Mommy, I never knew you, and the only contact I've ever had was coming out. I never got to hear your voice. I never got to see your face. I never got to see your smiles and laughter and never got to experience the good times with you. I'm sure you're a good person, a much better person than I ever came out to be. I—I'm sure you wouldn't want to see me. Not like this. Not a murderer."

Ghost knew Slithers was talking to her own genetic parents, not the parental units they each were assigned in their earliest memories. He had been dreadfully assigned the Nakamuras. None of them knew where they came from, nor what state they'd been born in. Any identifying records were lost. Ghost knew; he'd actually looked. There was nothing, as if just a blank slate.

Slithers sniffed her tears and snot back into her nose, then turned to Ghost and smiled. A smile; how cruel of a mask. It was like a bandage, a useless tourniquet. It covered up the wound, but the pain still remained. All the emotional baggage was hidden away behind the façade. Her smile was like the whitest bandage; pure, and utterly pointless. It was only a matter of time before nothing would remain of that bandage, except when it was dripping with crimson blood.

Slithers spoke. "Let's go. Let's go and make what's left of our lives count. We'll make it count for something, but for what, I don't know yet."

"To Area 51 it is, then," Ghost repeated himself, stone-faced. "If we die tonight, we'll make sure they won't soon forget us. If we die, we'll drag that base and everyone in it down into the depths of the blazing hot sand with us."

"We'll be walking into Hell," Butcher stated, resting her arms at her sides. She scanned the opposite side of the crater.

"You still don't see. We were born in it, destined to never leave," Ghost replied. His gaze narrowed.

The squad slowly climbed up the blazing hot crater. Ghost ensured that the radios would be silent. There was no longer a need to use them. The rest of Task Force 7 was dead, dying, or as good as dead.

Helicopters hovered in the air above, their blades spinning and dusting the sand in clouds. Soldiers in the helicopters aimed their rifles down toward the ground, as the choppers' searchlights swept the sand. The light was blinding in the middle of the artificial sandstorms caused by the helicopters' blades. The lights shone on Military vehicles and blown-up trucks. There was plenty of metallic debris stained with flesh and blood. A small unit of military vehicles drove through the sand, windows open, and rifles pointing out of them.

Ghost signaled the others to get on the ground. The heat was still getting to them, but they knew how to survive in worse conditions. They were completely buried underneath the sand, crawling through it like worms in the dirt. They proceeded to crawl due south, towards Area 51.

The humming of the trucks grew louder as they scratched their ears. The vibration of the earth pounded against their bodies. They managed to crawl over six kilometers.

Ghost inhaled *essence* from the air around, hearing a radio sound in the distance. "Task Force Seven spotted at Sector Eight." Immediately the vehicles revved up again, and many soldiers started whistling. The helicopters shifted direction, flying west. The vehicles started driving faster than before in the same direction.

Ghost waited patiently. The pressure was lifted from their bodies, and all the noises became distant. He immediately stood up from the sand, scanning the area with his rifle pointed down. Butcher, Slithers, and Ticker did the same.

"Well, that is lucky," Ticker said.

"That, or unfortunate," Slithers said.

"We need to start running," Ghost replied. "Our luck will eventually run out."

Ghost turned his radio on so he could listen in on the conversation between soldiers. He refused to say anything. They sprinted swiftly. He knew he'd see nightmares over and over again. No one made it out without any scars, seen or unseen. Their lives were all fated to be a tragedy, one with no moral, no hope, and fraught with disaster and a never-ending pain. Truly, the world would have been a better place had they never been born. Two years before that day, contracts and agreements between all the nations had been signed. Everyone agreed to it, Ghost was there. Two years since Task Force Seven had last been deployed. No one dared even to entertain the idea of bombing their neighbor again, not while they were in the picture. He'd done it. He'd achieved what most thought possible: world peace. And all it had cost was their lives, their futures, and an enormous amount of murder.

How many families did I destroy for it?

The radio chattered. *"They moved on to Sector Six. We need to move now and corner them there. They can't have much fight left in them."*

"How many do you count?" Another voice came out. Ghost recognized it as General Snells.

"Four, sir."

"How many bodies are accounted for?"

"Eight, sir."

"Ghost?"

"Negative."

"His squad is still alive somewhere. Watch your six."

"Roger."

That tells me what I need to know. Ghost sighed.

"Ghost!" Butcher exclaimed. "Sector Six is on the way."

"I know," Ghost replied. "They're going to be in the way."

"You have to be considering stepp—" Butcher began.

"I reconsidered it. Not worth it," he interrupted. "We need to focus on our own task. Even if there were four more, I have no idea what the numbers on the other side are. Even I can't predict that. Besides, we're all as exhausted as they are. Even with four more, we won't last the night."

"But—" Slithers protested.

"No buts. This is final. Look, we need to hide back in the sand. They will be coming here shortly," Ghost snapped.

The four of them buried themselves back under the scorching sand. They waited. Their hearts beat through their chests as the vehicles rolled back over the sand. The helicopters were churning their blades in the air, pushing the sand away as they hovered over Sector Six. The soldiers were making their way down the crater towards a large abandoned building, using the cover of some scattered debris.

Another officer called out on a megaphone.

"Task Force Seven. I know you're in there. You are surrounded, and we know you can't continue for much longer. Come out, and this won't have to get violent. Just stand trial for your crimes, and no harm will come to you until after the trial."

What crimes?

"What crimes did we commit?" said another voice. It was Viper. "What did we do? Tell us that and then we'll consider coming out! Otherwise, you'll just have to blow us up in here."

A feisty one she was. Ghost remembered her well. She was hard on the outside, but had a little soft spot for Ticker.

Ghost got out from the scorching hot sand. He scanned the area before hiding behind a mound of rocks. Ticker, Slithers, and Butcher followed silently close behind. They were concealed from the rest of the U.S. soldiers and could get a better glimpse of what was happening. The sand was stained red. The soldiers were still numerous, and too many for Ghost to guess how many there were.

He peered over the rock, down into a large basin with a square building. The building was abundantly surrounded, and the soldiers placed claymores around the exits. Machine guns were stationed around every blockade and protected with three-inch steel plates. In front of the building were four iron poles, freshly erected for the occasion. *How respectful. They really put a lot of thought into this.*

The silence was deafening. Ghost examined the incident scene, calculating all possible next moves, knowing that the wrong one would be the end of it and would mean that they wouldn't complete their mission. Task Force 7 needed to make a move, because the good old brothers-in-arms were willing to wait. After all, they had all the time in the world. Task Force 7 were the ones running out of time.

Venom, they can wait. You must do something. You and Viper.

Nothing happened. The soldiers began stretching, still cautiously watching the building. What appeared to be an eternity passed. And then it happened. Glass was broken from the windows. Guns, unprimed grenades, and knives were just tossed out of the window. The front door was kicked down. The soldiers immediately focused their attention on the door with their rifles aimed, their fingers just above their triggers.

Ghost clutched his chest. *They have given up and had enough.* He let out deep and measured but silent breaths.

Venom walked out with her hands up. She was weeping tears of anguish, and her face grimaced, shining bright with the flames. "Don't shoot. I'll come out. I just want a fair trial."

Viper hesitantly walked out, her hands behind her back. She glared at all the soldiers, baring her teeth at them. She let out a sigh before looking up at the sky. Tears streamed down her face as she grimaced. Her hands made angry fists behind her back.

Wraith came out, his hands atop his head. He glared at everyone, not letting anyone out of his sight. Ghost knew this wasn't going to be peaceful at all. They were utterly alone down there. Wraith stood behind Viper, never looking to the ground, never to the sky, and he didn't let tears swell his eyes, as if he held some small fragment of hope that there was the faintest chance he could survive, but it was clear that even he was jaded.

Finally, Metal came out. He was a little taller than the rest of them, but he was the youngest of them all. His hands were folded in front of him as he reluctantly walked forward. His steps were small, and his knees trembled beneath him. His head was bowed down low as he came out, grinding his teeth.

"We're out. You damn bastards! What was our crime?" Wraith demanded. "I want answers, and I want them now!"

"You will be tried. Cuff them," came the officer's voice. He was smoking a cigar and kept his left hand in his pocket.

"Not until we get our answers!"

"You will be cuffed, or I will light you up right here!" General Snells scolded. "With what you did, you're lucky you're getting that much. You've already been tried, traitor!"

This stifled Wraith.

Sixteen soldiers sprinted up to them. They kicked the backs of their knees. The Task Force Seven members cried out in pain as they hit the ground. They were cuffing their ankles and wrists. Knees were pressed into their backs, and they were crying—all except Wraith. He was scanning the basin for a way out.

Viper cried the loudest. Her screams were heard for miles like a dying banshee, waiting to be released from this Hell. She, Venom, and Metal were waiting for the sweet release of death, as Death had always been their one true friend.

Ghost couldn't look away, no matter how hard he tried to force his head down. It was as if his body refused to budge, like he was stuck in a single time frame while the rest of the world continued to move.

Venom, Viper, Metal, and Wraith were struck in the backs of the knees with batons, crying out as they collapsed forward. The batons swung wildly. The tried to move away, but these soldiers swiftly tied them with zip-ties. The soldiers beat them relentlessly, until blood spilled on the ground. The four from Task Force Seven just wept, unable to move. Satisfied, apparently, the soldiers dragged them through the sand, hoisted them up on the erected posts, and tied them firmly with rope, chains and duct tape. Ghost assumed these soldiers believed them to be monsters that needed to be as secure as possible, and that in order to kill one of them, they needed to be brutalized beyond repair.

General Snells paced back and forth. Their faces resembled those of mere dogs trapped in a cage by a master who'd beaten them so many times they anticipated the strike. The man was terrifying, and even more terrifying for a dog who was on its last legs.

"You want to know your crimes?" he said. "Treason."

"What did we do?" Venom sobbed, her face cringing. "We didn't do anything! What did we do to deserve this? We fought for you so that you could hide behind us! Your Medal of Honor is a disgrace! That belongs to us!"

Truth was, the only mistake they'd ever made was being born. Now they knew not to make that mistake again. The more he looked on, the more he saw the events unfold, the more Ghost felt unnecessary, and that his whole life had been a lie. One thing he slightly understood now, having Snells confirmed it: the reason this was all happening was because of something Task Force Seven had done, and it had been labeled as treason. But what was it? His eyes narrowed as Snells flicked the cigar out of his mouth.

Snells glared at them as he took multiple steps back. "Light them up."

"What?!" Wraith protested. "You said—"

His voice was abruptly drowned out by the roar of rapid gunfire. The four of them screamed as their eyes widened at the onslaught, the flashing lights of the guns coming for them. Their bodies were penetrated with bullets, ripping apart their uniforms and flesh. They cried out, but their screams were voiceless.

But one voice reached above the gunfire, only one voice. The voice of Viper. "MAMA!" she cried. Her left arm was completely severed, and blood came out of her mouth. She looked to her left. Venom was already dead, her head dropped down as her waist fell from her torso. Her cries became screeches as she was pelted with more burning bullets into her torso. She turned the other way, and saw Wraith. He was already dead; numerous bullets had made it through his skull. Her other arm was finally severed. And then onto Metal, who had it worse of all. His head had finally been sliced from his neck, and his chest was already opened up, his heart and intestines falling out of his torso like a drooling mouth.

"MAMA!" she cried, louder than before. Her eyes were stretched open as her chest started to open with the gun fire. "MAMA!" She could feel her waist coming apart. "MAMA!"

Ted woke up, springing himself up from his sleeping bag. His chest was tight. He crossed his arms over his chest, as if trying to hold on to something. A violent scream expelled from his mouth as tears streamed down his face again. He coughed, then sucked in air through his teeth, his eyes wide open, grimacing with his own torment.

He saw this in his sleep, again, and again, and again!

He slowly turned to his phone to look at the time. It read: 10:53 PM.

CHAPTER 6

Evasion

SAMANTHA WAS RUNNING LATER than usual. Her heart was pumping in her chest heavily. She could feel the sense of anxiety swelling over her like a plague. She sat in the shuttle, anxiously tapping her finger on the cold window as she watched the pedestrians. With every stop, ever moment the shuttle stayed still, she felt like she was going to be late to Park Street. She chuckled nervously. Such a silly thing to be concerned about, being late of all things. *Sam, you need to stop bringing work home with you.*

The shuttle dropped her right off at South Station. She walked up the stairs and stepped into the busyness of downtown Boston. Cars drove by, blasting their music with their windows down. Buses made their stops right next to her, letting numerous people off. She smiled at the people as they came off. Some were distracted with their phones in their hands, nodding off into some other world. Others seemed jaded, as if they were repeating the same routine again, and again, and again.

She walked west on Summer street. She paid close attention to the cars and the streetlights. She felt insignificant in a city filled with so many skyscrapers representing decades of hardworking individuals. She wanted that success.

She crossed the street to the front of a convenient store. There were several men there, some lively, smoking cigarettes or joints, with no care in the world.

Samantha had always been a people watcher, but not often did people stick out to her as much as the man sitting across the road on a side street. He was perhaps in his forties, with an ungroomed beard with white streaks in it. His eyes looked exhausted and in his mouth was a cigarette, and in his trembling left hand was a paper bag, held in such a way that she could tell plainly there was a bottle in there. Whisky, gin, bourbon, or some other cheap but strong liquor, as his breath reeked of it. Hanging around his neck were a pair of dog tags. His coat was tattered, with an American flag on the shoulder, also fading in color.

She sighed as she looked around the area for a bank. *No. That won't help him.* She walked into the convenience store. She looked around, speeding her way into the refrigerated section, and pulled out two bottles of water. *I might as well, while I'm here.* She turned around and looked around for something suitable and nutritious to eat, one where she didn't risk killing him because she didn't know if he was allergic to anything. She found a salad with chicken in it. *Better than nothing.* She didn't bother with any plastic silverware; there likely was none to be found.

She walked out of the convenience store with her purchases and walked down the side street: Arch Street. The man's eyes were fading out into sleep. She went up to him and placed one of the bottles of water next to him and left the salad next to that.

She left him to drift off in his sleep. Images and video clips flashed across her mind of soldiers laying on the street with nowhere to go, no one to call, just left abandoned on the street. *I wish I could do more; you all deserve so much more than this.* Sam assumed this man was one of the tens of thousands of veterans who'd been left abandoned by the country they'd sacrificed so much for. She had enough money to live off of, that was true, but she had little in the way of spare change. She hadn't had her big refrigerated-freight customer for very long, and she was waiting for her first commission check, which would allow her more freedom to help more strangers she ran into like this one. *But there is only so much one person can do.*

She walked up Summer street. She was in no hurry to get to the study on time, as the topic was indeed depressing, and she was already late, and she'd already decided this was a silly thing to be anxious about. Despite her rise in anxiety, she intended to walk ever so patiently. She walked through the streets, watching the lights flicker on and some summer performers playing around in the trafficless square that separated coffee shops, clothing stores, and Downtown Crossing over towards Washington Street.

The moon peered out from behind a veil of clouds from on high. She looked up as the blue mystic light shone down on her. She took a deep breath as she kept walking further on the street. Summer turned into Winter real fast. The moonlight was hidden by skyscrapers, but at the end of this street was Tremont. The corner of Tremont and Winter was decorated with the state flower of traffic cones. Parked behind was a police cruiser with an officer leaning against it, looking at the traffic. His eyes seemed emotionless as she passed by.

She waited with a score of people of diverse origins, waiting at the wide crosswalk to cross Tremont Street, the wide street that always had construction going for some reason or another. *It's been the same for years. What are they doing?* she wondered.

The traffic lights turned from green to yellow, and at last red. The cars came to a halt, except for one who was speeding through the yellow light and just missed it. Massachusetts drivers; you can't trust them. They're insane. The cross lights permitted her to cross the street. She ran across diagonally to Park Street because the window for authorized walking was limited. On the marble front steps of the church were people sitting, many with joints hanging from their lips. Their clothes were tattered and not well kept. There were flies buzzing around, and she wasn't surprised; one of them smelled like they'd soiled themselves, the rank odor reaching her nostrils. She assumed they were homeless, and this was the one place they could socialize, seemingly, without the police arresting them for loitering. Not wanting to be rude, she briskly walked up Park Street to the glass entrance of Café.

Her phone buzzed in her pocket. It was buzzing a lot these days, between high alert news, grocers and reefer trucks going out of business—which was good for her, but terrible for the competition. She felt bad for them, and that was the one part of her job she hated. She had to beat those rates down with the drivers, even if they were desperate to get out of Maryland or California; they'd take any rate. Today, the truck driver had been haggled so low, she was certain they'd taken a $200 loss taking the load.

She pulled out her phone and opened the email.

Samantha Harris,

Driver picked up PO 3840172 at Shed Baltimore, MD. 1834 PM. CI 15:34 PM CO 18:34 PM. Groceries. 30 pallets sideways. Outbound to Cincinnati OH.

Regards,
After Call.

She let out a sigh of relief. It was a close one. The load had never got picked up, but something was in Ohio, enough where the driver was willing to take a steep loss on it. He'd make up for it. She smiled as she walked up the street. Her phone buzzed again.

She looked at it again before turning to the glass doors, reading *Breaking news! China enters into Trade War with U.S.A.* As she stared at it, her hand trembled with the phone. She sat down on the stairs while she read the article.

News was filled with nothing but horror stories these days. Europe seemed to be in flames, and Asia was not far behind it, what with all the declarations of war and last-minute alliances that had occurred with the dissolution of NATO. *What were they thinking?* The United States seemed to be out of it for the most part. For that, at least, she was relieved. She didn't want to think about what a war with the U.S.A. would be like. As it stood, the U.S.A. seemed to have been out of everyone's conflicts for about ten years.

According to White House officials, negotiations with important nations which disbanded from NATO are falling through. The world is in shambles right now and the only thing that is certain is uncertainty. U.S.A is trying to maintain relations with nations formerly within NATO after what they call "a colossal mistake." Eastern and Western European countries are at war with another, and many nations in Africa have followed suit. Fortunately, the instability hasn't quite made it to the Americas, but White House Officials state that it is only a matter of time.

White House officials announced that America has entered a trade war with China. They implied that negotiations had gone nowhere, and that China was not cooperative with them. When asked further about the future with China, White House officials stated that the future is uncertain, and updates will follow. However, they are anticipating a declaration of war from China.

Opinion: it seems rather unclear why the U.S. would enter a trade war with China. It is even more unclear as to why they're anticipating war. It seems that nations are like dominos; once one falls, another tumbles after it. There is little information being revealed to us, and our nation's leaders are hiding something from us.

"Well, there's a surprise," she said sarcastically to herself. She looked up the sky, now empty. She grimaced as she put her phone in her lap. She bowed her head down as she began to pray silently to herself.

After her silent prayer, she looked at her watch. It was 7:27 PM. Large group was over or ending. She stood up and went inside and went to the welcome table. The receptionist was still very much disinterested, as he was paying attention to something on his computer screen. She pulled out a name tag, wrote her name on it, and placed it on her suit. She then took out a cup and put it underneath the cheap coffee machine, placed a coffee capsule in the machine and clamped it back down, waiting for the coffee to drip.

As her coffee finished pouring out, the rest of the members of Café were walking out of the fellowship hall and into their various small groups. Samantha followed as Jennifer came out.

"Hiii!" Jennifer called out, running to Sam's side. "Isn't it a little late for coffee?"

"Too late and coffee should never be in the same sentence," Sam answered, smiling back at her. Jennifer and Sam walked side by side like two best friends in middle school.

"Hey, you didn't by chance see Ted out there, did you? On your way in?" Jennifer asked. She still had that giddy smile on her lips.

"No. I can't say I have," Sam answered, her suspicion that Jennifer might have a thing for Ted confirmed. "Did he not show up?"

"No. Maybe it's nothing. Maybe he'll be here shortly. He did say he was coming back," Jennifer commented.

"You seemed to get along with him well last Tuesday," Samantha responded.

"Yes, I did. He seems pleasant enough, oddly romantic." Jennifer snickered as they turned the corner into the room which overlooked the graveyard, getting into their corner of the table and waiting for others to start trickling in.

"Well, you did say once you prefer a man in a candlelight setting. Like a romantic emphasis from a Jane Austen Novel. Which one did you want? Was it Knightly or Darcy? Is he a keeper?"

"If only I could get those Knightly qualities in someone like Darcy," she laughed. "Hard combination to come by. Ted could be Knightly," she joked.

"I get that," Sam replied.

"No Ted tonight?" Tim asked as he sat down next to them.

"Regrettably, no," Jennifer replied, looking him in the eye. "I was really looking forward to seeing him again."

"Don't you have his number?" Sam asked. "Text him."

"I'm not going to pressure him just yet." Jennifer smiled suspiciously. "You can't just push him to come if he doesn't want to. Look, if he doesn't show up, I'll text him and tell him he's missed."

"Fair enough," Samantha said. *She's totally into him*. And she was amazed at Jennifer's self-control, not texting Ted right away. Samantha turned to Tim. "Where's Michael?"

"He was with me a little while ago, but he said he had to go back to the office to check on emails. He got something breaking news or some bother that he thinks is going to affect him," Tim replied. "He said he'll meet us at Terri's."

"Did he say what it was about?" Samantha asked.

"Something to do with China," Tim answered.

"I see. He probably has to work another hour to read the room," Sam suggested, assuming it would take that long for Michael to get a grasp on what was likely to happen to his account at work.

Jack interrupted everyone. "Welcome to Café, welcome to connecting group. I see we still have a few stragglers and new faces. So, to let us all get a sense of one another, I'll start. Say your name, where are you from, what brings you to Boston? And the icebreaker, hmm." He scratched his neck and looked up to the ceiling. "If you could meet any person, living or dead, real or fictitious, who would it be? My name is Jack, I am from Houston Texas, and I work as a nuclear physicist at a nearby nuclear power plant. I came to Boston for work. If there is someone I would like to meet? Julius Robert Oppenheimer. I'm really interested in his thought process on the Atom Bomb. That's it; just your boring nuclear engineer."

They all went down the line, introducing themselves with elation, giving them their background information and locality. It was routine for everyone, but the differing perspectives always kept things interesting. Even though Sam had known Michael, Tim, and Jennifer the most closely, she couldn't say she knew everything about them.

The line finally made it to Tim. "My name's Tim. I am from Colorado, Denver specifically. I came to Boston for college, and I settled here over in Dorchester. If I could meet anyone, living or dead, I'd have to say Jesus."

"No! No! No!" Jennifer exclaimed, pointing at him. "No. Bad. Tim. Bad. No cop outs! We all want to meet Jesus. No! I *demand* a do-over!"

The room rang with laughter.

"But I really want to—"

"Tim. Bad. Bad Tim. No! No! No!" Jennifer exclaimed. "Give us something juicier than that!"

"Fine," Tim chuckled. "Hmm. Come back to me."

"Cheater." She elbowed him. "My name is Jennifer, I am originally from upstate New York, and I moved to Boston for a change in scenery. New York is terrible. I am a biological researcher right around the corner. If there was anyone I wanted to meet, dead or living? Real or fiction? Well, King Arthur. I've always loved his tales, as heavily fabricated as they are. He was such the romantic."

"Not Mr. Darcy?" Sam joked.

"Oh, please, Darcy and Arthur, there just isn't any comparison!" Jennifer said.

The room was filled with laughter. It was clear that Jennifer was the life of the group, or the class clown. Sam wondered how she behaved at work. She let her own laughter subside.

"Well, my turn! My name is Samantha, I also moved here for work after college. I am moving back. I was from Peabody, went to school down in Virginia, and was relocating back up here when I took a job as an account executive for a Logistics brokerage," she began. "If there is anyone that I want to meet, living or dead—and not Jesus since that's off the table—" There was another chuckle across the room. "—well, let's go historical, shall we? I've always wanted to meet Joan of Arc. Her story sits a special way with me."

"As you can see, we are a very diverse group of people," Jack said. "So, if any of you are new here, and I think there are a few of you, we just started Ecclesiastes. We are going into the second chapter, so without further ado. . ."

Samantha joined everyone at the back end of the bar of Terri Nation. It was a slow night. There was no one except the food runner and Scott, who seemed very happy with bright shining eyes and a smile behind his thick black beard. Samantha, Erin, and Jennifer sat together at the bar as Tim and Brian were chatting away behind them, not ready to get a drink.

"What are we having today? And, no Michael?" Scott asked.

"Nay," Jennifer began. "Well, the eccentric drinker should be coming in rather shortly, or so he said."

"He did, but Tim said that. And you know how spontaneous Michael can be. He might just not show up," Sam replied.

"Who did Tim say wasn't coming?" came a loud obnoxious voice behind them. Sam, Erin, and Jennifer looked behind to see Michael smiling down on them, his hands resting on Erin and Jennifer's shoulders.

"You," Jennifer said. "Dang it. And here I thought I was going to have a normal drink for once, like some brandy, a glass of wine, a beer or even some rum and Coke. Oh well. I guess my dream died early tonight."

"No one's stopping you." Michael laughed, turning to Scott. "Bartender's special! Whatever that is."

"You're stopping me." Jennifer smirked. "Make that two, and for God's sake, don't spit in it like you did three weeks ago."

"That was sweat!" Scott laughed.

"I was joking," Jennifer replied.

"So was I." Scott sneered as he cleaned the bar top and ducked down to get some glasses.

"Just the dark Crellic," Erin said.

"Cab for me, please," Sam requested.

"Make that together," Jennifer asked. She slipped her card over to Scott. "Close it out, if you would."

Scott hastily went over to pour the wine and simple beer for Erin and Sam. He sliced some cucumbers, mixing in muddled mint and blueberries, poured in some vodka and soda water and what Sam guessed was simple syrup, then started shaking them all together.

"I don't see Ted. I take it he elected to go home earlier today?" Michael asked.

"No, he didn't show up," Samantha said.

"Erin. You work with him, right?" Michael asked. "How is he?"

"I don't know. He made another big deal again. This was one of those one-offs and not likely something he's going to repeat," Erin said as she sipped her beer. "I don't know how he does it. He must be really lucky or have some insider information, but even if he did, there is no way he could accurately predict when something will just plummet. Even with inside information, he can't make those calls at precisely the right time. Yet, he is making those calls at precisely the right time. He seemed fine though, but when he made the deal, he seemed disappointed. None of this should even be possible."

"How much was the deal worth?" Michael's eyes widened in curiosity.

"Our manager clocked it in at $350K," she said. "I don't care who you are, no one can predict the market the way he does. He is consistently beating it, even with all of the uncertainty in the world."

"But why was he disappointed?" Sam asked. "Shouldn't he be happy with that?"

"I don't know. I know I'd love a deal like that! But I am nowhere near to his expertise actually," Erin explained. "He also has the nasty habit of leaving late and arriving early. However, he left earlier today, in the middle of a meeting."

Scott came back with the drinks. They were identical and had a foggy color to them. He slid the drinks along the table to Michael and Jennifer. Jennifer took a sip. "Wow, so this is what it's like to be on Cloud Nine. Tell me, you didn't spit in it, did you?"

Michael took a sip of his.

"Just his," Scott answered, laughing. Michael coughed and spat it out.

"Now, now, Michael, I'm sure he's joshing you." Jennifer sneered.

"Who even says that anymore?" Michael chuckled, and his smile lit up.

"I said what I said!" Jennifer took another sip. She licked her lips. "Not bad, this one."

"Hey, Scott?" Sam asked.

He was about to turn to another guest when he turned to her. "Yeah, Sam?"

"That man that we met two weeks ago, over in the corner. Has he been coming here often?" she asked.

"Yes. He usually just gets a glass of wine and some potatoes," he answered. "He is always pleasant. He didn't show up last week, though."

Sam knew that to be true. *Wait a minute.* "Last week? Do you mean he was here earlier?"

"Yes. He left fifteen minutes before you arrived," he answered, turning away to address the rest of his guests around the bar.

"That's not good," Erin said. "I'll try to talk to him tomorrow if I can. I have plenty of reason to."

"I can't say I'm surprised," Michael commented, sipping his drink, whatever it was. "After all, the discussion we had was depressing."

"And to continue it today would have been worse," Sam admitted.

"It is depressing if you don't finish the context," Jennifer commented. "The moral of Ecclesiastes was and always will be that if this world is all there is, and God doesn't exist, anything we do is pointless. Our friends are pointless, our family is pointless. Our accomplishments don't mean anything and even our marks on history are pointless as they won't stand forever." She sighed. "But that doesn't mean that we should stop trying to live our lives." She pulled out her phone and scrolled through her contacts. She started texting a message. "I just texted him. Hopefully, he'll say something."

"I'm sure it's nothing," Michael said. "Besides, the world is crazy right now. I wouldn't be surprised if he's just exhausted all of the time and needs a break. I haven't done stocks, but I imagine its exhausting work."

"Yeah, it is!" Erin said, taking a gulp from her beer. "You have to pay attention to everything that's going on in the world. Literally anything could affect the market. Good news, bad news, global news, a shipping company going out of business, or even the materials of certain commodities skyrocketing into the air. The more information one has, the better. The problem is, there's so much information to digest, and not every single thing is going to affect the market. Like, Michael, did you read about that trade war thing?"

"Yeah, that's why I wasn't at Café today," he answered.

"I read the same thing too," said Sam.

"Yeah, well, it's like this. Something like that is going to affect the market. It's probably going to crash. My assumption, of course," Erin replied, tilting her arm as if to illustrate a graph. "Now, let's say that trade war was between China and Russia instead of the U.S. There is a high likelihood that it would affect the market with increased commodity prices since we get a lot of business from China. There is no guarantee that *that* trade war will directly affect our market. Its effect on the market would be indirect to us over here in the U.S., but it would likely affect it, if not immediately. But there is no promise that it would send the market down. Many people would assume that it will, and then sell their assets, hoping to buy them all back when it goes below. This is called shorting a stock, but the way the market works, that kind of behavior may drive the value of the assets up instead of down, causing a lot of people to lose out on money. But since it's us, I'm sure the market is going to crash; it's just a matter of when."

Samantha was annoyed. There were way too many variables with finance, stocks especially, to care about it. Honestly, she'd never gotten into finance for that very reason, and she didn't care to have it repeatedly explained to her.

"Well, that is going to make my head hurt. I'll stick to my 401K, thank you very much," Jennifer said. "So, what's everyone doing Saturday?"

"I'm free," Michael said without skipping a beat.

Erin and Sam both nodded.

"Excellent. It's decided then. I'll see all of you Saturday, and Tim. Hopefully I can get Ted to come," Jennifer said, clapping her hands.

"What are we doing and where are we going?" Michael asked.

"Why, my house, silly." Jennifer smiled brightly at him. "Game night, of course. I have a little game we play there. It's a great way to get to know your friends."

"Okay. Time?"

"Noon is fine," Jennifer said. "I've got the refreshments already arranged!"

CHAPTER 7

Game Night

~It was all a mistake.

J ENNIFER WOKE UP SATURDAY morning bright and early. She stretched out as the sun beamed down on her face. She yawned and stepped out of bed and moved over to her nightstand. She picked up her phone to check for her text messages to see if Ted had responded. Her texts looked lonely on the screen: *Ted, we're meeting at my house for some games, Samantha, Michael, Tim, and Erin. I did invite a few more that I'm not sure if you've met or not. Text me later.* The text message was alone, like it didn't want a response. She stared down at it, contemplating what to do with it. She put the phone on the nightstand again and crossed her arms around her chest, violently tapping her arm with an intense index finger. "Tedward!" She finally decided to pick up the phone again and hit the call icon.

The phone rang, dialing the number that Ted had given her. *I really hope he didn't give me a fake number. If he did, there's nothing I can do.* The phone rang second time. *Come on, Tedward. Wakey Wakey!* It rang a third time before forwarding to his voicemail.

"You've reached Ted. I'm sorry I can't get to the phone right now. Please leave your name, phone number, and brief reason for your call and I'll get back to you as soon as possible."

Beep.

"Ted, this is Jennifer. I hope you're not ignoring me. Anyway, you're invited to my place for some games and dinner today—"

"Hello?" the voice on the other end of the phone picked up.

Jennifer was surprised, not thinking that cell phones would allow someone to answer mid voicemail. Her smile lit up her room, even though only she was in it. "Heeeey there, buddy! This is Jennifer."

"I know." He chuckled. "I memorized your number. How may I help?"

"So, I'm hosting a small group of friends—I'm not expecting more than ten of us—for games, drinks and food at my place today. We're starting around noon today, and I want to invite you here for that also." She brought down the excitement in her voice, speaking softly into the phone. "By the way, we missed you this week!"

"I see," he said, his voice going soft over the phone. "This is kind of sudden, to be frank."

"I texted you Tuesday about it. You never answered," she said back to him. "Come on, what better way to get closer to your friends than games and fellowship?"

"Uhm. I don't know."

"What? Do you have plans already?" Jennifer asked him.

"No."

"Then come on. Look, if it means that much to you, you can take me shopping next week," she joked.

"I don't recall making an active effort to take you shopping," he replied.

"Well, at least I got a full sentence out of you. Can you do me a favor?" she asked.

He chuckled on the other end of the phone. "What?"

"Do you have a pen and some paper?" she asked.

"I do."

"Take my address down. You're coming. I won't take no for an answer."

"What am I, your servant?" he said.

There was some silence on the phone. Jennifer turned her head and then back to the phone as if she were consulting an imaginary friend. *He might find this funny.* "Yes."

He burst out laughing on the other end of the phone. "As you wish, milady."

"There's the romantic Tedward I know." She laughed and gave him her address, certain that he was actually writing it down. "Ted, it starts at 12:00 PM. You can come early or come later. Or on time. That's cool too. Up to you. But you are coming! Or I'll track you down to the ends of the earth and feed you my amazing boxed macaroni and ketchup."

"Ketchup?" He sounded confused.

"There may or may not be cheese involved in some way, shape or form. I don't know. Maybe you don't have to find out, huh? Just come," she joked.

"Need me to bring anything?"

"Just yourself," she answered.

"I see," he gave his reserved, few-word answer.

"I speak for myself and everyone coming that you should also bring clothes. Yeah, that's a good idea. Don't come naked. That would make for a rude awakening, although a very comical story a year down the road."

He chuckled again, "Okay, I'll see you there. Is there anything else?"

"No. Just give me a time when you'll be here."

"I'll probably make my own lunch, so I'll probably be there around one."

"Okay, we'll see you then!" she exclaimed before hanging up the phone. She immediately started a group chat with Michael, Tim, Erin, and Samantha. *He's coming. He'll be here around 1PM today.*

She hastily went over to her kitchen and poured herself a bowl of cereal and milk. She started cataloguing the games she wanted to have available for them, as well as making the plans to order the pizza. She swiftly ate her cereal before arranging things around the living room, making plenty of space available for the "Acting Game." She didn't have the cards for the physical game, but it was a close substitute.

Hours passed. Jennifer had gotten everything ready, the drinks were in her cooler, and of course the pizza was on its way. She'd ordered four pies to be safe: pepperoni, chicken and broccoli, cheese, margherita pizza. That would satisfy everyone with their dictary restrictions. She didn't think any of them were vegans, god forbid, at least it wasn't clear; however, she did in fact know Tim was a vegetarian.

There was a knock on the door. She quickly glanced at her watch, which read 12:03 PM. She immediately went to the door to answer it. Samantha smiled as the door was opened. She entered the apartment. "Sorry I'm late. There was some problem on the red line today."

"What happened? Did it derail or something? I hate that line," Jennifer said.

Michael was behind her. He lived in the same neighborhood over by Davis Square, the place he called "Heaven on Earth."

Michael laughed. "When was the last time you heard someone say they liked the red line? It's like asking if a morbidly obese man likes the tape worm inside his own belly."

"Now that's a specific analogy if ever I heard one," Jennifer said, her face twisted in disgust. "I'm not touching any of the chicken now. By the way, the pizza should be here in about a half hour."

"Great, I'm famished." Michael smirked.

"It's barely noon," Jennifer mocked him. "I swear, where do you put it all?"

"Fast metabolism." He chuckled.

"Wow. I wish I had the ability to eat the things you do and not gain weight." She was about to shut the door.

"Waaiit!" came a familiar cry. Jennifer looked out of the hallway of her apartment to see Tim sprinting down the corridor. "I'm here. Don't start without me."

"Tim!" She smiled at him and placed her hand defensively on her chest. "I would never!"

"Oh, yes you would!" he shot back as he came bolting down the corridor and stopped at the ajar door. He panted.

"You're right." She laughed, tossing her hair back. "I'm a monster."

Sam and Michael had already taken a seat on one of the sofas. Michael's arm was around her shoulder. "Jennifer, did Brian say he was coming?"

"Yes, he did. And you know he'll bring you-know-who," Jennifer said. She looked at the watch. 12:10 PM. "But you know him. He probably went to bed seven hours ago, so he'll probably just be waking up, if he's even up already. He probably won't be here 'til closer to three. That's a man that knows how to show up fashionably late." She turned to Tim, who was still panting. "Tim, I have some bottled water in the cooler. Go get some."

"No thank you," he panted, while making his way to his seat. "You know—"

"Yes, yes, I know. Environmentally friendly and all that." Jennifer sneered. "Well, I have some plastic cups you can get tap—"

"Don't you have real cups?" Tim stared at her blankly.

"Tim! Do I look like some girl who wants to wash her dishes all the time?" she snapped at him. "Of course, I do." She walked over to her cupboard, grabbed a cup and filled it with water to give to Tim.

"So, I want to know," Samantha said to Jennifer. "How did you get Ted to agree to come?"

"Well, I called him this morning. He finally picked up the phone as I was leaving a salty voicemail." She put her fingers to her lips, but her smile never faded. "I talked him into going. He tried to push back, but I wouldn't let him get out of his corner."

"Well, that must be—" Michael began.

Ring.

Jennifer took out her phone and looked at the caller ID. *Erin.* She answered the phone. "You've reached the city morgue. You kill 'em, we chill 'em."

Tim spat out the water from his mouth.

"Hey, Tim! Tim! Tim! You clean that up!" Jennifer scolded him. "So uncivilized."

Erin chuckled on the other line. "Which door do I enter?"

"It's apartment number 58. I'm on the sixth floor. When you come out of the elevator, take a left. See you soon! Bye-bye now." She hung up the phone. "Tim, who gave you permission to spit water all over my floor?"

"You must have been the class clown," Michael replied.

"Oh, dear, dear sweet little carpet," she said. "That wasn't me. That was some guy named David. A terribly dreadful little creature."

"You read Jane Austen last night again, didn't you!" Sam accused, shaking her head.

"You know it! Jane Austen a day keeps depression away." Jen laughed. "Or was it something to do with apples? I don't know. I'm not a doctor. I'm just a researcher." There was a knock on the door. "Erin, or Pizza?"

"Erin," Michael answered.

Jennifer went to open the door, and Michael was correct. "Welcome in. Excuse the spit, Tim did it. Tim, are you done cleaning?"

"Yes, I am." He was cleaning it with a washcloth. He hated paper towels.

"Good grief. I give you my glorious tap water, and this is how you repay me. Some friend!" The room was filled with laughter as Erin walked in. Jennifer was confident around her friends, but it did take some people some time to get used to her. She knew that. After all, she came come off as an unlikeable jerk, but that was her love language. *And that's the way I like it.*

She looked at her watch again; 12:20 PM.

"Pizza running late?" Michael asked.

"Not yet," Jennifer said.

Jennifer lounged next to Tim on the couch. Michael had his arm wrapped around Samantha's shoulders, and Erin was poking about Jennifer's bookshelves, looking at the impressive Jane Austen collection in a variety of different editions. Jennifer smiled as Erin petted the spines so casually, especially the leatherbound editions reprinted in '08. "I recommend *Sense and Sensibility*, that's my personal favorite."

"Jennifer," Erin said, gazing back at her, "how many times have you re-read this collection? And why do you have so many?"

"I re-read the collection yearly. You might call me a hopeless romantic."

"Ted bug?" Erin sneered.

Taken aback, Jennifer turned her head to the side, and her cheeks blushed red. "Maybe."

A half hour passed and there was another knock on the door. "That must be it." She opened the door, paid the pizza man and brought the pizza to the island. There were numerous paper plates that had come with it. Of course, Tim scoffed at them.

Michael went over to get a slice. "Get your frail hands away from that!" Jennifer slapped his hand away from the paper plate. "Now, now, my sweet little carpet, we are waiting for Ted. I can reheat the pizza in the oven if I need to. Twenty minutes isn't going to kill you."

An hour passed. It was 1:50 PM in the afternoon. There was not another knock at the door. Jennifer felt discouraged. She was a little concerned by Ted not having shown up yet, and there was no communication from him indicating he was going to be late. *I hope he didn't get into an accident.* She sighed. "Well, I guess you all can eat now."

Why did I feel it necessary to make them wait?

Tim, Erin, and Michael immediately went over to get some pizza. Jennifer was tired of listening to Michael complain anyway. She felt Samantha's hand on her shoulder. "It'll be fine. I'm sure he got caught on something."

"I suppose." Jennifer took out her phone and sent another message to Ted: w*here are you?* She put the phone back in her pocket and slouched her shoulders as she walked over to get a slice of pizza on that dreaded paper plate.

"Hey, Erin, did you ever follow up with Ted the other day?" Michael asked as he took a bite of his pepperoni pizza.

"Yeah, I did. He only gave me few-word answers," Erin replied, taking a bite of her chicken alfredo. "He said he was fine."

"Well, you know when someone answers that way, they're insecure," Sam said. "That's what my boss tells me when I say I'm fine."

"I'm sure it's nothing," Michael said. "As he mentioned before, he works in world markets. I wouldn't be surprised if he was still working and had some remote meeting he'd forgot to mention."

"Seriously, Michael, how much does he have to be working if he's doing that?!" Jennifer exclaimed, gritting her teeth. "Erin, didn't you say he was one of those come-in-early-leave-late kind of guys?"

Tim frowned.

"Yeah," Erin replied.

"That isn't unusual for someone in a high-pressure job," Samantha explained. "I do that frequently too."

"So do I," Michael said. He scratched his chin as he was chewing on his crust. "But if I had to guess, he was probably working close to sixty hours per week."

"That isn't unusual," Jennifer admitted. "And if he works on the weekends, he would be closer to seventy hours?"

"Perhaps, and that's a little extreme," Michael admitted. "I would never choose to work that much, unless maybe he has a reason."

"Maybe he just really likes money," Tim said. "I mean, if he's in stocks, that's usually the reason."

"No, that's not it. He admitted that he only does it for something to keep him busy, like he enjoys doing it. He said he has more than enough for him to live off of," Michael replied.

"Honestly, that's impressive. He doesn't seem to be much older than any of us," Tim said.

Another hour passed. Jennifer had received no confirmation from Ted that he was coming or that he was running late. It was two hours later than when he'd said he would show up. Had he lied to her just to get her off the phone? She couldn't discount that possibility. She felt like her heart was heavy. *Did I push him too hard?*

There was a knock on the door. Her smile lit back up again. She rushed over to answer it. She opened the door with a smile on her face. When she saw who was on the other side, her emotions fell heavily upon her heart, like she was chained to the ground by large boulders and she couldn't move or risk having the weight crush her. Being the polite host she was, she exclaimed enthusiastically, "It's Brian!"

"Yeah! It's Brian!" he repeated in the third person, nodding his head enthusiastically. "Sorry I'm late."

"Don't fret, my sweet little fox, come on in. The pizza is here. I was just about to pull out the wine," she said, ushering Brian, Steven, and his little friend Rosa in. Brian was the oldest of them all, nearing his mid-thirties.

"Oh, excellent; plenty of time for drinking. I brought my own wine, actually. It's from the Valley up over in Westford."

"Wait. Really?" Samantha asked. "I love their wine; it's something about their grapes. Their wine is of the best quality."

"Yeah!" Brian walked over to the island in the kitchen and placed two bottles of wine on it. He put the corkscrew in one of them and immediately opened it. Brian, Steven, and Rosa went over to the others and started talking about their week. No one brought anything depressing into the conversation.

Jennifer was happy they were able to have such a good time in such a small apartment. The games hadn't started just yet, but she was beginning to lose hope that Ted would be showing up tonight. *You could have at least told me you just didn't want to come. But maybe I shouldn't have put you in that position, forcing you to either lie or hurt my feelings.*

She pulled out all her wines out onto the island and started pouring cups of wine into wine glasses and delivering them to her guests, smiling as she handed each one off. She saved Brian's wine for last. He usually bought the expensive wine, anyway.

"Hey, whatever happened to that newbie?" Brian asked. "I don't think I ever succeeded in getting him out. I haven't seen him in a while."

"Are you referring to Ted?" Michael's head tilted in response. "The one from two weeks ago?"

"Yeah, that one," Brian took a sip of his Cabernet. "What happened to him? Did someone scare him off?"

"I don't think so. Actually, he was supposed to be coming tonight, but he hasn't shown up yet," Sam replied. The curve on her lips faded.

"Well, it's probably nothing to worry about," Brian said, unconcerned. "A pity, I wanted to meet him. I never got a chance to say hi to the new guy."

"Maybe you'll get that chance still tonight, or—"

A heavy knock at the door interrupted Samantha.

Who was that? Jennifer thought. *It's way too late for it to be Ted.* Of course, at this point she assumed he was no longer coming. "I've got it." She walked over to the door. Her hand gripped the handle and turned it. She opened the door wide with a smile as she looked to greet whoever stood behind it.

Jennifer breathed heavily as she looked at him in the doorway. She felt her smile drop to a frown as her heart raced, and she couldn't quite make out the emotions her heart was trying to feel. Was she angry? Upset? Excited? She couldn't tell, but her hands trembled at her sides. She grimaced at the man as his presence suddenly made her angry.

"You know, Tedward, when you tell me you're going to be here around one, I expect you to be here around one. Maybe fifteen minutes late or so, but around one. It is four o'clock! I already told everyone you would be here at one. Would you make a liar out of me?" she said with an uplifted chin.

The laughter-filled room went deafeningly silent. Jennifer scratched the back of her neck.

He gave her a polite bow. "My apologies, milady. For you see, I just couldn't bring it upon myself to come to some kind of party without bring something of value to my beloved host." He spoke very smoothly, and he was not at all flirtatious; he seemed very sincere. He took out a large bottle of red wine made of fine glass, the price tag ripped off.

Jennifer's eyes lit up as she immediately grabbed the bottle from his hand and read the label. "This is Colossus' Rome Red Ca'habielli!"

"What?" Brian called over. "Ca'habielli? Jenn, put my wine back in the fridge. You can't get much better than that!"

"Ted, that's a $1,200 bottle of wine. Where did you get this? More importantly, why would you give it to me?" Jennifer knew the value of such a brand of wine was only reserved for the finest of occasions, and not something easily obtainable in the United States. This was strictly imported from the wineries of Rome.

"Eh, I'm not going to keep it around my house," he replied. "It's much better shared among *friends*." His voice dropped a little at the sound of the word.

An expensive vintage such as the Ca'habielli, imported from Rome, was meant to be enjoyed slowly. Yet, such a gift should not be squandered. Jennifer found herself wondering why in God's name Ted would think to bring such an expensive wine as a gift. That bottle of wine costed more than some of them paid for rent. She was not going to squander the gift, lest he feel offended, despite the social insult of providing such an expensive guilt. She also took special notice of his sudden tonal change in the word "friends." She couldn't ignore that. What exactly did he mean?

"Come on in!" she invited him in, immediately changing her tone from ire to a sense of joy. "There is pizza. I know you said you ate already, but it's here if you want it."

"I appreciate the sentiment," he answered as he walked through the apartment, scanning the room as if to read the reaction of each person.

Samantha walked up to him. "I'm glad you came."

"I'm glad I made it." He smiled at her; the bags under his eyes were puffy.

Jennifer put one of Brian's unopened bottle of wine in her cooler, pouring out his bottle into several wine glasses. She uncorked the bottle of Ca'habielli. She placed it on the counter where she would let it breath for an hour. This was such a gracious and unnecessary gift. *Ted, why?* Feeling self-conscious, she delivered the poured glasses to every one of her friends in the room, including Ted, who she considered a friend despite not having known him for very long. *Ted, why did you hesitate?*

The party drank all of Brian's wine and allowed the entirety of the hour to pass by, speaking until the Ca'habielli was completely breathed.

The party grabbed their now empty wine glasses and got into a line. Jennifer poured Ted's glass first. He smiled that impeccable smile; there was something soothing about it. Like the genuine smile of someone who knew no pain, who knew only the kindness of the world, and was sheltered from the many horrible, physical, psychological traumas from the world. He was always in a safe place.

Jennifer poured the wine into the empty glasses, filling them halfway so she could distribute it equally to everyone in the party. The party stood around in a circle, and Michael raised his glass up.

"A toast to friends all under one roof; some we have been with since high school, and others who are newer to us," he said with a smile, specifically looking at Ted. "And let us not forget to thank Jennifer for hosting us this evening! For we wouldn't be here without her, and I doubt Ted would have made it without her. Cheers."

"Cheers!" the rest of the party repeating in unison.

They all took a sip for the Ca'habielli. Jennifer let the wine sift through her lips before tasting the sweet and bitter arrays of the beverage. It was without a doubt the finest wine she had ever laid her lips upon. She had spent her years drinking a number of wines, but all paled in comparison to this legendary bottle shipped all the way from Rome. *No wonder this wine is so pristine.*

CHAPTER 8

Raw Brutality

~Prepare yourselves. You've picked a terrible person to jump. Don't give me that look when I know you don't have the stomach to sit through raw brutality.

HOURS PASSED, AND AFTER the last of the bottles of wine had been consumed and the final game had been played, Ted moved around to one of the windows, staring out of it down at the city lights illuminating the empty streets. He could hear some background chatter as Tim and Brian were leaving Jennifer's Seaport District apartment. Jennifer was engrossed in a conversation with Michael, and they seemed to be getting along quite famously.

Samantha walked over to him with another glass of wine. He turned to her, thinking he mustn't let his guard down around her; after all, she was the one who'd gotten him involved with them initially. She could pry out of him secrets he wanted to remain hidden. He didn't want to know them himself. She joined him, sitting on the wide windowsill. She returned his smile back to him. He thought the smile was genuine, with authentic happiness and sincerity. She said, "Ted, I have a question, and I hope I don't come off as rude. I hope you don't mind."

"I don't mind at all. The moon is out, the wine is delicious, and any matter of question is allowable." He smiled, and yet he felt exhausted. "But just because a question is allowed, it doesn't necessarily mean I'll answer."

"Okay," she replied.

He could tell she was put off by his answer. *Perfect.*

"We didn't do anything to upset you two weeks ago, did we? We were concerned that something might have happened to you afterward when we didn't see you. And we were especially concerned when Jenn told us you would be here at one and there was no response when you were late." She let out a nervous laugh. "I think Jenn thought you might have died on the way here."

"Well, as you can see, I am here now, and not dead," Ted replied. "I don't mean to cause concern, as I hadn't come to think myself to be part of this—how does she put it?—part of this 'dysfunctional family.' As such, I didn't think my absence would play a major part in your day's concern, as you and I only met three weeks ago."

"Okay." Sam nodded. "Then, do you consider yourself part of us, then?" She looked at him seriously. "Answer me honestly. You have a hiddenness about you. I'm having a hard time reading you."

He smiled. "I don't intend to keep anything from you, but I will speak on such matters required for our relationship and nothing more. I am difficult to read, so you say, and this is the first time I'm hearing of it."

"Because you're unusual. All I really know is what you do and where you are from. I don't know what your likes and dislikes are. Does anyone?" Sam continued, pushing for some unambiguous answer.

"I suppose I like working. I guess that is one thing—" The volume of his voice dropped.

"About that," she interrupted him. "How many hours do you work? From what I hear, you are something of a workaholic."

"I suppose one could say that." He chuckled, looking at the ceiling. "I work about as much as one-hundred and sixteen hours a week."

"What?" She repeatedly blinked. She couldn't believe her ears. "Can you repeat that?"

"One-hundred and sixteen hours a week," he answered. He was careful to retain that smile.

"I thought that's what you said. How can you possibly maintain that?!" she exclaimed. "Do you even sleep?"

"I sleep enough." He smiled.

She realized something: underneath his eyes was the jaded expression of a man who knew little sleep. "Ted, how much do you sleep?"

"I sleep enough," he replied.

No wonder he can just go out and buy a $1,200 bottle of wine. "Why do you work so much? Do you even have something you would consider fun?"

"I find work fun, and it keeps me occupied," he answered.

"You're avoiding the question," she accused.

"No, I'm answering the question. The truth can be so hairy. Like I said before, I will answer your questions and reveal some of myself as necessary for our relationship." He kept his smile, but his tone lowered a step.

"That—that's not the same thing!" she exclaimed. "It's not the same thing. You are avoiding the—"

"Miss Harris, I believe you might have had a little much to drink," he suggested. "Might it be time to retire for the night?"

"Perhaps you're right." Sam looked down at her glass, which was now half empty. "I'm sorry, Ted, I shouldn't have said anything. Can you find it in yourself to forgive me?"

"I'm afraid I cannot. There is nothing to forgive. There is no reason to be sorry. Humans are humans." He smiled at her.

"I will leave you to your scenery, then. Will we see you Tuesday?" Sam asked.

"Time, I suppose, will tell, assuming I don't have any fires in the market to put out," he answered.

"But look, I know that we just met you, and us going out of our way to make you part of our little group may seem off-putting, and for that I apologize. I hope you will see that we mean you no discomfort." Sam stopped speaking for a moment to allow him a moment for a response. Seeing that there was no response, she said, "That will have to do for now." She took her wine glass and went over to Michael, who wrapped his arm around her shoulder again.

Ted took to the window again and looked out at the black, empty sky. The darkness was familiar to him. It was like the murky waters of the Dead Sea, filled with nothing but hopeless void. His eyes were beginning to droop, and his attention shifted to his hand. His hand was not twitching as was common this time of night.

If it is all meaningless, as you say, then why don't we all just lie down and die?

Why are you not trembling? What is different?

The door closed behind him. He turned to see only Jennifer in the room. She smiled at him as she brought her glass over to sit with him and stare emptily out of the window, down at the city lights. She let out a sigh of relief.

"Well, that was fun. Did you enjoy yourself, Tedward?" she asked him.

"Well, it certainly wasn't dull, and I'm sure I have you to thank for that." He smiled back at her. The moonlight was oppressively pushing down his spirits.

"So, tell me, Tedward: what is one thing I don't know about you?" she asked him. "Answer, and I will reveal something about myself."

He hesitated.

"So, there is something human about you after all." She laughed. He could have sworn there was something sinister behind her watchful gaze.

"Well, I suppose it's been a while since I've played twenty questions, but I can't help but think that's not how it works." He chuckled. "I suppose you'll have to ask me something specific. Isn't that how it goes?"

"Okay," Jennifer smirked. "So that's how it is, you sly little fox."

"I think I am much closer to a wolf," he joked.

"Perhaps a wolf raised by foxes." She let that sink in. "Well, my dear—"

"So, I'm a deer now?"

"You are whatever your sweet self wants to be. You be a deer, a fox, a wolf, or any other woodland creature. So, here's my question, and forgive me if I already asked, but I cannot recall: have you any siblings?"

"There are those that I would have called brother and sister," he answered.

"Well, were they half siblings, full siblings, adopted?"

"I suppose you could say they were adopted siblings," he answered coldly, retaining his smile.

She smiled, satisfied with the answer. "Now, Tedward, I believe it is your turn to now ask me a question. As reserved as you are, surely you have a question."

"I have many questions," he replied. "Sadly, very few, if any at all, involve people."

"Then I beg you to make a question for me. What would pique your interest about me?" She leaned closer to him.

What are you doing, Jennifer?

"I suppose this one I can ask: what do you find peace in?" he asked, revealing nothing else. He merely retained that smile as he asked it.

"I suppose I haven't given it much thought. I suppose if I found anything that gave me peace, it's that I can be of some help to someone along the way with this very short life I've been given. Like many, I will not live for very long. Humans do not live very long lives. As they used to say—what was it?—before they all started digesting liquid detergent—'YOLO.' You only live life once." Her face went dark. "I guess I find the opposite to be true. You live and die just as many times as the other, and they equally plague us. Like both are a disease that must be vaccinated. But life's vaccination is death, and death's vaccination is life."

"How very Tao of you," he said.

Her smile returned as she laughed sheepishly. "Then it is my turn, then. What do you find peace in?"

"I'm not sure if I like that question." He snickered. "And was it not the same question I asked you?"

"Yes, it is. Is this question a little too revealing, Tedward?" She laughed like a little cat tugging on its yarn of string.

I asked you that to find an answer for myself.

"You could say that, but I also know you will not like the answer," he replied.

Her face went graven again. "Look, Ted, I will decide if I like the answer or not. If I like it, then you would be pleased you were wrong. If I don't like it, I suppose you'll be satisfied knowing you were right all along. But I will accept whatever answer you give me, as it was my question that I asked. The point of this was to get to know some facet of you that is hidden underneath that shell. They say darkness loves company, but it hates what's on the surface, as the surface is where truth lies."

"Well, they say darkness can't live in the light," he said.

She smiled again. "That is something true you just said." She paused. "Now, might I have my answer?"

"Well, I suppose it doesn't matter if you would like the answer or not, so I don't have a reason to deceive you." His voice dropped.

"Tedward." Her voice dropped, and she tilted her neck. "I know you may not think that we know you, and you're right, we don't know you as well as we would like, and I suppose you don't have a reason to trust me, but I trust you. I might not reveal all my little secrets just yet, but I trust you."

He let out a sigh, but he kept on smiling. "I suppose I don't find much of anything peaceful. I work a lot, and don't leave myself time for such luxuries." His voice dropped as he broke eye contact with her.

"Ted?"

"Do you know why I chose life as a stockbroker?" he asked. He didn't let her answer. "It is the one job in the world that I can think of that will let me work around the clock. I barely sleep. I am lucky if I sleep more than thirty minutes at a time." He paused, looking back into her eyes, trying to analyze her reaction. She patiently waited for him to finish, looking him in the eyes, nodding. "I have no peace within myself, so I drown myself in work, hoping to keep my mind occupied."

"Does it work?" she asked.

"Yes," he replied.

"Is it worth it?"

"I don't know," he replied. "I think I've spoken enough of myself for one night. I think it is time for me to go back."

"Home?" she asked.

"That is such a funny word," he said, standing up and leaving his wine glass on the nearby coffee table. "I've been in many countries and moved countless times. I don't think I've ever been to a place I would call home."

Jennifer frowned, her eyes glazing over. "Ted, that is so sad." She went to grab his hand. He pulled it away. "Look, before you go, and I know you must be eager to leave—perhaps it was wrong for me to push you to come tonight. Perhaps it is my fault, and this was wrong of me. I didn't know that bringing you here would bring back so many memories, painful, and reminders of what you once had, or never had, and may never get the chance to feel again." She sucked on her teeth as she looked him carefully in the eye. He took a step back. "Iah—I know that I can't imagine what it is you missed, because I don't know you and I'm not going to pretend I do. I will say that I want to know you. Now, I am sorry for pushing you to come, and Iah—I hope you can forgive me. I want to know you more, and I hope that I've made it clear that I want to be your friend, and I'm not going to push you anymore to tell me what you don't want me to know."

"I thank you, Jennifer," he answered. "I must be going."

He turned around and walked to the door.

"Ted, will we see you on Tuesday?" she asked, just as the door was still slightly ajar.

"Time will tell," he answered truthfully.

As the door shut behind him, Jennifer's hands trembled. She walked over to the door to lock it. She started picking up the paper plates and threw them in the trash with the now empty pizza boxes. She placed all her cups in the dishwasher before making her way to her room.

The room was large, and her bed looked like it was freshly made and patted down with the utmost care to avoid any wrinkles. She crawled into her bed and lifted her knees to her chest as she stared blankly at her bedroom door. Tears started to stream down her face, because she remembered something. The look in his face was all too familiar. She remembered the same look on her uncle's face, the same overtired look, the baggy and swollen eyes. The one-word answers, and a fake smile while giving a genuine laugh, laughing at his own misery.

She remembered her uncle being elusive with the truth. Not exactly lying, but he wasn't telling the truth either. The man was a hardened veteran who'd seen his fair share of battle, and the fatigue showed with the lack of interest in anything. The last night she'd seen him whole, well, he'd been hanging from a ceiling, his torso stretching. No one knew, or no one made known how long he'd been hanging there, but if he was stretching, Jennifer knew it had been quite some time since anyone had made the effort to check in on him. It was long enough, anyway, that no one seemed to have missed his sudden absence.

Even if just for a moment, she saw the ragged look on her uncle's face to match perfectly Ted's face, and then she knew that Ted was hiding something that he wanted to keep hidden. Some mischief, regret, trauma, but the Ted she knew was not Ted as he truly was. He wore a fake smile, the social bandage to put on a show, to show everyone he was fine, but it was nothing more than a mask, and underneath that façade was a festering wound, and it hurt. *Damnit. It hurts.* She felt a part of her heart in agonizing pain. She wanted to do something, but what?

Ted gasped, gritting his teeth as he leaned against the back of the elevator all the way down. He started breathing heavily as the elevator lights blinked from floor to floor. He glared at the lights as if they were mocking him. His fists clenched until he reached the bottom. The elevator bell shot through his head. He took a deep breath and again hid his misery. The double doors slid open, and he crossed the threshold.

He went down the stairs and opened the last door to enter the empty street of Seaport Boulevard. The streetlights were blinking. The cars were empty, and the street was devoid of all humans. Just the little pieces of trash that flew out of the public trashcans. He parked all the way towards Government Center. He walked west, following the many empty buildings, burger joints, coffee shops, ice cream parlors, and fisheries.

The moon beat down on him, and not a star was in sight. He held that same defeated smile as he walked down the boulevard. He took deep breaths through his nose until he passed the bridge across from the Boston Tea Party Museum. He smelled something foul in the air. He looked behind him, and he could smell the stench of something that was all too familiar to him: blood.

He turned around in the middle of the bridge and he could see cascading purple, pink, green and blue lights flaring up from the end of Seaport, getting much closer to Black Falcon Avenue. They looked like short-fused fireworks without the noise.

He turned around and walked away from the lights. Whatever it was, he wanted no part of it. If someone was getting murdered in an impressive array of fireworks, he didn't care. Besides, even if he did get involved, he'd only end up killing someone, and get caught in an endless loop of violence and murder. That was the last thing he wanted. He continued on in the moonlight, the lights behind him ceasing. He crossed the bridge over the water, walking beneath some trees as he arrived at an intersection and waited for the crosswalk. There was a large skyscraper in front of him, and a hotel; the dark side of the hotel, with the only windows of the tenants. The entrance was on the other side. There were no lights here. The lights in the skyscraper were shut off, as there was no one working on it this evening.

He heard the breath coming from some bush. Someone with foul intentions. He sighed and turned to the bush. A man came out of the shadows. He could sense six other men coming out. The one in front of him pointed a pistol at him. It was a 9mm. The other six had makeshift melee weapons. One of them a bat, another a two-by-four. The others carried miscellaneous metal apparatuses: a crowbar, a pipe, and two machetes. *I wonder where they got those from.*

"Empty your pockets!" the man with the pistol said.

Ted raised his eyebrows at him.

"Do you think this is a game?! I'm not playin'! Empty your pockets, or I will shoot you dead!"

The man's hand was shaking. Ted knew the man had never held a gun before in his life, especially holding it like that. He knew the pressure of the gun would never make the intended target. He said nothing.

"Do you think I'm playin'?"

"You're not going to shoot me like that." Ted smiled at him. "Did you really intend on robbing me with such a shaky trigger finger? You're not fooling me, so if you would kindly let me be on my way—"

"Hit him!" the man with the gun said.

He could hear the scurrying footsteps coming from behind him. Ted laughed as the crowbar struck him in the leg. He never reacted to it. He turned to the man who'd hit him and smiled, mocking the man just as the moonlight mocked him.

"You see, I don't want to kill you. Don't turn me into that monster," Ted said.

"Again!" the man with the gun ordered, his voice shaking as if this was his first time trying to rob someone. Or perhaps this man had robbed many people before—just not with a gun—and this was his first time encountering someone who didn't bother to budge to his demands, and even mocked him.

The man with the bat struck Ted in the side. It sounded like some ribs were cracked. Ted shrugged it off and stepped forward. It was not his ribs, but the barrel was splintered. The man with the gun got his grip and pointed it at Ted, looking at him with hatred in his eyes.

"Oh, don't even bother looking at me like that." Ted's smile changed, finally showing his teeth and mania and bloodlust in his eyes. "I know you don't have the stomach to handle raw brutality!"

Ted sprinted toward the man with the gun. The man opened fired with the silenced pistol. Ted's eyes scanned the trajectory of the bullets, seeing each one leaving the chamber, hearing the clicks from the gun, precisely knowing the moment each round would leave the barrel. Just as he'd predicted, the man didn't know how to shoot the gun. Ted followed his bullet lines to avoid being hit. He heard the footsteps of the two running behind him, trying to stop him from getting their ringleader.

The gunman's face contorted, clearly surprised. The clicking trigger of an empty gun being repeatedly pressed was like a count down. The ejection port was pushed back, and the inside of it was smoking. He dropped the gun and stepped back; his face turned to that of a scared old man.

"I'm sorry. I was jo—"

"Fat chance, and you're too late!" Ted was right in front of him.

The warmth left the air, and everyone could feel it. His left fist and arm revealed blue veins that glowed in the dark as he came to swing a haymaker, and with his right leg, he kicked around to the side. The gunman was spinning in a cartwheel in the air before hitting his head on the sidewalk. The blue veins appeared along his leg as he brought his foot down to the skull of the gunman, crushing it instantly, blood and bone smeared on his shoe and the sidewalk.

He swiftly jerked to the side, turning around and avoiding a swing from the crowbar. The man with the bat swung at Ted again. He caught the splintered end with his now glowing hand. He kicked the man's elbow with his right foot. *Crack!* The man's forearm broke, causing him to let go of the bat. Ted swiftly snatched the bat from the air, turned it around and snapped it in half before stabbing the man in the shin with it.

The crowbar came swinging again. Ted moved to the side to avoid it and kicked the man hard with his left foot, sending him into the street.

The two men with machetes were close, swinging them in unison to either side of him to cut him off from dodging to the side. Ted looked closely at them. He moved off to the side, grabbing the machete from one of their hands, stabbing the other with it and pulling it down until his guts spilled onto the ground. He took his bloodied hands and put them around the other man's head and twisted it backwards.

He missed the other man with the crowbar running up at him from the street. "You bastard! You killed them!"

He swung the crowbar furiously in many directions. Ted sighed as the man came in grabbing distance. He heard the disturbance in the air of the crowbar parting it in front of him. Ted wondered, if only for a moment, if this could kill him, but then why should it, when everything else failed? His heart pumped blood to his head. He snarled at the man. He sidestepped, deflecting the crowbar. He heard the rev of an engine. His eyes scanned the street, seeing a parked car turn its lights on. He ignored the car and returned a hateful glare at the man. *Death surrounds everything I touch.*

His left arm lit up with grey veins. The crowbar swung downward, and Ted blocked it with his arm, and the man's arm was jerked back with the impact as the crowbar vibrated violently in his hand until he dropped it. His eyes were bulging out of his skull as Ted's hand seized him by the throat, lifting him up. The grey veins turned their color back to blue. The man could feel the strength of Ted's fingers digging into his throat. He clawed at Ted's hands to get free, but Ted's strength was beyond human.

The car's tires screeched. The man's life was fading. Ted's eyes shifted towards the car speeding its way to him. He snickered as the man's arms dropped down, lifelessly. He smiled, sneering at the car. "If you intend to run me over with that, you better be wearing your seatbelt!"

Ted's blue veins glowed from his hands, crawling rapidly into the corpse of the man he now held. This man was like an extension of his hand.

The car sped towards him, the wheels moving round and round as it screeched, staining the pavement with its black rubber tires. He smiled as he thrust the corpse into the front of the car, crunching the hood, blood spattering everywhere. The car came to a screeching halt as the front of the car dented into the axel, sending both front tires spinning off. The crunching metal filled the air as countless shards of glass started falling through the air like sweet, bloody snowflakes where the driver had been ejected through the windshield.

Ted picked the flying driver out of the air by her neck as he let the other man fall from his grasp. The car flipped over him and crashed into the road, slowly scraping and sparking down the pavement, followed by a trail of streaming gasoline.

The woman was still conscious, still in shock. She tried to grab hold of his hands to release herself. There was nothing she could do. The veins entered his right hand again. He squeezed her neck tighter. She tried to cry out, but her windpipe was crushed, and she could feel the man's grip touch her spine. Her eyes gaped as her mouth desperately tried to scream.

There was one man left, too scared to scream, too horrified to run. He squinted as he tried to pull out the splintered bat from his leg. He grunted. Ted briefly turned. It seemed this other man wanted to help his driver. Ted curled his lips, seeing the despair fill his eyes, because there was no fighting against something or someone who even Hell rejected.

Crack. Buckle.

Her arms and legs fell lifelessly. He squeezed her neck tighter until her eyes were pushed out of her sockets, hanging on by the retina. He threw her to the side. She rolled over like a ragdoll. He started laughing as he stood with blood on his hands and feet. Whoever they were, they had picked the wrong man to try to rob.

"That was oddly therapeutic," Ted said, smiling up at the empty sky. "I should probably be doing this more often." He turned to look at the petrified survivor. "Whenever you find a man filled with murder in his heart, you stand aside."

Ted's shoes lit up with his veins and he sprinted through Seaport Blvd at an inhuman pace.

CHAPTER 9

Façade

*~As everything fades—the music, the laughter, the smile, the
bandage, the makeup and the masks— once it is all removed,
we find out for ourselves that we were never okay.*

TWO WEEKS LATER, SAM was back on Park Street on a Tuesday night, walking out of the church. Everyone around her had umbrellas in an array of colors and sizes.

The air felt cooler when the breeze passed through their clothes, caressing their skin. The rain was falling down ever so lightly, as if the heavens were undecided if it wanted to rain. The steady *drip drop* could be heard as it fell in puddles on the sidewalks and streets. Cars were driving by, their wheels spinning out water, drenching unsuspecting pedestrians who'd been too careless to bring an umbrella.

As Samantha had been leading the study that night, she'd wondered if she might find Ted at Terri Nation. He hadn't been there last week, according to Scott, and had seemed to avoid them the week before that. She also noticed as she spied Jennifer that she seemed a little down today, not her usual self. Truth was, Samantha hadn't seen Jennifer at all since the game night she'd hosted two weeks ago. Samantha looked down at her feet as her shoes splashed in the small shallow puddles on the sidewalk.

Did something happen between him and Jennifer after we left? she thought.

She hurried up and hooked Jennifer's elbow, startling her. Samantha saw something in Jennifer's eyes that she hadn't seen before, and it filled the air like a stench of regret. She should have known something was off. Jennifer hadn't been her usual joking self these last two weeks, and the last time she'd seen Jennifer as herself was at the party, before she'd left her and Ted alone in the apartment. *He didn't try to hurt her, did he?*

"Hiii!" Jennifer exclaimed. Her face lit up with her bright smile again. "What brings you to my side on such a rainy night?"

Sam needed to speak to her privately. Fortunately, they were far out of earshot from everyone else following them that night.

"Well, I was thinking, I haven't seen Ted in a while. Have you heard of anything?" she asked.

Jennifer sighed through the rain, and sucked the air through her teeth, hissing. "I can't say I've heard from him," she answered, turning her head away from Sam. "I haven't heard from him since that night."

"Have you tried calling him again? Or texting?" Sam was suspicious and couldn't help but fight this feeling that Jennifer was hiding something.

"Yes," she answered. "I started getting abrupt responses again."

"What did he say?" The curve in Samantha's lips became less prominent.

"The last thing he told me was that he wasn't someone I wanted to get close with. Whatever that means." She exhaled deeply. "Oh, well. Nothing we can do about it, right?"

Jennifer's smile returned to her face, and the rain grew heavier, pounding her umbrella with tremendous force, as if handing its burden onto her. *Ted.* Samantha followed Jennifer through the bar, waving at Scott as they entered.

Jennifer sat at the bar and took out her purse. Sam sat next to her. They were alone for the most part; the rest had yet to catch up to them. They did manage to see the four foreigners drinking to themselves in the corner again. She was not going to bother them tonight.

Scott asked Jennifer, "Having the special?"

"Not today, Scott," she answered, smiling at him. "I'm afraid I'm not in the mood for an adventure tonight. The House bourbon on the rocks is fine by me. Just for tonight."

"Who are you?" Sam asked, joking with her. "I'll take a merlot."

"Big spender today, aren't we?" Jennifer joked with a half-enthused smile.

"You could say that." Sam turned to Scott and slid her card across the table. "I'm buying today." Scott's eyebrows rose as he disappeared behind the bar top. Samantha turned back to Jennifer with a smile. "I got my commission check last week. And you always buy my drinks; it's time I returned the favor."

"Why, thank you so much!" Jennifer exclaimed.

Scott came by with the drinks in hand, including the receipt. Samantha took the receipt and wrote in a generous tip. Scott's eyes popped. "Thanks, Sam." He sped off to check on the foreigners.

"What's wrong?" Sam asked.

Just then, a surge of people came in, flooding the bar. The noise came in like a rushing wave. Out of the corner of her eye, she could see the foreigners getting uncomfortable with the noise. The hostile man she'd met two weeks ago sneered from across the room. *Or was it last week?*

"Iah—" Jennifer began.

"Hey!" Michael's arm draped over Sam's shoulder. He waved down Scott. "I'll take the special."

Scott smiled back at him. "Whatever that is."

Michael looked down, smiling at everyone, until he noticed that Jennifer was *not* drinking a strange concoction. "Not feeling adventurous today?"

"Can't say that I'm up for an adventure." Jennifer smiled back at him as she took a sip from her glass. "Maybe you can use this as an excuse to finally coerce Brian into drinking some of Scott's lovely aromas."

"But I like my drinking buddy," Michael jested. "Oh well, maybe next week. I need to catch up with him anyways."

"Tata for now!" Jennifer laughed. Sam sensed the reluctance in her laughter as Michael scurried off into the unusually large Tuesday night crowd.

Brian was real busy today.

"So, Jennifer. What's wrong? I can tell when you're not yourself."

Jennifer smiled at her as she took another sip. "Why, nothing out of the ordinary."

"Jenn. Your laugh is half genuine. I can't tell if you're actually happy right now," she said, placing one of her hands atop Jennifer's on the bar top and looked her in the eyes. "You can pretend to borrow Ted's smile, as wide as it is, but it can't hide your laugh. You have a unique laugh. I love your laugh. So, out with it, please. What's wrong?"

Jennifer let out a sigh and placed her drink on the counter of the bar. "It's Ted," she said. Her smile began to fade, and her eyes watered. "He showed me a part of him, a part that he kept hidden. He is not what he seems."

"Did he hurt you?" she exclaimed softly. "Don't—"

"What, no!" Jennifer corrected herself, turning abruptly to Sam. "Don't even mention the idea. He is not like that! He may not be what he seems, but he's far from a monster that would hurt someone in her own apartment!"

"What did he show you?" Sam lowered her voice.

Sam looked into Jennifer's eyes, those cold, trembling eyes glimmering in the bar as golden light reflected upon them like the emission of little flames. "I saw nothing but agonizing pain. Just that. Pain, and nothing else. He is restless and suffers from what I can only imagine is the most extreme form of insomnia I have ever heard of. He sleeps not more than thirty minutes a night. It's like he's hiding pain that just wants to get screamed out, but when he tries, he can't."

Sam remembered asking him a question that may have touched upon his insomnia. She recalled that he'd only given her vague and brief replies that never really answered the question. *The man is mysterious, and a tough nut to crack.*

"We talked a little about peace, in our little conversation there. In there, I found that he does not hold any peace in his heart. He has never known a home. Or so he said. He has some siblings, but he talked as if they were just part of his past, and nothing of their relationship remained." Jennifer took another sip of her cup as it trembled in her hand. "A man like that can exist, but the mere act of living brings nothing but pain to him."

"Do you think he's suicidal? Because if so, we need to get him help!" Sam's smile was gone.

"Someone once told me, 'The brightest smiles bring us the greatest of joys. The loudest laughter is like a grand orchestra, and the most beautiful faces are covered in makeup, because we are okay, and everything is fine. The brightest smile is like a bandage, it looks okay, but inside the wound still festers, asking to be cut off. They say laughter is the best medicine. And the mask is our way of making ourselves look more beautiful, to reduce our flaws and hide our scars. When the smiles fade away and the bandage is ripped off; when the laughter is silenced and the music stops, when the makeup is washed away, and our mask fades, we find that we were never truly okay.'" Jennifer ignored the question.

"Oh my God!" Sam covered her mouth with her hand. She understood the imagery loud and clear, even if Jennifer never actually said she believed Ted to be in danger of suicide.

"Iah. I just wished I thought of it sooner," Jenn said. Her face went blank, as if staring at something that wasn't there.

"When was the last time you got a response from Ted?" Sam asked.

"Last Friday," she answered. She put the glass down. She buried her face in her hands. "Sam, if you would, leave me alone for a minute. I just can't. I can't." She choked on the last phrase.

Sam patted her shoulder. "If ever you need to talk. . ." She found herself choking on her words. "You know I am here, and you know how to get in touch with me. You know this."

Samantha went into the crowd, searching for Erin. If anyone had had contact with Ted, it would have been her.

Samantha caught sight of Erin straight away and walked up beside her, elbowing her. Erin looked up, sipping from her cider. "Well," Erin said to her, "you made me spill by drink."

"I'm sorry." Sam hesitated. "I needed to ask you something. Has Ted been showing up at work at all?"

"Yes. Still the workaholic. What is it with you and Ted? Aren't you and Michael dating? And I thought Jenn had the hots for him." She turned on her stool and took another sip of her cider.

"What?" Sam stepped back. "No, I'm not dating Ted, but that's not the point. Look, it's just that, it's just that he's new. I'm not romantically invested in him at all. Here he is in Boston, by himself, and he doesn't seem to have any network of friends of family here. He comes off as a loner," Samantha replied. "Did he seem off to you?"

"I can't say that he has," Erin answered. "I mean, he comes around like clockwork. His behavior doesn't really change."

"What about after Jennifer's apartment the week before?" Sam said.

"No." Erin scratched her chin.

Sam felt defeated. She was trying to piece together who Ted was, and knowing now that Jennifer was emotionally invested in him, she felt a wave of concern fall upon her heart. Ted was like a painting, vibrant in color, but the artist was unknown, and the strokes of the brush were unknown, hidden by layers and layers of paint, layers of layers of different personalities, all competing for dominance on one canvas.

"Wait," Erin said, her voice dropping a bit. "Actually, I suppose this was a little unusual. On that Monday, he seemed very energetic, more so than usual. It was like he'd had a good night's sleep or something, or accidentally inhaled some speed. That would have been cause for concern, but he was back to his usual self the next day."

"I see."

"Did he disappear again?"

"I suppose you could say that."

"Look, Sam, a man like that sells himself to his work. For him, it's like nothing else matters or exists outside of it. Trust me when I say this: you may see him again, you may not. He may readily move across the country tomorrow if he thought to. He isn't the type of man to keep friends. At least, that's the vibe I get from him."

"That's a sad life to live." Sam's voice dropped.

"He seems satisfied with it, all the same." Erin sighed. "As much as I would love to have his level of success, I mean, that is a ton of money, I wouldn't trade my friends and family for it."

"Satisfied does not mean fulfilled," Sam reasoned, but what if he didn't want to be fulfilled?

"I don't think he wants a fulfilled life," Erin gave her rebuttal. "Look, people get into stocks to make money, and to make a lot of it. Ted, as far as I can tell, has never lost anything so far. His portfolio, and the portfolio of his clients grows exponentially. He doesn't seem happy with it, like he goes through the motions." She let out a deep sigh. "It's like, whatever he is going through, that he's just stopped caring. He doesn't seem to care about the money at all, and he's raking it in every single hour. My suggestion, if you don't see him again, is to just let it go. Just let him go."

"I see." Sam didn't feel like talking about this anymore. She was concerned, as if something was pulling at her heart. "Thank you for that."

"Look, Sam, I'm sorry." Erin looked her closely in the eyes and put her free hand on her shoulder. "For what good it is worth, I completely agree with you, and I don't think it's a healthy path that he's walking on. And I don't know if this is going to help you get anywhere with him, but I asked him about that last big deal he brokered out, and why he didn't seem satisfied with it. It was because he knew the answer. It's like he wants to be wrong, as if there was one mistake in his life that led him to believe everything was inevitable. Like being wrong would undo that mistake."

"Thank you for that, Erin. That's more than I could have hoped for." Sam smiled, but she couldn't say she felt happy about the answers she'd received tonight.

Samantha left Erin to continue whatever conversation she was having with Brian. She understood that Erin spoke from a place of matter-of-factness, and with little empathy. Of course, she meant well, and certainly no malice was ever intended, but it didn't always come across that way, especially with this. She certainly was upfront about things, and blunter than Michael. Sam worked with truck drivers; she should have known how to deal with this by now.

She walked back over to the bar where Jennifer had been. Her glass was empty, but her umbrella was still there, leaning just underneath the bar. Jennifer's coat was gone. *Maybe she got a call from Ted. That is highly unlikely at this point.* She sighed.

"So, did you finally make your rounds?" asked a very smiling Michael.

"I did." Sam looked up to him. She finished her glass of wine. "I'm worried."

Michael's phone buzzed in his pocket. "Why are you worried?" he asked as he picked up his phone to read something he found enticing on the web.

"Ted. I feel like we made some headway with him, but—"

"You get the feeling he never showed us who he was and are now concerned that something might have happened to him. You are concerned because you feel like he was growing on us to the point where he would consider himself to be one of us?"

"Well, yeah," she said indignantly.

"I wish I could think like that." Michael laughed, and his face immediately went dark as he read the headline of a news article. "The reality is that we often don't know ourselves well enough to read into others, and we think we can read into others so easily. There are those who protect themselves with an unbreakable wall." He sighed. "Do you remember that philosophical question, 'what happens when an unstoppable lance meets an immovable shield'?"

"I remember the question. I don't remember the outcome," she admitted.

"The shield won. The lance shattered and its rider came tumbling down," he replied. "Look, some shields just can't be broken, and some walls won't come down, no matter how hard you smash against them. There is only one way through, and that is around." He pointed his finger in the air with a half-raised hand and moved it in a circular motion. "Hoping there is some kind of crack in there. You can only make it through the crack."

"So, in other words, pain." She came to the sudden realization that only pain would make it through. She could only talk to Ted through pain, and that was the only thing he truly understood. Or so she thought. She focused on Michael's phone. "So, what has your eyes so captivated when I'm right here?"

"The suicide rate just spiked up," he answered. "We are beating Japan."

"Great." Sam sighed. *And Ted might become a victim of that.* "As if the world didn't have enough problems. That is not something we need to be beating Japan in."

"I guess, in part it is our fault," Michael said.

"How do you mean?" she looked into his eyes with concern.

"How busy are we? We constantly move and move and move, never slowing down for a second, never checking in on our own mental health. It is inevitable that we will follow the same road, down our own broken-down insanity. How many times do we see the same thing on the streets? How often do we turn our eyes against those who are struggling with their own strife, never lending out a hand?" He locked his phone and put it back in his pocket. "How many times have we seen someone, and not offered to help them? I'm guilty, Sam. Every single day. I wish there was more that we could do in the world, you know, something that's more than giving someone a meal, more than giving them our spare change that we know we'll never use. Our spare change, is it really giving it to them? Or are we merely just discarding that which we think is already garbage? Our scraps, we have many, but to those who have nothing, to those born with nothing, those scraps are like mounds of gold, piled up. We, as Christians, need to be doing more than whatever it is we've been doing. Our inactivity is what is killing us inside. It's like every single one of us is living off borrowed time and we don't know it."

"Michael," Sam immediately thought of Ted again. "Do you think Ted is—is at risk?"

"I'm afraid I don't know him well enough to answer," he replied, shaking his head. "I feel the only one who may have some inkling of an idea of how he feels is Jennifer. I don't have an answer."

"I'm going to go," she said, her face turned graven. She put the rest of her wine on the counter and left it.

"Do you need me to walk you to the T?"

"No," she answered. "I'll be fine. I just need to clear my head."

He smiled at her as she turned away, walking out of the back of the bar. She made it down the stairs and walked over the red carpet, aware of everyone around her, waitresses with artificial smiles walking with empty glasses on their trays. The people in the pub were laughing and smiling, without a care in the world.

Are they hurting somewhere, deep inside? Sam wondered. *Are they all patched up with those bandages, and are their laughs singing? Did they remember to wear their masks and put their makeup on?*

She turned to ignore them. She was relieved to find that it had stopped raining outside. There were puddles on the ground and Jennifer sat on the side of the curb, her knees up to her chest and her head buried in her hands, just like Sam had left her. She was only in a different place not far away.

She sat down next to her; the puddle soaked her bottom as she wrapped her left arm around Jennifer. She said nothing. Jennifer raised her head, looking up at the top of the building in front of her. Her eyes were swollen as tears continued to stream down her face. She leaned into Samantha's shoulder. She tried to stifle her own sobs by intermittently sucking in the air through her teeth.

"Iah—I wish there was more I could do. I can't. I can't do it anymore!" she cried.

Sam's heart was forlorn as she leaned her head against Jennifer's. She found herself weeping with her. Jennifer sniffed the snot back into her nose. She offered no words; she knew her friend didn't need words, only an ear to listen to, a lost art in the world. Most people were quick to console their wounded friends with words, with the best of intent. They only poured salt on the wounds. Not Samantha. She listened, and offered no words of encouragement, for that would be undeniably worse than rubbing salt into a festered wound begging to be cut off.

"Why can't I be better?" Jennifer sobbed. "I know I'm not perfect, but I could stand to be a little better. A better person. Perhaps if I was more like you, Sam, then perhaps Ted would still find it in his heart to come back to us. I saw—I saw pain, undeniable, unspeakable pain in his eyes. Eyes are like the door into the human heart, his human heart! That isn't something you can easily hide, at least—at least not for very long. Why must I talk so much, without much listening? Why couldn't I have been more like you, Sam?"

Sam rubbed her tears from her own face with her right palm, twisting the tears out. "Because then you wouldn't be you. My gift is listening, but you have something I don't have. Together, we are a complete person. Our friendship is something few can claim. You are a great observer, and you can see pain, where I can't. I just can't." She sobbed with her. "I can listen, but even I can't hear pain. Listening is only good when someone talks to you. But no one can hide from the eyes, no matter how hard they try."

"But if only I—"

"Jennifer. It is possible Ted only spoke to you because he knew you were a talker, and that I am a silent listener. He may not speak to me or open up to me. A man like that doesn't miss anything, not even the smallest detail will slip past him." She sighed. "I must be going, now, Jennifer." She stared at the empty puddles. "Look, God will make a way, even when the gates are completely closed. If God wants him, He will make a path for him to follow, to alleviate his pain."

"And if He doesn't?"

"Then I'm afraid we've done all we can, and all we can ask for." Sam took her hand and pulled Jennifer's head to hers, kissing her forehead. "Good night, Jennifer. We can offer prayer. That's all we can do now. It is out of our hands now. Come, let's get you home."

Home.

Samantha took her hand and pulled her up from the sidewalk. They walked the streets towards Park Street Station. Samantha consoled her as they got on opposite sides of the red line, Samantha taking it towards Alewife, and Jennifer taking her train to Ashmont.

Samantha looked overhead at the announcements of the next train towards Ashmont, while not ignoring Jennifer who was sitting on a bench on the other side. Samantha kept thinking to herself as she waited, and she heard a loud screeching noise coming from the subway bound for Ashmont. She covered her ears with her hands as she watched Jennifer disappear behind the subway. The subway started off again, and she could see a large number of people exiting the station. Jennifer was no longer there.

Her thoughts drifted off into emptiness, and couldn't shake Ted's face, and his happy smile that seemed so genuine, but now she wasn't so sure; in fact, she was certain the opposite was true. And another thought plagued her mind: at this moment, he was a man of mystery, of which she knew so little, and yet she felt compelled to bring him into their friendship. Even when there didn't seem to be any rational reason for it. *He needs help.*

She said a silent prayer to herself.

There were bright lights in the tunnel. She looked down the tunnel for the train that was coming her way. The T was never presentable, at least not this late at night; cans and bottles rolled on the floor, used napkins glided across it, and crumbs littered the seats. The train screeched as it came to a halt, and the doors slid open. No one came out, but there was a full train. She stepped onto it, grabbing hold of one of the rubber straps secured to the metal bars at the top.

She stood over a woman, maybe in her forties, her right palm planted firmly on her forehead, her face turning red with the passion of some unknown negative emotion. Sam might not have been able to see all pain, but this woman was in dire need of a friend, someone to assure her that everything was going to be all right; just a little more encouragement in the deafening roar of everyday city life in Boston.

If only Jennifer was here. She could be that friend. You were always the talkative one, and the reassuring one. Why can't I be like you too?

Would things have been much different if your and my personalities were switched? Would we be asking the same questions?

After each stop on the red line, more and more people got off, and fewer and fewer people boarded to replace them. Eventually, after Harvard Square, she found herself utterly alone in the car. She stared out at the blackened tunnel.

To her, Ted was as much a mystery as many unknown things in the world, like the hostile man, the tall man with a strange name she didn't remember. Ted seemed happy, but she knew now that he was not at all what he seemed. He was more than a happy person, excited about all things, but she knew something deeper than his skin, some layer he'd revealed to her when no one else was worthy in his eyes.

The light to Davis Square lit up. She stepped off the subway car and walked up the gray stone stairs. Samantha stepped underneath the roof of the station, gazing out in front of her at the square filled with bars and now-empty restaurants. The rain picked up again. She was about to step outside when she noticed the luminescent light coming from above. Looking upwards, she could see the moon gazing down with its light, shining on the streets, glimmering in the puddles. She sighed, taking a step forward, pulling out her umbrella to shield herself from the torrential rain and oppressive moonlight.

The air, it's different tonight. The moonlight, it is different also; alien.

It was like there was some toxic gas in the air from a nearby leaking oil drum, just ready to be lit on fire and spurting its gasoline all over the place, setting fire to everything around it.

The stop at Davis did not release too many passengers, and she started to feel like the only one. She was alone in the dark street, like a lamb or sheep drawing in a pack of wolves to devour it.

She walked on the side street, heading up on College Avenue towards her apartment. The rain kept coming down, harder and harder, splashing bigger puddles in the streets. A late-night car was driving down the road. Its wheels turned, splashing Sam with a large wave of dirty water.

The tears of the heavens were strong. Whatever cause they had for weeping, they'd kept it in too long, bottled it deep down, never talking to anyone about their problems. The heavens had been silent, keeping and holding all the pain in until finally their flood gates had broken open, revealing the insides of their turmoil.

She walked up to the path to her apartment. Her door looked blue in the peeking moonlight. Out of the corner of her eye, three houses down, she saw a man fumbling through his keys to open a door. She looked down as she creaked her door open. Taking a better look at the man, she recognized him, and that bright, smile. *Ted. You were this close to me all this time?*

The man opened his door. Sam closed and locked hers. She walked over to the sidewalk and made her way to his house. He entered his house; he shut it firmly behind him. She made it to his door and heard the locks.

First, she could hear the tumbler being locked with the knob. The second lock she could hear was the deadbolt. And the third and final lock was a chain. She knew she needed to be secure in her own apartment, here in Somerville, but three locks seemed too much.

The door shook in front of her. She stifled a gasp, covering her mouth. She placed her hand ever so lightly on the door. The door was stilled, and she heard Ted cry. His cries started as stifled and intermittent sobs. Then, as just a little time went by, the cries went louder. The cries, to her, were like those of a child.

Had he had a childhood of grief? Had he been exploited or abused? Was he the victim of relational rape? Had he lost his family? Or perhaps had he been a child who was born with nothing and wanted nothing more than the experience of children who had even the minimalistic comfort? Was he once a child without innocence, or was that innocence stripped away from him? If so, why did he enlist in the Army, where such things would only break him under the surface, never leaving him?

Samantha took a small, bated breath and turned away from his stairs. Tears filled her eyes. *Jennifer, if only it was you instead of me. Then, then perhaps it would be different, and maybe there would be a little less pain in the world, and a little more peace. Maybe things would be different.*

She returned to her stoop, bringing her keys back to the door. Her roommate was sleeping peacefully, naked on the couch.

Her roommate was not Christian like her, and she did not share in the same ideals. Sam wouldn't have said she was particularly fond of her roommate either, as she tended to leave things messy. Especially when she knew Sam wouldn't be home until well into the night.

Samantha walked into her roommate's bedroom, yanking the blanket off the bed to tuck her in on the couch her naked body was laying on. Walking into the kitchen, she pulled out some light cleaning gloves before walking back into the living room to clean up the bowl of half-eaten chips and collect bottles of beer which were scattered throughout the room. She wasn't afraid of the beer, but she dared not touch the discarded semen-filled condom on the ground with her bare hands. Picking it up, she discarded it into the trash.

She pulled her gloves off, discarding them in the trash, and went to the sink and washed her hands. She walked into her room and changed into blue pajamas. Her tears became swollen as she stared up into the ceiling. Her thoughts drifted into an old story that she now felt she had to contemplate. It was one she'd read numerous times before, and was a case for inspiration for her, especially when things got difficult. The story of David and Goliath of Gath. She re-read the story to herself in her head, told within the first book of Samuel. She went over the entire tale, thinking to herself, *Why is this coming to me now? And at a time like this? I need action. Not some story about some hope when I live in a world without any.*

And then, it finally came to her. In that story, it was not man who held victory that day. David was nothing more than a tool. The battle was already won, as was constantly drilled into her brain at Sunday School. But though God never required the assistance of man, He wanted it. God was like a father who asked his six-year-old son to help change the tire of the car on his day off. Of course, He didn't need the help, and with the help of a little boy it would only make the task more difficult, but it was an excuse to spend time with His child, because after all, that tire never needed to be changed. And so sometimes, action was required by humans.

So, Lord, that is what you ask of me.

She pulled her phone off of her bedside table. She opened up her calendar and went to the coming Saturday.

10:00 AM Saturday, Brunch with Ted.

Just hang in there, Ted. Just a little while longer. Please, just a little while longer.

CHAPTER 10

Steel Trap

~When Hell's Gates were opened, the friendliest faces were demons and monsters. When Hell's gates were opened, what was left of humanity became nothing more than soulless husks.

IT'S JUST BRUNCH, SAMANTHA tried to calm herself. Besides, she had to think about any additional questions Ted might ask, like, how did she know where he lived? Perhaps the truth wasn't as creepy as she thought it might be; after all, it was incidental.

She walked down the stairs. She opened the door, and her phone rang. She took it out. It was Tim. She picked up the call. "Hey Tim, it's Sam."

"I know." He laughed. *"I called."*

"Yes. Yes, you did." Samantha wasn't exactly amused. She sucked the air through her teeth. "What's up?"

"Michael, Erin, Jenn and I are going out for brunch in thirty. Wanna come with?"

"I can't. I'm actually in the middle of something," she replied.

"What? Already on a date?"

"No. Michael is with you; it should be obvious that it isn't a date," she scolded him, and she shook her head. "Look, I don't have time as I'm in the middle of doing what I'm doing. I'll talk to you all about it later. I just can't do it right now."

"Have you considered not doing that and coming with us instead?" Tim pushed her. She knew he wasn't serious this time. *"I'm curious though—excuse me while I'm putting my shorts on—this seems important to you. What is it, if you don't mind me asking?"*

"Ted," she answered. "Turns out, he doesn't live far from me."

"Sam, I know you and Jennifer obsess over him. Give him his space. He'll come around," said Tim.

"Shut up, Tim," Samantha scolded.

"Fine, but be careful." Tim's tone dropped. *"Remember, if something happens, text us."*

"Don't worry, I'm not going to get into trouble of any sort," she snapped. *At least, I hope not.*

"Just be careful."

"You know I will. Okay. I gotta go. B—" she interrupted herself. "Wait, make sure to tell Jennifer. I'm doing this for her."

"I'll pass it along. Bye-bye." Click.

Jennifer, I'm doing this for you. You weren't yourself that night, I can tell, and I have my suspicion it's because of Ted, not because of anything he's done, but what he revealed to you that he showed no one else. He's a man that needs help but is afraid to ask for it.

Sam put the phone back into her pocket, opened the door and crossed the threshold into the warmth of daylight. She took a deep breath as she closed the door behind her and locked it. She walked down her stoop to the sidewalk. Her heart pounded with every step, filled with anxiety. She stood straight, making sure to at least look like she was confident, when the reality was that her heart trembled inside her chest.

She walked three houses down and up the steps to his door. She took a deep breath. *This is it. Please, let this be the right thing to do.* She knocked three times on the door. She kept silent, listening for any footsteps or movement. She searched the windows to see if anyone would open or curtains would move. She heard nothing and saw nothing; her smile faded as she feared the worse. *Don't tell me, Ted. You didn't do it. You didn't do it! Please be alive.* She knocked three more times. She waited again. Just like before, she heard and saw nothing change. She waited again nervously as her gaze trembled on the door. She bowed her head down, letting out a long sigh. She knocked on the door one last time and waited.

At last, she heard the chains from behind the door moving. She returned the smile to her face and stood up straight. The dead bolt came undone. She let out a sigh of relief. Finally, the tumblers inside the knob's lock became undone. She stared right at the edge of the door where it would open as the knob slowly turned.

Ted opened the door with that bright smile of his, looking at her, and seemed not at all surprised to see her. He was wearing the same cargo shorts and fatigues she'd first seen him in. "Good to see you, Sam," he said to her in his smooth tone.

She looked at his brown eyes to see if she could see the same thing Jennifer could see. All she could determine was that he appeared tired, with bags underneath his eyes, as usual. "Yes, it is good to see you also, Ted. It seems that you've become somewhat of a stranger of late. We missed you."

"And I suppose you tracked me down to find out if I would come back?" His eyebrow raised.

"Not exactly. Well, I didn't exactly track you down. I just simply noticed on Tuesday night that you lived here. I live a few doors down. And since I only live a few houses down, I thought I might invite you out for breakfast," she replied. "I think it might be nice to share a meal with you."

Share a meal? Really? Sam! You're better than this!

"No thanks," he replied, passing through the threshold, closing the door behind him. "I already ate."

"What did you eat?" Sam asked. She managed to peek at the floor behind the closing door, finding it to be bare. *Clearly, he knows*

I'm not leaving without him, but he's still hesitant. Perhaps this is the closest to asking for help he's going to give. Otherwise, he'd slam the door in front of me.

"Food," he answered.

Abrupt replies again. "Okay, how about a cup of coffee, then? I'll eat breakfast."

"I have coffee. There's literally no reason for me to come out of my house for that." He chuckled.

Why are you like this!

"Ted," she said. "I'm going to be blunt. You need friends! You can't be isolating yourself like this! We appreciated that gift of wine that night. Really, we did. We appreciated not because it was expensive or of the highest quality, we don't care about things like that. We cared about it because it came from a friend. *You* are that friend, Ted. I know you can't see it, but we want you to be our friend, and we want to understand what's going on in that thick noggin of yours! I know you don't wear your emotions on your sleeves, I get that." She peered into his eyes, those cursed baggy eyes, and there was a shimmer of light in them, like a candle refusing to burn out. "Why would you tell us when you've only known us for a short while? You wouldn't, but it's your fault for not getting to know us either. It's like you don't want to get close or risk having your heart shred to a thousand pieces."

She clenched her fists at her sides, sighing. "You can't hide your pain from me." She felt tears swelling in her eyes. "I came to this door, and I heard everything. Jennifer is hurt because of whatever it is you said to her, and she was emotionally distraught. Are you afraid of us hurting you, or of you hurting us?"

Ted never once changed his facial expression. He continued to smile that dastardly fake smile. *Damn this man!*

"Look, I can tell I'm not getting through that steel trap of yours. You know I'm not great at talking. Jennifer is excellent when it comes to talking. I'm good at listening, but, so help me God, I am not taking no for an answer." *Damn you! I came here to listen, not talk, Ted! Why are you making me force a monologue?!* "I don't care if I need to come into your house to drink a cup of coffee with you. I will. But you and I are having coffee! I said no to brunch to Michael and Tim *and* Jennifer for the purpose of talking with you today, and I'm hungry!"

"Well, sorry to disappoint, but I don't have any food in my house." He opened his palms to his sides. "I have coffee, but if you're hungry, I'm afraid I have nothing to offer but an ear."

"And I don't want your ear, I want your words. I'm offering my ear!" She stamped her foot. "Ted!" she hissed. "Alright, that's it. Give me your hand! I'm taking you to Joe's Bagel Bin. It's a mile this way. At the rotary, you know, where College Avenue turns into Broadway!"

Ted shook his head. "Fine, I guess I'll begrudgingly grant your request. After you."

"Chivalrous as ever," she scoffed. "Give me your hand!"

"No," he sternly spoke. "I will walk with you to get your breakfast. You may not hold my hand."

"Ted! Why must you be so difficult? Seriously, how am I supposed to know you're not going to just run off when we get to the rotary?"

"You don't," he replied. "Now, Samantha, let's go. The sooner we get there, the sooner I can leave. Upon my *honor*, I will not leave you until I've heard everything you have to say."

"I came here with the sole purpose of listening." She shook her head. "Come!"

She led him along the sidewalk and to the rotary, passing underneath many trees, shaded from the warm and overwhelmingly bright rays of sunlight. Neither of them spoke. She just led him with the unrelenting force of someone fueled with anger and indignation.

They crossed the crosswalk into the rotary and turned around the bend into a coffee shop that looked like a fancy place for breakfast, apart from the large bagel that loomed over the sidewalk, shielding the pedestrians from the oppressive astral rays.

Ted sat across from her in the diner. She crossed her hands over the table, and her ankles were also crossed over each other. Sam felt proud she'd got him this far, but insecure not knowing how the rest of this conversation was going to go. She noticed Ted observing everything in the room. His eyes scanned every moving person, and spectacle. He seemed to be looking for an exit through all the windows and ways in and out.

"Are you done?" Sam asked, irritated.

"My apologies," he said as he turned his head to look at her, never losing that smile. Nor did it seem to curve even a little less on his face. It was like he really was just a portrait.

"Ted, seriously, sometimes you just need to calm down. You're scanning the room as if there is someone out to get you. All the time. I noticed it at the party when you first came in," she admitted.

"Welcome to Joe's Bagel Bin. How may I help you?" the waitress spoke to them. The waitress had dirty blonde hair tied behind her. She was skinny and had a cheerful smile, probably fake.

"Two coffees." She pointed at Ted. "You're not skipping out on this! I'll have two eggs, scrambled, and a side of home fries. Ted, what do you want?"

"I'm not hungry. I told you I ate already," he admitted.

"I've never met a man who didn't think with his stomach," she said.

"Surprise me."

The waitress left and returned promptly with two hot mugs of coffee. The steam poured out of the cups as they were placed in front of the drinkers. Sam took a sip and returned her gaze to Ted, softening up her irritation. Ted still had that stupid smile on his face.

"Where was I?" she asked.

"I believe you were berating me." He chuckled as he took a sip.

That stupid laughter. He did it way too much for it to be genuine.

"Yes, now I remember. Do you hate us? Be honest. It will be easier for you, and me, and everyone involved if you spoke the truth. I don't want your riddles or deflection. I am directly asking you! And I will ask another direct question until I get an answer."

He placed the coffee down and gazed into her eyes, maintaining that smile. "Someone once asked me a question. Her smile seemed innocent at first. She was a lovely person, or so I thought. She asked me this: 'Tell me some things that you like, some things that you hate.' Well, looking back on it, my answer was very childish when an answer escaped my lips back then, and I guess it's similar to the question you asked. My answer was this, back then: 'I like my friends, but I hate violence.' Such an odd concept, and a childish answer for someone like me, someone who joined the Army, and did things contrary to my nature. If you were to ask me the same question today, I suppose I would answer it like this: there are many things that I hate, and I'd be hard pressed to find anything that I didn't hate. And I don't particularly like anything." He paused and let her think about what he said. "Is that enough to satisfy your curiosity?"

"So, you only hate us because you hate everything," she repeated. "Even though we've done nothing to you."

"Those icebreakers, as Jack calls them, are dangerous things. They reveal personal information, information that one can hold onto, and use, and twist. When you give out that information, you're just asking people to stab you in the back."

"You're a man who has no trust in anyone, or anything," she commented. The food arrived in front of her. Ted's plate came with a heaping portion of scrambled eggs. "What about your family, or friends?"

"I had people that once held my confidence," he answered.

"And?"

"They're all dead." His tone dropped, but he retained the façade.

Sam eyes stretched open, and her fork trembled between her fingers. She felt there was a great silence at the table, as if the two of them were in a soundless bubble where even screams couldn't escape one's lips. Her expression went from irritation to sorrow, her eyes watering as she took a bite of some of her home fries. "And your siblings?"

"We aren't on a talking basis." His tone dropped again.

"I see," She replied. "You said most of the people you held your confidence in were dead. What about the rest of them?"

"None of them can be trusted. I was foolish to trust them. But I did thank them for everything they've done for me. It is through them that I knew I only ever had fifteen friends. No more than that. Now I have none." His voice dropped even lower, and his smile faded. His eyes dropped down as if they themselves were exhausted. "Funny thing, really: a soldier, a sailor, a marine, a guardsman, coast or national, they all join the service to sacrifice for the greater good, to fight for honor, to fight for peace and our freedom. They would like to say that they would lay down their lives for peace, freedom, and honor, but I know the truth. Not one of them will question an order if it comes from the top. Every single one of them will commit genocide and not bat an eye, just because it's an order. They'll do it." He sighed as she continued to listen and eat. "I'll tell you what I told Jennifer, and now I realize it was a mistake on my part giving her my number: I am not someone you want to be close with. I'm not someone anyone should be friends with. With everything that I've done, my name will appear in the history books, but not next to Martin Luther King JR or George Washington. Not even President Lincoln. No, you'll find me in the history books, but not compared to them. The only people you could compare me to are Hitler and Stalin."

Ted, why would you compare yourself to them? The worst people who ever lived. Surely it isn't that bad. What did you do that made you feel this way?

He continued, "You asked me the other week why I felt I needed to work so much. Honestly, I want to be working more than I already am. I don't need the money. I don't want it." He waved his hand. "What am I going to spend all that money on? I *need* to work. I need to drown myself in it. It's the o—" He covered his mouth, tightly gripping his jaw. The light in his eyes faded. "It's the only thing that's drowning out all of their screams. It is the only thing that is masking all of those faces." He gritted his teeth. "They said that Saul killed his thousands and David his tens of thousands. I, on the other hand, would be lucky if my numbers were nearly that low. I'm nothing but a cold murderer."

She put her fork down to the side of her half-empty plate and looked down at it, trying to determine the meaning behind his words, or if he was lying to her. No man, no matter how cruel or sinister, would willingly admit they were a monster. A man who would call himself as such would be a dangerous man. But could there have been something else behind those words? A hidden meaning, perhaps? Was this true? Was any of it true? Or was it just a mask, a façade to hide the truth? *No. Ted, why are you lying to me, or perhaps do I not completely grasp the situation?*

"Ted." She looked back at him. *Why are you like this?* "It would be better if you didn't lie to me. I can't imagine what it is that you're going through, or how it tugs on the strings of the heart. I can't imagine a man would compare himself to Hitler, and yet you've done that. I don't doubt you have done things you regret doing, but that is something we all have done. That is what makes us human. Yes, we lie sometimes. Yes, we betray our friends' trust. That is who we are." She sighed and leaned back in her chair, relaxing with her arms crossing her chest. *God, please put in my mouth the words to speak. I'm lost.* She continued, "I have no doubt that you have killed in the service; that is to be expected. I don't believe you killed more than tens of thousands of people. I believe you may feel the rotten stench of regret for the things you've done. I know you must see the nightmares. When I found out where you lived, Ted, I walked up to your door and almost knocked after hearing all the locks clicking shut. And I heard a man removing his bandages, removing his laughter, and removing his mask. I'm sure you suffer from guilt and trauma, but you cannot do this alone, no matter how hard you try." She sucked in air through her teeth as she tried to stifle a cry, but she already felt those tears streaming down her face. Her spirit felt jaded with melancholy. *Is this how you feel? Am I making it worse?* "You can't do this alone, Ted. You need friends, and we are offering it to you. There are no conditions attached. All we want is you. That's all we want, that's all Jennifer wants. We don't want your excuses, we don't want your lies, we don't want your laughter or your jokes, or even that smile that you and I both know isn't real. All we want is you and your friendship. Maybe it isn't even fair of me to ask this, but what happened that turned you into this?" She'd seen enough war movies to recognize the symptoms of PTSD, and it was clear he suffered from it, but that wasn't all he suffered from. There was more, much more he was hiding underneath the surface. That steel trap was far more complex than she'd realized, and she couldn't crack it alone. She was the spear, and he was the shield. The shield might crack, but she was at risk of falling off the horse.

"Well, it appears that you have found a way to tug on something that I forgot was there once," he answered. "But I can't tell you what happened. Everything that happened is classified above top secret. I will hold this in, bottle it in forever, and never talk about it to anyone at any time. Because I can't. You don't understand. I want to talk, but I can't. And I can't even tell you why I can't talk about it."

"But if you keep doing that, this bottle is going to explode!" she whispered.

He deeply sighed. "I'm afraid that bottle has already exploded. And it was pieced back together, much to my dismay. That bottle won't stay broken, as much as I want it to."

"What are you talking about?" She leaned forward on the table, her elbows propping her up.

"In all my years of living, twenty-three regrettable years, I have but one regret: not hanging myself with my own umbilical cord. Now I can't even die right."

Sam shifted uncomfortably in her chair. He was obviously trying to redirect the conversation away from how he was truly feeling. She knew he must feel that way, but she hadn't expected him to come out and say it. Or for it to be so unsettling. *He is suicidal.* "Ted, what did you try to do?"

"Everything I can think of," he answered grimly. "And nothing works!"

"If nothing works and you are a living husk, why not try to bring life back into it? Why not try to make friends with what you have? If nothing works, something is trying to keep you alive, or you're not quite ready to go." Sam waved the waitress down. Ted merely smiled at her, mocking her as if she had fallen off her horse, and that shield remained uncracked and unbroken.

The waitress came by.

"I'll take a box for his eggs and the check. I'll pay for it," Sam said.

The waitress nodded and left to fetch the box and print out her check.

"You barely touched your eggs," Sam commented.

"I can't taste anything. I haven't tasted anything in over fifteen years," he replied. "Eating for me is like putting fuel in the car; it's tasteless. It's nothing more than a careless chore. There." He smiled again, the façade which he knew wasn't fooling anyone anymore. The smile seemed sarcastic. "Now you know a lot about me. You can believe my tale or not, but that is me. A bitter man filled with nothing but hate and regret. Tell me, then, Sam, would you really want a man like me as a friend, when taking life seemed second nature to me? Or am I just a tool to you, a project for you to work on to make yourself feel better?"

Sam pointed a stern finger at him. The box came with the check. She gave the waitress her card. "Ted, I'm going to ignore that, and forgive you. Why? Because I know you don't mean it. I think you revealed to me much more than you intended, or you are the best poker player alive. You are making yourself look like the Devil, like I'm sharing breakfast with Satan to make me feel better for breaking a friendship with you or any kind of bond, and that I would be free to do so easily. That doesn't work on me, for the Lord taught me better than that. My friendship, as well as Michael's, Erin's, Tim's, and Jennifer's are still on the table. We want you to be part of us. Now, will you come with us for the Fourth of July Canoe trip?"

"I'll dec—"

"You will accept this invitation."

"I will think about it."

"You will come."

"I said I'll—"

"And I said I'm not taking no for an answer, Ted," she replied. "Unlike before, I now know where you live. I'll drag you on the canoe if I have to."

"Fine. You've got me. Heaven knows even I can't relocate fast enough for that." He snickered.

"You better not even think about that!" she said. "Are you taking your eggs?"

"No."

She packed up his eggs into the box. "Well, I'm not about to let this go to waste. Are you coming on Tuesday?"

"I'll think about it," he replied.

"So, no," she said. She knew what his 'maybes' or 'think about its' meant. They were the polite way to decline an offer. "I'll see you Saturday. We meet at Kendall Square at 4:30 PM. You will be there then—no. I expect you there at 4PM. If you are not there at 4PM,

I will assume you're trying to escape, and I will drive to your house and pick you up myself!"

"I see you don't trust me," he said, returning that forsaken smile upon his lips.

"I trust you, but I also trust that you will try to avoid it using any means necessary," she said. "I know you don't trust us, and I'm not going to pry any further." She picked up her purse and stood up. "I will trust that you will be there at 4:00PM. If you are not there, I'm dragging you here myself."

"I understand."

CHAPTER 11

Ducks

TED TOOK A SHORT walk, crossing the street to Nathan Tufts Park. He walked upon the shaded path to the tower. He took a brief look at it, making it look like he was even marginally interested in it. He investigated the blank, empty gate that went into the tower. It was locked. He walked down the path to find an unoccupied bench. Looking around, he made sure that no one else was there, so he could relax a moment. Satisfied, he sat himself down on the bench.

He looked out toward the empty street. The sun gazed down through the clouds and through the tree line. He leaned back into his seat, crossing his legs and relaxing his arms behind the back of the bench. He sighed deeply before retreating into his thoughts.

"Why? How cruel can you be? You will not let me part from this world, and that is the only thing I want. I don't want friends, and don't want or need a family. I entered into this world with very little, and what little I had was violently ripped from me and left me to ponder the cruelty you left me in. And God, here you are, mocking me, trying to give me hope when I can't see past the tunnel," he whispered softly to himself, barely audible beyond his lips. Even he hardly heard those words, mildly distracted by the chirping birds up in the sky and the ribbits of the frogs nearby. "You have shown me the light in the tunnel, but as with all good things, I can't trust it. You know I can't trust it. You know I can't trust You. How cruel can you be?"

A warm summer breeze brushed past him. He caught the sweet aroma of wildflowers in its wake. The scent of pine was pungent, and assaulted his nostrils, but he didn't care. It was one of his favorite smells. Funny, he'd lost his sense of taste, but not his smell.

"By some fluke chance, I missed something. I let my guard down once, for just one minute out of a desperation to get in my door, and now *she* knows where I live. Was that—" he stammered. "—was that Your doing? Lord, are you trying to tell me something? Are you really trying to tell me I should be giving this cursed life one last chance before cancelling out a subscription I never signed up for? This was something I didn't want. I never asked for any of it, and yet You forced me to pay a price higher than any have paid."

Ted was not a praying man, nor was he a spiritual man. He had never been given the opportunity to tell his friends how he felt, to process his grief, nor could he trust a therapist. Yet, here he was, praying to nothing, just talking to himself in a public park like a deranged fucking lunatic.

"By some fluke, you want my heart when it is garbage. It is filled with scars. You stabbed it. You shot it full of bullet holes. You cast it into the furnace. You crushed it with buildings. My heart is beyond repair and it is dead, and yet, because You stubbornly say so, it keeps beating and powering up this soulless husk. I feel just like Frankenstein. I didn't ask for the life my Creator gave me, yet I'm cursed with this cruel existence. Even for the very purpose I was thrust into that life. Ten years ago, the wars stopped. Ten years ago, there was no further need for me to kill anyone anymore. You knew that. And yet, you forced me to kill nearly two hundred thousand men in the blink of an eye, and every single one of them I would have called my brother, or my sister. Now, I know better. What do you want from me? Why won't you just let me go and let me die? Your forgiveness can't reach me, and I am cursed to go to Hell, and for a monster like me, there is no better place to be. Just let me go and let me—"

His train of thought derailed when a little flock of ducklings, led by their mother, walked in front of him. He counted the flock, and the flock was large for ducklings. There totaled fifteen ducklings and the mother. There was a duckling in the back that caught his eye. The little duckling had a few black spots on its feathers, and it waddled with a little limp. The little duckling squeaked.

Ted's watched its little webbed foot, and it appeared that something was not quite connected right, as if the poor little creature had been born wrong. Would it be a mercy killing to put the duckling out of his misery?

He leaned over and placed his hand on the ground, his palm facing the sky. The little duckling turned its little head to him. As if everything stopped, and as if the little duckling knew something, he waddled over to Ted's hand and climbed on top of it. Ted raised the little duckling to his face and petted it. He smiled as the cute little feet stamped on his hand like a marching band. Ted investigated the black, empty orbs in its skull.

The mother duck stopped waddling and looked at Ted as he petted her little duckling. She quacked, flapping her wings erratically, waddling towards Ted, who simply traded a gaze, lying even to her. He returned her gaze and placed the duckling down, no longer considering killing it. The little duckling returned to its flock and went back in line as the mother duck led the way into whatever paradise awaited them, a paradise *he* was banished from.

"I'm glad you haven't lost your soft spot yet." He heard a familiar voice right next to him. The voice was so nostalgic that he lost his sense of location. The voice of so many memories—the good ones—swept over him. He turned to the left to see a teenager, aged if he remembered right was fifteen. She was the youngest of them all, and she'd been the closest one to him. She wore torn black cargo pants and a black long-sleeved shirt with her vest draped over it. Her black hair was down, and one blue eye was hiding behind her hair, while the other one had blood smeared over it. Just below her abdomen was bleeding black blood. She smiled at him, that same playful smile he'd fallen in love with. It was full of energy and hope, and the love to match it.

He frowned.

"Suh—Slithers," he gasped. He didn't mean to. She looked real to him, as if he was looking at an actual person, and not the ghost his mind had conjured up.

"Ghost," she answered, smiling as blood dripped down her head. "I miss you. We all do."

"Iah—I love you." He choked on his sobs. He knew he was overdue for this, but he hadn't expected it to hit him out in the open, exposed.

"Ghost, I love you too. We all do." She smiled back at him. "Tell me, have you lost your tender heart already? I don't think you have."

"Every morning, *every* morning it breaks a little more. Every single day. I dream these nightmares as they cascade over my insomnia, oppressing me far more than *they* ever could. I am stuck in the past, and I want to leave it behind, but I don't want to leave it behind," he sobbed. Tears streamed down his face, and his smile faded, and his face was cringing. "I know when I wake up, I'll never see any of you again. I'll never see any of you again."

"The life we lived was cruel," said Slithers. "We were all tormented inside, especially with everything that we had to do. We were darkness. We were bitterness. We were hatred. But you taught us all something, before the end. Do you remember what you said to me?"

"I can't remember," he sobbed. "I can't remember."

"That the odds were against us. But if there was a chance, a sliver of a chance that we could succeed in doing something good, in leaving some kind of legacy for humanity to follow, just one chance, it was worth it. Whatever it was, even if that chance was infinitely worse, it would be worth it for a chance to get this Hell undone," she answered. "Ghost, we were darkness, and when the darkness was too oppressive, you were our light. You were our Captain, our moral compass. It was through you that we never killed anyone innocent. It was because of you no civilians were ever killed on our watch. That was something, wasn't it? Was it worth it for even just that?"

"And everything we fought for is being undone now as we speak," he sobbed. "Our sacrifices were all meaningless."

"Was it, Ghost? Was any of it meaningless?" Her hand touched his. He felt the warmth of blood touch his hand. She grabbed it and brought it to her cheek, and his hand felt her flesh, as it was before the last fires raged eight years ago. The flesh was so real in his hands. She took her free hand and pulled out a ring, a scrappy ring at that. The ring was nothing more than a few nails welded together, and embedded in the ring were fragments of bullets.

He recognized that ring. He'd looked, but had never found it. The ring he'd made for her over eight years ago. The ring that he'd made for her was akin to that of a marriage, something he'd picked up from listening and watching his parental figures, Major and Lieutenant Nakamura. Whatever it was they'd had together was what he'd wanted with Slithers, and he'd nearly had it.

"Was this meaningless?" she said to him.

"No." He sucked in the air through his teeth, gasping as he tried to stifle more sobs. But this was not normal for him, for the tears never stopped, like a river dammed up with a dam that had finally cracked. "I—it was worth everything. Everything was planned. You and I were to be together that Saturday, but you never got to see that Saturday."

"I know," she said. "I know. I know our parents wouldn't have wanted to see us like that. But that wasn't for them to decide. No, we were born with a purpose, and our tale ended. But yours still goes on. Ghost, if there is a sliver of a chance to undo this Hell, if there is a sliver of a chance, and if that chance is infinitely worse than it was back then, it is still worth it. Our time is over. Your time is still moving forward. Time stopped for me, and it kept going for you." She leaned toward him and looked at his now swollen eyes. "We all lived a cruel existence, but you gave us light. Who else can you bless with your light?"

"How can I, when I see only darkness? The mask faded, and it's not all okay. It's not okay anymore." He knew she referred to her biological parents, the ones she'd never met. Ted didn't know who his parents were either, only the dreaded Nakamuras.

Her forehead touched his. "You say you're not okay. You say that all you see is darkness around you. That's okay. Because that was once my reality. You broke the darkness, and the light forced its way in. The light is there, Ghost. It is right there! You know it is. You must let it in. Just let it in! We can't stand seeing you like this. Just let it in."

He opened his eyes, and he saw Slithers with her hair pulled back in a ponytail. She smiled at him, shading his face with a white sunhat that hadn't been there before. Her blood-stained uniform faded to a blue sundress. "Just let it in. You need to let the past stay in the past, Ghost. I know you don't want to forget us, but this pain isn't doing anything good."

"Maybe—"

"Maybe, Ghost, the reason you can't seem to really kill yourself is because you know that doing that will kill all memory of us," she said. This cut through his heart, and he could feel it bleeding inside his chest. "You gave us hope when there was none. Now, it is time for someone to share that hope with you. I love you. We all do."

She kissed him gently on the lips before her body changed into a wind of flowers, flying like petals as his hallucination burned away. His hands trembled uncontrollably and the light reflecting upon his eyes shimmered. His body felt weak as he leaned forward.

He curled himself up on the bench, holding his knees tightly to his chest as the tears swelled in his eyes, streaming onto the bench, making a waterfall drip onto the pavement of the path. He felt like a soaked sponge being twisted and wrung dry and then cast carelessly to the side of the sink.

"Juh—Jennifer," he stammered. "Why do you look like her?"

He couldn't deny the similarities between Slithers and Jennifer. Granted, Jenn was older than Ted, by perhaps five years, assuming his estimation of his own age was accurate. They had the same build, the same-colored hair, the same colorful and playful smile and laugh. Even the smell seemed the same; the smell of patience and care. It was something that he didn't smell much of in the world. No matter how bad things got, or how hopeless, Slithers had always smelled like there was an abundance of patience and care.

Maybe, just maybe, it was time to let it go.

CHAPTER 12

Fireworks

*~To fight for peace, that kind of courage requires a specific
type of person. You are not that person; I am that person.
And I hate it. Let me tell you something, if you want to truly
fight for peace, and if you want to be that kind of person,
I'll tell you how: you have to kill yourself, again, and again,
and again, until what's left of your humanity is dead and
you become nothing more than a murderer. You'll bear the
burden of all the hate and discourse of the world, but you'll
save the world from itself. Can you bear that burden? I
thought I could. No one can.*

SAMANTHA HAD PREVIOUSLY ARRANGED for everyone to be at
Kendall Square at 4:00PM or a little earlier. That would give
her enough time to track Ted down in case he bailed, *again!*
She looked carefully at her watch as Michael, Tim, Erin, and Jennifer
were sitting down on some of the benches. Jennifer peered diligently
down the stairs of the subway station.

There were droves of people coming up and going down under
the red signs reading "Kendall Square." Samantha and her friends
were shaded by numerous trees and banners hanging on the sides of
the brick shops and restaurants.

Jennifer's fingers interlaced with one another on both hands, one hand squeezing the other tightly. She had a white visor that covered her face in shadows, khaki shorts and a black shirt. Samantha walked over to her as she was alone, isolated by herself, clearly bored of all the finance talk. Obviously, Michael led most of that conversation, with his confident demeanor, owning that salmon-colored shirt that less secure men would not wear.

"So, what are you feeling right now?" Sam asked Jennifer, sitting down next to her, wrapping her arm around Jenn's shoulders.

"Well, I suppose I'm feeling overjoyed that I might see him again. Thank you, Sam," she said cheerfully. Sam felt relieved Jennifer returned to her usual upbeat self. "And I'll be relieved if he doesn't show up," Jennifer continued. "I am satisfied either way. Of course, I'd like to see him again, but I will no longer force his friendship with ours. It is—"

"Sometimes, we need a friend to be an enemy," Sam said, looking up at the sky, looking for an answer, and something genuine to say. "Only a true friend will insult us to our face. Only a true friend will call us out on all our shit."

"Sam!" Tim called out. "Language."

"Sorry, Tim!" Sam called back. She was grateful for him holding her accountable, "Look, I can't say what I heard on that night when I forced him to come." She glanced down at her watch; 3:57PM. "But I know what he needs. He doesn't need that soft and passive friend. He needs a stern but active friend. I didn't know that was something I could be, but I think we all need to be part of that. We all need to be active, or else we'll all lose him."

"There are times when we need a stern hand. There are times where we need a motherly caring hand, and the occasional whip up the butt with a wooden spoon." Jennifer chuckled. She'd taken enough beatings with that wooden spoon before. "I read something before, back when I was doing my undergrad, that a man who grew up in a violent household responds best to order and direction. Such a man is responsive to those who lead them, for fear of being punished. Such a man doesn't respond well to a passive friend because they can't offer that guidance."

"You have no idea how right you are," Sam commented, looking back at her watch. 4:02 PM. "Can you call Ted? Ask him where he is please. Else, I'm driving to pick him up."

Jennifer took out her phone. She hesitated before forcing her thumb violently down on the touch screen. She brought the phone to her ear, listening to the dial tone.

"Why don't you put that on speaker?" Sam asked, eager to hear the tone of his voice.

Jennifer nodded and placed her phone on speaker, holding it away from her ear. Her free elbow rested on her thigh as her chin rested on her palm, her hair dropping to the side as her head tilted. The phone rang three times.

"Hello?" came that familiar smooth voice.

"Tedward!" Jennifer cried out; her face lit up with excitement. "It's me, Jennifer."

"Oh, I know." He chuckled softly into the phone. *"I have your number in my phone, remember?"*

"It's good to hear from you again. Are you coming? Where are you?"

"Oh, you know, around," he joked.

"You've certainly got that Bostonian sarcasm," she jested.

"Oh, please. Bostonians do it better."

"Don't threaten me with a good time."

"Jennifer! I would never!"

"So, where are you?"

"I told you; I'm not threatening you with a good time."

"Tedward!"

"Open your eyes."

Jennifer was looking at an empty subway station. She blinked repeatedly and took one hand to wipe away any sleep from her eyes.

"What am I supposed to be looking at?"

"An empty subway station."

"What?" she turned her head around and found Ted standing on the other side of the street, right in front of the Merlien Building on One Broadway. He waved and bore that smile. "Tedward! What are you doing? Get over here!" Jennifer found herself yelling at him from across the street, but it was apparent her voice carried over his phone as he pushed it away from his face.

"Well, that's a relief," Sam said, taking a deep breath as she turned her head towards him. He was wearing his wrinkled fatigues and khakis. His hair was still a scruffy mess. "Now I don't have to go chasing him down." She felt a major burden being lifted from her chest. She smiled as Jennifer met Ted at the crosswalk. *Thank you.*

She went over to Erin, pushed her to the side of her bench and wrapped her hand around her waist. "So, what do you think?"

"I didn't think you to be much of a matchmaker. I mean, how long did it take for Michael to give you the slip?" She chuckled, elbowing her in the side.

Sam looked at her awkwardly.

"Jennifer would have said it better." Michael laughed.

"Sh! Sh! Sh!" Tim put his finger to his lips. "You don't want her hearing that. Last time someone made that assumption—" He shuddered. "So many accidents."

"That was completely unrelated! The pipe in the room burst!" Samantha teased, chuckling.

"Yeah, it didn't help we were on the top floor." Michael scratched his chin as he tilted his gaze skywards. "Oh well, not like she caused it."

"So, where's this canoe place?" Erin asked. "Oh, and I suppose I know him a little better, but even I have my hesitations. They seem a good match. Way to be an *Emma*."

"Oh, please, I get enough of that from Jennifer. I don't need that from you, Erin." Samantha scowled at her. "I'm not a fan of Jane Austen, personally."

"Before you go off some unnecessary tangent that is likely to make us late—" Michael began.

"You're one to talk," Sam replied sarcastically.

"For the record, I came early today." Michael shook his head as he pointed an index finger at her chest. "It's about a fifteen-minute walk."

"Michael, I'm sure we'll be fine. We originally planned to be here at 6:00 PM in case something happened. Then Ted happened. And he was on time; contrary to popular belief, it was either on time or not at all. We have plenty of time. Fireworks don't start until later. Which reminds me, food," Sam rebutted.

"I'll go grab something. Anything in particular we want?" Michael asked.

"Didn't we plan this—forget it. Go to the store, get some snacks, soda, and anything else you can think of. Fortunately, some of us had a late lunch." Sam pointed at herself.

"Come on, Tim." Michael grabbed Tim as they went along the opposite side of the street to a nearby convenient store.

"So, you finally came on time, or even at all," Jennifer said, smiling up at Ted. Jennifer relaxed to the lovely melody of walking and chattering noises. The background noise was like music to her ears, reminding of her violin playing days. She felt the warm rays beat on her skin. She saw cars driving by, merging onto different lanes on the busy street, some honking because some inconsiderate tourist had cut off a driver. She shook her head; whoever that tourist was, they'd clearly ignored the *no turn on red* sign. "What changed? I didn't think I'd see you today, or at all ever again."

"I hope my sudden surprise was welcome." Ted smiled, but this smile wasn't as wide as all the other smiles he'd given her. There was *something* different about it, but Jennifer couldn't quite place it.

"It most certainly is." She smirked, her eyelids dropping a bit like she was planning something. "Honestly though, I was going to be content in whatever happened. Although I would say I wouldn't have liked to have not seen you again, I don't think my sensitive little eyes could take any more of that. And don't dodge my question, you sly fox, you."

"I wasn't planning on it." He let out a small laugh that came out more like a cough. "I know something's changed: I haven't quite determined what yet."

"So, are you going to tell me something pleasant about you? Unlike that dreary excuse of an explanation the last time I saw you?" she asked.

"I—I think I will save that for tonight. I have to think of something that you don't know about me that is pleasant," he answered, his tone dropping at *pleasant*. Jennifer could tell his smile lessened about a few centimeters. She found herself relieved that to her, he couldn't maintain that façade, or perhaps was willing to trust her of all people with something precious. "It is—hard for me to find something pleasant."

"Then, think on it. But don't filter yourself, Tedward. If you must, give me something precious, and I'll give you something precious." She poked him.

He paused, rubbing his chin. "I don't think any of that came from a Jane Austen Novel."

"Nope!" she cackled, pulling her head back and letting her hair fall. "I came up with that cheesy line myself. If it was pulled from some fake crap romantic novel with unrealistic expectations, this was purely coincidental."

"I see. It seemed a little dry for Jane Austen."

"I'm not Jane Austen," she defended herself.

Ted went with all of them to the rental, where they rented three canoes. Of course, they didn't originally plan on filling all the canoes with passengers; this was something Ted picked up on. One of the canoes was meant to be for storage for food and snacks while they were out at sea.

"I still think a whole canoe is too much space for this," Erin said as they tied the canoes together with bungee cords. "I think two was enough."

"Well," Samantha said, putting some bags of snacks into the canoe she and Michael shared, "we did think Brian was coming. He flaked last minute."

"Typical Brian. He's probably with you know who," Jennifer quipped, loading the canoe she and Ted would share. "Let us be off! Very important business!"

Ted watched Jennifer as she stumbled into the canoe. Ted and Michael pushed the canoe out from the shore and hopped in. Tim and Erin helped balance the sudden weight in the additional canoes to prevent them from tipping. All of them rowed out and waited for the sun to set.

The skies were clear, and the sun was finally setting over the western horizon of Boston as the darkness was swooping in over the east. The lights of the city at night came on, taking away any light from the stars from above. Jennifer and Ted shared a canoe.

"10:28," Samantha said. "The pop concert should be ending soon."

"Why did we come out here so early?" Tim complained. "I have to pee."

"Bro," Michael said with a laugh, "you have a whole ocean."

"That's not sanitary, what about the fish? I don't think they'd like that," Tim replied.

"You do realize they pee in the same water they swim in, right?" Michael said. He reached out to grab an empty coffee can. He tossed it over to Tim. "Use this if you're concerned. My Uncle Jack used to road trip with these things. He'd never stop even to use the bathroom. He just kept driving."

"Uncle Jack," Tim said. "How fitting."

Tim swiftly turned around, using the can as his toilet. Ted noted how careful Tim seemed to be with it, trying to hide his private parts from the rest of them.

"You better dump that out, Tim!" Erin exclaimed. "If I'm sharing a canoe with you, I don't want to have to smell it the entire time."

"But—" he started to protest.

"Dang it. Just give it to me!" She smiled and took the bucket and dumped the urine into the water. She rinsed the bucket out with the same water.

There was a loud whistling in the air. They all jerked their heads and pointed at the white billowing streak following the rocket in the air. Sam, Erin and Jennifer leaned back in the canoe as they pointed. Numerous lights lit up the skies and shimmered in the ripples of the water.

These three seemed to Ted to be the most like children—that is, how he would have expected children to behave.

The first boom of distant tank fire echoed in his ears, the cannon blowing up, overwhelmed by the enormous pressure of the exploding powder, sending flares and flashes of white. The noise sent ripples between the canoes. Ted could feel the weight being shifted in the canoes. Again, and again, and again, the lights would flash blue, red, green, and white, sending debris into the ocean.

His fists clenched at the sides of the canoe. His eyes flared as the beautiful exploding lights lit up the blackened sky. The loud bangs concussed his skull. He took numerous soft, measured breaths as his hands dug into the sides of the canoe.

He ground his teeth as unwanted memories began to assault his mind:

Afghanistan, August 13th, 2012.

The air was dry, the moisture was gone, and the sand scorched.

Ghost sprinted in the sand with Viper behind him. Ticker was to his left, and Butcher to his left, her katana drawn. Her height made the katana look like a five-foot Odachi.

Their legs sprinted through the sand, through the whistling howls of the tank fire aimed directly at them. Ghost saw and jumped to the side, and Viper jumped in the other direction, just avoiding the impact. Sand went everywhere, pelting his body like bullets.

More shells of tank fire followed; the whistling never stopped, as if the tanks themselves were the form of their hated oppression. Ghost took a good look at the line in front of them. The tanks kept firing, and the buzzing of bullet fire came, obscuring their vision.

"Ticker! One hundred-thirty-six meters!" Ghost yelled as two bullets grazed his cheeks. He ignored it. Pain was all too familiar for him to bother with it anymore. "One o'clock!"

"Ten-four," Ticker replied.

He could hear the rapid sprinting of Ticker, the little soldier sprinting faster and harder. Not more than fifteen seconds later did he hear cries and a loud explosion.

The sound cleared.

Ghost saw the right most tank was nearly toppled, but completely ripped to shreds. Afghan soldiers were dying near the tank, from gunfire, explosive debris, or even the flames themselves.

Ghost, Butcher, and Viper picked up into a full sprint, leaving clouds of sand in their wake. They jumped behind the sandbags. Ticker swiftly blew up another tank. The Afghan soldiers were in complete disarray. It was like they were surprised that they stood over a foot and a half above their enemies.

Ghost let his rifle fire; he constantly pulled the single shot trigger numerous times as he aimed down the iron sights. His gun ripped through the second-rate bulletproof vests the Afghan soldiers were wearing. One of the other men threw his rifle at him. Ghost was briefly distracted as he sidestepped from the man's swing with the pulwar. A second swing was made. Ghost pulled out his knife. He grabbed the man's hand and twisted him down to his height. He thrust his knife into the man's chest, twisting the knife and ripping apart the man's chest.

Ghost watched as the man's corpse collapsed to the ground and watered the sand with its blood,

More fireworks started firing and whistling in the air. Ted realized he'd drifted off in an experiential nightmare and attempted to return his smile to his face. He released his grip on the canoe. He stared out at the open sea and the lights of the city. There were many canoes and other boats with people smiling happily at the bright exploding lights.

His breaths were still short and measured. He needed to control himself, or something worse would happen than these sudden flashbacks. He bowed his head down. *They can't see this.*

He gasped. His eyes were wide open as he felt something warm touch his hand. His hands started trembling, but he was much too afraid to do anything. His gaze suddenly shifted to his hand and found a warm mass of flesh covering his trembling hand. He looked up at the arm from which the warm, gentle hand was attached. He found himself looking into the concerned eyes of Jennifer, who held his hand firmly.

"Ted," she whispered. "You don't have to go at it alone. That's what friends are for. That's what we're here for. You don't have to live life alone."

She drew him further inside the canoe, still holding his hand over the side. His smile faded and his eyes trembled in the exploding lights. He leaned back, breathing heavier.

No! Stuh—stay away!

She came closer to him. He leaned into the back of the canoe.

No! Stuh—stay away! You don't know what I've done.

As if reading his thoughts, she said, "No, you don't have to go at it alone. That's what friends are for."

Jennifer, stay away. Please. You don't want any part of this—of this monster. No. I am not a monster. I am something—something so much worse.

She lunged her body softly into his chest and threw her arms around him, her chin resting on his shoulders. "Ted," she whispered. Her trembling voice spoke volumes as he felt this alien embrace him.

He felt darkness all around him. Her voice, that *damn* trembling voice, it couldn't be trusted, no matter how much comfort it brought to him. The smiling face of Slithers entered his mind. She smiled at him in the darkness, as if Slithers lived on in Jennifer. He closed his eyes as he stifled sobs from within. He took a deep breath with her body leaned so close into his. *How cruel. How cruel can you be, forcing me to look back into memories that I know I can never relive? What would I give to have that again, even just one last time?*

"I can't begin to understand what you're going through, but Ted, I want to understand it. I know you're in pain, and this life, or whatever it is, it can be Hell. But it is like that for everyone." Her tears streamed down on his shoulder. "I know you want to bear this alone, we all do, but we can't. We just can't. No matter how hard we try, we can't do it alone. Share the load!"

He felt a weight on his chest, as if his heart was in his stomach, crawling its way up through his throat, restricting the air he could let in and out. "I—I can't.," he began to whisper. "I can't tell anyone. Jennifer, the less you know, the better."

"Then tell me what little you can. Tell me how you feel. If you can't trust any of us, trust me or trust Sam. But you can't grow unless you open up more, or at the least, come out more often. Ted, we consider you a friend. Even if that feeling isn't mutual. I don't know what must have happened to you when you can't trust anyone."

"What I went through is classified," he stammered. "I am not allowed to talk about it, and it would only place you in harm's way, even if you believed it."

"Then tell me something about you. Something I don't already know. Something precious," she requested. She leaned back from him and looked him in his watery eyes. "Anything. Tell me what makes you happy. If you can't manage that, tell me what makes you hurt. Just give me something."

"There used to be a girl. Her hair was black, and her smile lit up the sky, even when there was no sun to illuminate the darkness. She was always happy. You could say, given our circumstances, we were class sweethearts. We were even—what's the word for it?—engaged. It was going to be held on Saturday. We were going to invite our little, small group of friends."

"What happened?" she asked, gazing deeper into his eyes. He sensed that while they were worlds apart, she understood that, and she was trying to understand him in whatever way was possible, pushing and applying pressure when needed, and releasing him just at the right moment.

"For her, Saturday never came. For them, they never got to see that Saturday either," he answered.

"I'm so sorry."

She placed her hand on his shoulder and grasped it firmly to console him as the whistling of the fireworks continued. They continued firing at a rapid rate, the grand finale arriving with innumerable explosions, filling the air with multiple different colors.

"But what bothers me the most about it is I can't talk about what happened, and that—and that you look so much like her, it's uncanny. It's disturbing," he said, feeling he needed to desperately push her away. This was all too familiar, and it only went one place: pain. Either for himself or her. If he let her into his life, no matter how small of a part she could play to him, he would hurt her, and she would hurt him. It was only inevitable. But he also knew that if there was going to be any shot at providing peace to the turmoil in his heart, it would be through her.

"Well, I hope I can bring back some of her memories if that is what will keep you grounded," she said, leaning back. "Now, it is my turn, but I'll show you."

She leaned back from him and pulled up the sleeve of her left arm. She showed her wrist to him. In the faint light, he could see something all too familiar: scars. There were faint flesh-white scars slitted in x's across her wrist. She smiled at him as tears escaped those slitted lids; well-meaning, sincere, he was sure of that.

What is she thinking? She's just handing me this information! Jennifer, are you stupid?! I could—I could use this to harm you. You know this! But you have no reason to believe I would use this against you. Why? You know how cruel people are; why are you trusting me, a stranger with the scars of your heart?

"Why are you showing me this?" he asked. "This is frail info—"

"Because, my dear Tedward." She smiled and looked into his glimmering eyes. "I know you don't trust me, but something tells me that you will never do anything to hurt me."

He let out a sigh. "Perhaps you're wrong. Perhaps you're right."

The fireworks were over. Sam whistled as she saw Jenn and Ted cozying up over in the other canoe. They immediately moved back to where they'd been, hoping no one had seen anything. But Sam saw. She saw the whole thing, and it left her with a smile.

The six of them returned the canoes. They all made it to the Kendal MIT train stop, outbound to Alewife. The subway was crowded, and they all huddled around in the corner of the back end of the large subway car. There was a lot of talking and commotion in the subway car from rolling bottles and cans; it filled the ears of all the listeners.

Michael started engaging in a serious conversation with Ted, asking him about markets. Ted answered his questions in depth, keeping his mind busy from the demons flying around inside his head. Sam said little until they all got off on Davis square. Jennifer and Erin lived closer to Boston, but they were spending the night with Sam, and Tim was planning on crashing at Michael's house, which was not far off from College Avenue.

Ted held onto his smile, looking up at the near empty sky, filled with little stars, and that old oppressive moon beating down on him. The weight of the light was heavy as they walked up towards College Avenue. Michael and Tim waved their farewell as they took a right on Morrison Avenue. It was now just Ted, Erin, Jennifer and Sam. Of course, seeing as Ted's house was only three houses further down the road, they might as well have been going to the same place.

Ted's fists clenched at his sides, and his right hand trembled underneath the pressure he put them under. He tried to maintain that fake smile, but now, he knew it had become less of a mask, as there were two people who could see through it. And they knew it, and he knew it. He felt naked before them.

And yet, the damned majestic moon beat his spirit down as they walked down the sidewalk. *Just a little further, and I can close the door behind me,* he thought to himself. He kept his pace as his heart felt like it was beating through his chest. The breaths became more rapid. He resorted to breathing through his nose to limit his noise as they walked. Erin, Jennifer, and Sam were caught up in some conversation that Ted had tuned out. He didn't want to be bothered by anything useless. *What good is it? Everything is pointless.*

At last, he could see his beautiful, peaceful, and empty house. He was close. The three women moved up the stoop to the apartment building. Ted waved good-bye briefly before picking up his pace.

"Tedward!" Jennifer called.

Damn it! "Yes?" He turned his head towards her and greeted her with his smile.

"I'm sure I'll see you Tuesday?" She brushed her brown hair out of her face.

"I haven't given it much thought," he answered vaguely.

"Will you come?" Her smile faded into a stare much more sincere.

"Time will tell. It always does," he answered.

"Yes, or no?" she asked again. "No more dodging the question."

"I don't know if I'll come or not. I'll think about it," he replied, lowering his voice as his hand began to tremble.

"Don't make me text you in the dead of night again."

"I wouldn't dream of it. Good night."

He turned around and started walking back down the sidewalk at a brisk pace. He could feel visions flashing before his face; the nightmares were not far behind. They never were. He could hear the opening of the apartment building behind him, and Sam, Erin, and Jennifer started walking inside.

Suddenly, he couldn't move another step. It was not as if his legs were heavy, or that he'd suddenly lost all energy to move; it was like his body had lost the will to move. He grunted as he tried to move something, but his body did nothing. Even the willpower of Task Force Seven was not enough to move anything. He could feel his knees getting weak again. *Not here. Damnit! Not here! No! No! NO!* His knees buckled and he tumbled forward, catching himself from hitting his face on the concrete.

He could feel the darkness coming in around him. The oppression from the moonlight pushed him further into the darkness and deeper into the prison inside his own mind. His whole body trembled.

He gasped, breathing heavily. His eyes closed as he started choking by the pressure inside his own chest. Grief overtook him again. And he couldn't hold it anymore. He shrieked; his mouth opened wide as tears streamed down steadily down the sides of his face. His sobs turned into agonizing screaming.

Jennifer's hair stood on ends, and goosebumps rose from her arms. She turned from the door before closing it, running outside. She ran towards Ted and gasped, seeing him on all fours like a beast, sobbing and choking on the tears of his sadness. She sprinted over to him and tried to place her hand on his back. She tripped forward. Her hand passed through him like a ghost. She turned around immediately, catching herself. She looked Ted in the face, his eyes open, but swollen with tears. He looked straight through her, but not at her, like he was in a corner, staring at a wall. His sobs, she recognized them. These were not the sobs of a man, but those of a child.

I—I passed through him? No. I must be imagining it. She walked back over to him while he continued to sob. He didn't move at all. She went to place her hand on his back, and it passed through him again, touching the ground. She retracted her hand. Her hand trembled, she felt her heart growing heavy, and she found it hard to breathe as the air chilled her throat. She looked at her hand, and it was solid, and there wasn't anything wrong with her, but—*I didn't—I didn't imagine it. What is going on? Is he real?* She heard Erin and Sam's footsteps behind her. Both were wide-eyed. Tears entered her eyes as fear sunk into her heart and she clutched her chest. "Ted?"

There was no answer.

"Ted."

He continued to sob, moving from his tones to that of a child, to something even younger.

"Ted!" Sam exclaimed. "What is going on? Answer me!"

"Tedward!" Jennifer cried.

The wind started howling around them. Jennifer looked beyond Ted, looking down the rest of College Avenue seeing nothing out of the ordinary except that the road didn't end. It kept going, and going, and going, as if she found herself in some figment of another reality; a reality of endless despair.

Ted continued to sob. There was a pool of tears beneath his face.

Walking up briskly to Ted, Samantha placed her hand on him, only it passed through him, as if he was an empty hologram. She felt the darkness coming in, swirling around her. Her vision saw nothing but blackness, and the temperature dropped drastically, forcing her hairs on ends. She placed her hand in front of her face and saw all five of her fingers, bright as day, but everything else was dark. She found herself utterly alone in a black pit.

"Ted! Jenn! Sam! Get up!" Erin cried out.

She was not about to touch Ted. She reluctantly stepped forward, in an attempt to shake Jenn and Sam up. But she couldn't touch Ted. *Is he some kind of wizard? Why are they like this?* Her heart thumped inside her chest, and she was flooded with a ton of thoughts that wanted to be turned into questions, for she didn't fully understand what was going on. Why Ted, Sam, and Jennifer seemed to freeze up, Ted first, and as Sam and Jennifer touched them, they seemed to pass through him, but merely found themselves frozen still in place, as if time itself was frozen still around them. She didn't understand it, and that mysticism cut something in her faith in God, for a world with magic did not exist. Erin touched Sam on the shoulder. She shook Sam out of her trance, and she was weeping.

"What was that?" Erin looked down at Ted in his shocked state as she pulled Jennifer away from him. Jennifer was not weeping when she woke from the trance.

"I don't—I don't know. It was like—" Sam began.

Ted gasped and his weeping stopped. His arms stopped shaking as his head focused on the end of College Avenue.

"Ted! What is going on?" Jennifer went back to him, despite the protests from Erin. "Answer me!"

"Jenn, I don't think—"

The temperature dropped again. "Jenn, get back!" Sam pulled her away from Ted. The three of them took large steps back, keeping their eyes fixed upon Ted kneeling on the ground. His hands grabbed the sidewalk, and they could see blue veins rise up over his skin. The blue veins crawled over his shoes and clothes, emitting a black light from them. The girls were wide-eyed as they tried to comprehend what they were looking at.

Ted? Jenn thought to herself.

Ted pushed himself off the ground in a sprint, and within a singular stride, he landed nearly two hundred feet away. He sprinted off another stride, and another until they couldn't see him anymore. There was silence in the air, and the summer heat returned.

Sam and Erin started walking back into Sam's apartment. Jennifer could hear them speaking in flustered tones, discussing specifically what it was that they had seen, and the sensation of absolute darkness and the sudden chills. Jennifer couldn't hear any more of what they were saying, but she imagined their reaction would be as much the same as hers: confusion. Veins on the skin were not usually so prominent, and she was unaware of any new scientific discoveries about an additional circulatory system. Those were veins—she recognized them—but they weren't supposed to be black, or change color, nor should they have been able to climb and crawl on the skin. She sighed heavily and clenched her fists at her sides, feeling the tears stream down her face.

Tedward, my Tedward, what did they do to you? Is this the source of all your pain? If it is, I don't even think I could forgive it. This is inexcusable. I'll let you go for now, but I will find you again.

CHAPTER 13

Hedgehog

~Humans don't take their own lives because they want to die. Every day, every day they wake up in this nightmare. Every single day, I wake up to see the lives of those whom I killed. I see them every waking moment, and in my sleep. I can't escape from them. We take our lives because all we want is for the pain to stop. Is that so much to ask? Is that really so terrible?

FOUR WEEKS LATER, SAM and Jennifer had lost hope for Ted. He never answered the door. He'd stopped answering phone calls and text messages. The mail in his apartment never left the mailbox; it just sat there, as if no one ever bothered to take any of it out. Even Erin didn't see him at work anymore. When she inquired, Ted had simply left. He was no longer part of that brokerage. His porch grew dust, floating and clouding every time a small gust of wind would blow into the house. He was gone. Sam assumed he'd packed everything up and just left.

Samantha knew Jennifer had high hopes for him. He'd seemed to have come a long way that night, July the fourth, but had it been too far? Had he been pushed to the brink, where the only option for him was total isolation? Did he live in that house anymore? Sam couldn't be sure. But every single Saturday and Sunday morning, she would knock on his door. There was never an answer. *Did we treat him like a project, and not a man? Is that where we made a mistake?*

She still didn't understand what she'd seen that night. Ted had showed veins, glowing in the dark in numerous colors; she couldn't even tell how many shades of green she thought she'd seen on his body *and* his clothes. Not to mention that inhuman stride. She, Erin, and Jennifer had all seen the veins and agreed amongst themselves that they should never mention what they experienced to anyone else, for fear of being labeled as insane.

It was a whole month ago. Perhaps she was just imagining things, but that was the first time he'd showed his pain openly to them. It was not something to take for granted. *Ted, we tried. We failed. I'm sorry.* She placed her hand on his door, one last time. *I just hope—I just hope you're alive. If you can't find help from us, find help from somewhere. Please.*

This was the last Sunday she would choose to knock on that door. Perhaps constantly badgering him with texts and phone calls did seem rather stalkerish. She should have known; if a man at her office had started doing it, she would have felt the same way: isolated. As alone as he intended to be, perhaps their attempts at friendship had finally driven him off, leading him to leave everything behind. *Should we have brought him there? Perhaps the fireworks were the worse thing we could have done.* Forcing a military vet to fireworks should set them off. *I'm sorry.*

She removed her hand from the door that Sunday, never to knock on that door again.

Tuesday came around. It was the last Tasty Tuesday, and Sam's load had been picked up early and without delay. She was enjoying her commission checks, but made sure to put plenty of it aside. She walked up to the church and grabbed a cup of coffee in the fellowship hall nice and early. Granted, the coffee from the coffee

Machine with the pitiful excuse for coffee capsules was disgusting. Still, it was better than nothing.

There were volunteers coming in and out from the side kitchen, bringing in plates of cheese and crackers; some were even gluten-free. She leaned against the pillar, watching as people came by, talking with one another, often with full mouths or in between bites. She sighed as she bowed her head down, drowned in her own thoughts of isolation.

She felt an arm wrap around her shoulders. "What's got you in a slump?" Michael frowned.

She came to and looked up at him. "It's Ted."

"I don't think Jennifer or Erin's heard from him either." He took a bite of some sliced cheddar. "I suppose it's time to let go."

"I know, I—I just—I don't even know anymore. I just, from what little he let us in on, I just know he isn't going to get help. Michael, I don't even—I don't even know if he's alive." She started tearing up a little, bringing her hand to her mouth. "Can a man really live with all of that darkness?"

"You and Jennifer knew him better than I did. All I could really talk to about him was work. I did my best, but his walls were up around me also," he answered. "But I think that we've done all that we can do. I don't think there's any more we could have done."

"But there must have been something more, something else," she explained. "All it takes is one more good act. All it takes is to know someone is there. You said it yourself, we as Christians need to do better, but how can we if we can't even do this?"

He let out a sigh, "You're right. *We* can't. We can't do anything. Only God can, and perhaps this is exactly what needed to happen." He let out another deep sigh as he swallowed a cracker. "Have you ever heard of the hedgehog dilemma?"

"No."

"These little creatures wear quills outside of their hide as a defense mechanism. Whenever they are cold, they try to huddle with each other for warmth, but can't because whenever they get too close, they hurt each other with their quills, making it painful and dangerous. Effectively, they don't want to get too close for fear of hurting themselves or others. So, none of us know what happened to him because he won't tell us. He seems withdrawn to us, because he's afraid of being hurt. He feels that the closer someone is to his heart, the harder it is going to hurt."

"That makes sense. I think I understand now. He hides behind his mask, the smiles, the laughter because he doesn't want us to know how he actually feels, because he'll be giving a part of himself over to us, or other people. It is easier for him to live in a life of solitude than it is for him to trust others."

"I think someone, or probably many people stepped on his toes and betrayed his trust numerous times, to the point where he has no faith in any person. He doesn't trust anyone."

"But Michael, he needs someone to help him carry the load. He needs help."

"He won't accept it. It is a cruel reality. I can't help but wonder exactly what he went through in the military. Maybe, just maybe, inviting him to the fireworks was a bad idea."

"Maybe," she admitted. "But we would never have known unless we tried."

"You truly are trying to be a new kind of hero, aren't you?" Michael smiled.

Park Street Church emptied into the street on a dark, dreary night. Fog rolled in, rising from the ground and filling the air with the aura of decaying mud and sadness. Sam felt its oppressive weight in her lungs. She let Michael lead her up Park Street toward Terri Nation, with the group following closely behind, enveloped by the heavy, oppressive fog.

Amid the miscellaneous chatter around her, Sam found it difficult to breathe in the mist. Her heart felt heavy with every step.

Something was missing. But what? What was the one thing she could have done differently? Or was this opportunity lost forever? Was Ted lost forever? She remembered the veteran she had bought food for a few months ago, sitting carelessly on the sidewalk, unable to function in civilian life, leading to a life of destitution. No one cared for him. No one loved him or helped him off the street. Would Ted end up like him? *I'm so sorry.*

She knew she had to let go, but something kept urging her to try, just one more time. She took a deep breath, her thoughts filling her heart again. *If I have to knock on that door all day Saturday, Ted, I will. So help me, God, I will keep knocking until you answer the door, or my knuckles bleed.*

Samantha held Michael's hand as he led her through the threshold of Terri Nation. As they walked, Samantha paid special attention to the faces around her—the smiling faces. Not one showed a grimace of despair. These genuine smiles told her there wasn't a care in the world, especially if it concerned someone they didn't know. *So cruel,* she reflected, frowning. A world filled with smiles, hiding the fact that the world was full of smiling devils and kind hearts destined to be broken, anyone with a kind heart was doomed here. The cruel, smiling little devils would bury them all.

They turned the corner into the back of the bar. Sam's eyes scanned the room, searching for Ted, clinging to the faintest hope that he might be there. Maybe he would be like the hedgehog in the anecdote Michael had shared, and make an attempt to connect with them. But she wasn't sure if he even felt he had a reason to. This, of course, assumed he was still alive and hadn't taken his own life. She thought of Jennifer and her relationship with Ted—oddly romantic, yet one-sided. Jennifer would take it the hardest, if she hadn't already accepted it. Ted was gone.

But then, something else caught her attention: a half-drunk glass of red wine, with a beverage napkin resting on it. There was no one sitting in front of it.

Sam let Michael lead her to the bar. Jennifer and Tim were not far behind, still engaged in quiet conversation. Jennifer seemed both depressed and mildly angry, her face set in a frown, eyes staring blankly at the bar top. Sam could tell Jennifer had likely concluded that Ted might have taken his own life, though Sam herself remained uncertain.

As Jennifer walked behind them, she swayed slightly, her gaze fixed on her feet. She wasn't angry at Ted—how could she be when she didn't know the full story? Morbid curiosity made her want to know the whole truth, locked away in a steel trap. But now she understood that she would never get an answer and would never see Ted again. Whatever had happened, whatever or whoever had caused it, must have been so terrible that it had led him to his perpetually hollow existence.

Scott took their orders and brought over the drinks: a glass of wine, a cider, and two mystery drinks for Jennifer and Michael. They stood in silence, staring into their drinks, waiting for the ruckus of the bar to start. Sam didn't pay much attention to what was in the mystery drinks. She twirled her cup absentmindedly, watching the endless ripples in her glass.

"Well now, let's not let the gloom get us down, shall we?" Jennifer forced a cheerful smile. "Life is frail and fleeting. Let's not dwell in bitterness, but instead remember what we've been able to do for others while we're still here." She raised her glass, her hand trembling, tears streaming down her face. "To my dear sweet Tedward. May you find some hope in this fragile world."

"To Ted," Tim echoed, raising his glass.

He looked at Jennifer with compassion before bringing the bottle to his lips. Samantha hesitated, her lips hovering over her glass as she observed Tim shifting uncomfortably on his stool. Of course, he'd feel awkward—Jennifer had just forced a eulogy in the middle of a bar.

"To Ted," Michael said, raising his glass with a frown.

Samantha found it surreal to be toasting someone they didn't even know if they would see again. It felt like saying goodbye. She raised her glass and echoed softly, "To Ted." *Goodbye, Ted. Until next time, if there is a next time.*

They all took a sip of their dismal toast, surrounded by a bar filled with happy faces, none of whom seemed to have a care in the world.

Sam leaned into Jennifer. She knew that, out of all of them, Jennifer would take it the hardest. Ted seemed to have had some sort of hold over her; intentional or not, Sam couldn't tell. She wrapped her arm around Jennifer's shoulders, swaying gently with her as they drank. They exchanged few words, simply drinking together in the middle of their quiet mourning for Ted, however long ago his departure had been.

Sam glanced around the bar again, noticing the friendly faces of people oblivious to the pain surrounding them. *They don't care.* They didn't care about anyone or anything. Those smiles, those faces, were like silent agreements, a superficial contract of respect, giving the illusion that they truly cared—but everyone was always violating that unspoken contract. Only through this experience, and only through Ted, did she understand this bitter truth. Even though Ted was no longer here, she realized he had taught them all something about the frailty of the human mind and the inevitability of mortality. Who could truly be trusted?

"Scott, I'll take another," a loud voice called from the far end of the bar.

It sounded familiar. Sam turned toward the voice. Excusing herself, she walked in that direction, weaving through the groups of people. She followed Scott as he delivered another glass of red wine to the other end of the bar. When he set it down, she arrived at the same spot.

"Ted! You're here!" she exclaimed as the man took the glass of wine and looked at her.

"You again? What the fuck do you want? Get out of my face! No one wants you here," he snapped.

"I'm sorry, I thought you were someone else," Sam mumbled, lowering her head as she turned to leave. *Culain,* she remembered. That was his name. "My mistake."

"Yeah, keep better control of your friends, bitch. I don't want to talk to you again," Culain snarled.

The name *Culain* didn't exactly roll off the tongue. Sam frowned at him but turned away, letting him enjoy, or at least attempt to enjoy, his lonely glass of wine. She realized something: that man carried himself a lot like Ted. Though he outwardly seemed happy, his rude demeanor and those empty eyes told a different story. Had he also experienced a life filled with misery or despair? Could he relate to Ted in a way she couldn't? It wasn't fair for her to judge him. Reflecting further as she walked away, she wondered if Culain, like Ted, was a veteran with a rough edge, pushing people away because he knew how society often viewed him. Maybe that's why he lashed out, much like Ted, with poorly constructed threats, including that bizarre limerick about killing her and Michael—or at least that's what she thought it had been about.

Finally, out of earshot of Culain, she reached a quieter part of the bar. Her eyes landed on a man leaning against a large wooden wall connected to the seat he sat on. His face was hidden behind a menu, but his smile was eerily familiar. In front of him was a plate of mashed potatoes with only a single bite taken out of it, and a glass of water resting on the polished wooden table.

"Ted?" she asked.

"Hmm?" He looked up at her and smiled, but there was hesitation in his eyes. He hadn't yet decided if he was relieved or disappointed to see her. Emotionally torn, he didn't know how to express himself to others. He kept his feelings buried, though deep down, he did want a friend. But with everything he had done, he feared he'd only bring them pain—or worse, end up with another knife in his back. "Oh, it's you. How have you been?"

"That is a painful question, and not one that I need to answer right now. Where have you been? We thought you were dead! Your mail, it's still sitting there!" Sam exclaimed, taking a seat next to him. She pointed a finger at him to emphasize the rage she had in her facial grimace. "Are you okay?"

"I'm about as okay as I'll ever be," he answered. "I'll not get any better. I'll only get worse."

"How much worse can you get?" she said. "Look, I'm still not sure what I saw, and I'm not going to make you tell me. I'm not. If you want to talk, I'll listen. But damnit, Ted, you need help."

"I know I need help." He continued with that accursed fake smile.

"You know?!" She was angrily sarcastic. "If you know, why don't you get help?"

"I don't trust therapists, and there is no one living I can trust. Sure, some people experience emotional pain." He let his smile fade, growing weary of the mask he was forced to wear. "Some deal with grief, or depression, some deal with loss, and others deal with lack of trust, others feel guilty. But it is rare that they must put up with more than two or three of those at a time, and not near to the extent that I feel." He frowned, and finally she saw tears watering his eyes. "My heart is always heavy. It's broken, and it's nothing more than a ball to be played with, filled with scars and bullet holes. This heart is broken, and the body hasn't caught up yet. Besides, I'd hate to be an inconvenience."

"The only way for someone to understand is for you to talk about it. You don't let anyone try to understand. You keep pushing us away by your little disappearing acts." Her tone became soft. "Look, Erin isn't here. Michael, Tim, Jennifer and I just did a little eulogy because we thought you were dead, or at the very least none of us would see you again."

"I've told you before." His voice dropped down to the whisper, his eyes angled to hers. "I'm a murderer. I see the faces of the dead around me when I'm awake. The faces come back full throttle in my dreams. I hate sleeping because of this. I have nightmares every single night, and I wake up in the same condition you saw me in that evening. What you saw is me every single night. Every. Single. Night. There is not a day that goes by without it. I don't take vacations because of it. I don't rest because of it. My only hope is to work myself to death until I can no longer see these things."

"It's hard to imagine that you're still alive if your life is as tragic as all that," she asked. *I choose to believe you think yourself a murderer, but you're not a murderer!*

He showed his wrists. There were no scars. "There should be scars here from me cutting. They're gone. I've tried drowning, driving a car and locking myself in while driving into the ocean. I failed that. I tried hanging myself, and all I did was hang there until I passed through the damn noose!"

"Why don't you ask for help? Ted, you need it!"

"You don't understand! I'm not human!" He gritted his teeth. "I don't deserve help. Besides, in the end, who would want to help a monster like me?"

Then what are you, Ted? That I believe. God, just what did you put him through?

"What I told you that day, and you thought I was exaggerating, was the truth. Yeah, sure, I believe in God, a God of forgiveness and mercy, but so does the Devil. I have killed too many people for Him to even consider forgiving."

"Te—"

"No!" He jabbed her in the chest with his finger. He grabbed his wallet and dropped a c-note on the table. "No, Sam! You know something? They told me the first kill was the only one that mattered. And it broke me! And they lied! They all fucking lied!" His knuckles struck the table. "The first one wasn't the only one that mattered.

Every single one mattered. I remember every single face. Every face! And I was never given a choice. Not one! Sam, I know the monsters and demons aren't hiding in the closets or underneath our beds. I'd be lucky if they were that far away. No, they're running amuck in our heads. And they are restless." He stood up and started walking away.

"Ted!" Sam called, trying to grab his hand.

He snatched his hand away. "No, Sam! I'm not—I'm not worth saving." Warm tears streamed down his face. The ruckus of the bar ceased, and everyone turned. Jennifer put her drink on the bar and stood up, keeping her hands at her sides. "I would like to believe," Ted said, choking on his tears, "that a person like me would be welcome into Heaven, because that's where I believe them to be. But I can't. I have too much blood on my hands. I'm not welcome there, and why should I be? I only have a handful of good memories, and what I wouldn't give to have that again, but the nightmares never stop. It haunts me when I'm awake. It haunts me when I'm asleep."

Sam looked deeply into his eyes. Finally, though she suspected as much, he'd admitted to the reason those bags existed. She took measured breaths, hoping to make them subtle enough. *Just listen, Sam. Just listen. That's all he needs. Just let it out!*

He continued, "I came into this world with nothing. I still have nothing. Everyone I have ever loved is dead. Everyone I ever trusted is either dead, or dying, or has betrayed me, and those that betrayed me I murdered. And I would do it all over again. I came in this world with nothing, and what little I had accumulated was ripped from me. I will die with nothing. I'm not even going to get a tombstone. None of them ever got a tombstone. They served their country better and with more honor than anyone flashing that damn flag ever has and ever will and they were all thrown away for something they didn't do. If I could go back in time, I would, and I would get into those hospitals and strangle each of us so we wouldn't have to live and face the cruelty of this world. It would have bee—it would have been better had the thirty-two of us never been born."

Is he referring to his friends? Thrown away for something they didn't do? Treason? Sam felt like there was a rock in her chest. *The truth has finally come out.*

"There. Are you happy now? There's my heart. It's out in the open. Now why don't you do with it what you want and dissect it like the science project you think I am? I'm done!"

Turning away, Ted felt his ears fill with screams and gunfire. He could feel the hot gun in his hands, ready to fire. The faces assaulted his mind again, the bleeding and desecrated faces. He couldn't hear the swift footsteps of a weeping woman sprinting behind him. He felt pressure on his chest as the woman wrapped her arms around him and held him as tight as she could.

Ted gasped, and he came to, realizing he'd been crying all this time inside the back bar of Terri Nation. There was no sound except the deafening sobbing of this woman in front of him. He reluctantly scanned the room, sobbing still. All eyes were on him; many people who had seen him in passing, many of whom he didn't know nor care to know. He looked down, and it was Jennifer who was holding him.

"Ha—how were we to know the pain you were in? The guilt, the shame, the hateful regret, despair and utter isolation. Any one of them can be as heavy as a mountain. And you bear all of them. Your spirit is crushing underneath all of that weight!" Jennifer sobbed. "Why do you do this to yourself? Why? You can't—you can't keep living like this. You just can't! One mountain is enough to kill a man, crush his spirit. And you bear all of it. There's no need, none, to go at it alone."

She buried her face into his chest, feeling the warm tears down his shirt. He felt her embrace, her arms wrapped firmly around him, unwilling to let him go.

She continued, "You need to stop not wanting to burden yourself to others. I know you feel like we won't understand, because we don't know what you're going through. I know you feel like we would sooner stab you than help you. You can't keep living like this, Ted. Not when you have—you have friends to help. You may not see it, and you may not accept us as your friends, but here we are, trying to help you." His body was still and firm, like a petrified dead fish. "We want to help. You can't go through life like this alone. Let us help you!"

He gazed passively at the bar top, filled with another traumatic memory he found himself trapped inside. His eyes watered again, as if he saw something absolutely terrifying.

"I know you don't trust us, but we trust you to make the right decision," said Jennifer. Her hands clutched the back of his shirt.

"The—the last person who put trust in me died," he sobbed.

She looked up at him with sobbing, swollen eyes, and she smiled through the pain. "Then let us be a light that your darkness so desperately needs. Let us fill that empty hole. I will help you bear this burden, Ted. We all will. I will be your light, and I mean it." She rubbed her tears on his chest again. "I will—I will help carry that pain. You don't need to do it alone anymore. You say you've lost everyone you cared about, but we're here. And you may not care about us, but that feeling isn't mutual."

She sobbed into his chest, still holding onto it tightly. He tried to move his arms up to push her off him, but then the most peculiar thing happened. Even his will was not enough to move his arms, no matter how hard he tried. They just wouldn't move, as if his very being refused to let go of this woman, who provided something to him.

She continued, "Even in the handful of times we've gotten the chance to hang out with you, your absence will not go unnoticed. You say you no longer have a family. Let us be that. I know you're in pain, and hate yourself for living, but damn it all Ted, life is too short to be bitter about the past. Give yourself a fighting chance to enjoy what little life you have left. Give yourself a fighting chance, if—if not for your sake, then for mine!"

She released him, only to wrap her arms around his neck. "This is—this is what you forgot: the world is filled with so much uncertainty. The world is filled with darkness, and is contaminated by the poisonous rot of humanity, and at times we may think that life is not worth living. But what is certain is that while the darkness of the world may be like murky waters, and impossible to see through, behind the veil of darkness is light."

"But the darkness has a way of snuffing out the light. I don't want to do that to you," he stammered.

"If that is what it takes, I accept that risk."

"No—"

"At the cost of my own light," she repeated.

Why does she talk like her? Damn it, why is she so much like her? I don't want this. Why can't I just die in peace? Why must I be flooded into ancient memories of the past that must be buried, and buried properly? Jennifer, if I let you in, I can never let go. Do I—do I even want to let it go? Slithers, you were always there. Slithers' face crossed his mind. He could see her smiling at him with the sun radiating behind her, and that beautiful meadow with the ducklings crossing to the lake. *So cruel, forcing me to look into the past; as real today as it was, but it is only a mask. It's not real, but does it—does it really matter?*

Seeing Slithers in Jennifer, he was emotionally overwhelmed, weeping as the strength of his arms returned to him and he embraced Jennifer. He wept into her shoulders, berating her with all his pain, all his trauma, all his grief, all his depression, and all his isolation. Lord knew he had those in no short supply.

Sam's tears streamed down her face as she approached him from the side and hugged them both. Her head was buried on Jenn's shoulder. No one could hear the steps of Michael and Tim who made it to the other side. Tim hugged Ted from behind as Michael placed his hand on his back. Tim was much more affectionate than Michael.

Ted saw the bar begin to empty. The citizens of the bar left, one by one, leaving the huddled mass of people just standing there, moving like water around rocks in a stream. Some glanced at the crying mass but gave it no more thought than that of curiosity, not sharing a shred of care in the world for the broken man, the man who wanted nothing more than to die but could never follow through with it without killing what remained of his squad's memory, the memory of his only true friends and family.

He saw one man walking right by him, and unlike the rest of the bar, he took notice of Ted, sternly peering into his eyes, daggers stabbing into him. He was a tall man, and like Ted, seemed all alone in this world. Ted didn't recognize him.

Jennifer rubbed her face against his chest again. "Ted, will you come with us on Tuesday?"

"Yu—yes," he replied. "I'll come. I'll come. You don't need to find me. I'll be there. You don't need to call or text. I will be there."

CHAPTER 14

The Hunger

~Innocence was murdered that day. A true friend will kill his friend, because only a true friend would bear the burden for him. A true friend wouldn't let another friend live in rotting regret.

HE REMEMBERED SEEING THE snow season four times. That isn't to say he couldn't have seen it once or twice more.

It had been a long week. He waited in the bright white room, sitting in a grey steel chair, watching the room with his ever-watchful eyes, listening with those sensitive ears. There was a large speaker in the ceiling and a large one-way window. He sat at a pristine white table. The door creaked open, and his brother was escorted into the room, dressed in camouflage, walking proud and mighty like a hero. His brother was about his age, perhaps a little older, and just a little taller.

His brother was friendly. He didn't have a name yet. He was sat right in front of him. He was happily sitting down, turning his head and marveling at the bright lights with a large smile and beautiful brown eyes. He swung his feet back and forth, just waiting for whatever surprise they had next for them. They were all good kids. They'd earned some kind of reward. He looked at the boy's shirt, which had merely the number "2" written on it, not a name. He turned down to his, looking for something to identify himself with: "7."

"This is exciting!" Two said, clapping his hands with elation, like a child who knew without a doubt that something good would happen. He could barely restrain his excitement. "Seven, what you think they gonna gif us?"

"I dunno." Seven shrugged, leaning forward, looking at the room suspiciously.

"Maybe ah, ah, ah, one of those thick brown things the rest of 'em eat. That looks good!" said Two, drooling.

"Or maybe a glass of that white stuff," Seven replied.

Two's blue eyes glistened with elation, and his blond hair glimmered in the light. "Somethin' nice and sweet wash it down!" He continued to clap his hands erratically.

Another soldier opened the door and came in. Seven read her name tag, J. Nakamura. She had the gold-bar insignia. Seven paid attention to this. She came in with a plate, a single plate carrying a piece of a bread, just a slice. The white bread was browning, with green mold growing at the side of it. The bread was crumbling on the plate. Nakamura placed it in the middle of the table, directly in between the two.

Number Two looked down at, sighing heavily into his hand as he covered his face. A moment passed before he turned around in his chair. "Mom, is this it?"

"Yes, it is." She sneered.

"You dun feed us a week and this all we get?" His face was downtrodden.

"Affirmative. Now, do be good, sweet little boys and don't touch it until we say so," she answered. She closed the door behind her, locking the locks from the other side.

"Well, sucks this!" Two cried out, slamming both of his fists on the table. The reinforced table trembled. His face cringed and tears streamed down it. His hands grabbed at his hair as he leaned forward on the table. "I hungry. Mom, I so hungry." His stomach growled.

Number Seven joined in, staring at the food. Even the mold looked good enough to eat. They were all hungry. He couldn't think how much longer he could wait. They were starving to the point where Seven, at least, would gladly have eaten dirt. He was not so sure of number Two.

The bright light went out. Both leaped from their chairs and backed into the walls. Flashing red lightbulbs came on, twirling on the ceiling. They were both startled, their hearts pounding against their chests. They huddled close to the walls. The intercom came on, and a loud, painful alarm went off. They both screamed, tears streaming down from their wide eyes as they covered their ears tightly with their hands. Even that was not enough; the oppressive sound pushed them to the ground as their backs slid down the walls. They wept, crying, "Momma! Make it stop!" That was who J. Nakamura was to them. "Mom. Stop it! Please!"

The alarm stopped, and the white lights were turned back on. The intercom clicked on again. "I think it's time we play a little game. How's that sound?" said the voice of Lieutenant Nakamura. "That sounds like fun."

Two and Seven were still stunned on the ground. They panted heavily.

"Don't be like that. Do I have to sound the alarm again?"

They immediately crawled to their chairs again. They pulled themselves up with relative ease. They sat straight in their chairs, both scanning the room.

"So, do you want to play a game?"

"Yes!" As if he had nearly forgotten about the alarm, Two sounded elated yet again. Seven was instead apprehensive.

"You see, the door is locked and will only open from the outside. You have a plate with one slice of bread on it. Only one of you can leave. Decide for yourselves. You can both starve or fight for the bread. This is a winner take all game. You've got this!" she exclaimed rather enthusiastically.

They both looked at each other in disbelief. "Se—Seven, are they—are they makin' us fight?"

"I dun wanna," Seven protested. He crossed his arms and turned his body away from the bread. "I dun wanna!"

"That's the name of the game," Nakamura said over the intercom. "You live or you die."

Two stared at the wall, pushing his legs back and forth in the chair, ignoring his hunger. He ignored the growling in his stomach. "Seven. I'm not doing it. I'm not."

"I'm not doing it either. Cross my heart hope to die," Seven replied.

"Then decided."

Two went into the other corner of the room and sat there. Seven moved from his seat and sat in the opposite corner. They smiled at each other from across the room.

Hours passed. Neither of them moved. The hunger inside their tummies grew, eating away at them. Seven pulled his knees to his chest, propping his elbows on them. He scratched his cheek as his palm covered his mouth. Two did the same thing. They both breathed deeply, sucking through their teeth as they kept their hands on their tummies, applying pressure in the hope that it would alleviate some discomfort.

They both were in so much pain, they couldn't fall asleep. All they could think about was not fighting, and not eating that disgusting moldy bread. They both toppled to the side, curling themselves up with their knees to their chests, grimacing and crying.

The intercom turned on. "Congratulations!" Nakamura exclaimed from the other end of the mirror. "You've passed. You both can leave. Just make sure to finish the bread first."

They each felt a new energy sweep over them. They crawled to their chairs. They both sat, and number Two excitedly took the piece of bread and ripped it in half. He held both pieces in his hand and told Seven, "It okay! I knew we do it. Here."

Seven smiled at him, taking the smaller piece. They both smiled and nodded as they ate the moldy bread. It was bitter, dry, and unbearable, but it was food. They could hear the door mechanisms come free. "Seven! We can leave!" They both got up from the table together, walking side by side. They reached for the handle of the door, smiling.

Click.

Two's eyes opened wide, as he exhaled heavily. The handle turned but the door wouldn't open. He ground his teeth. "Hey! Momma! What gives? You says we can go!" He pounded on the door with both fists. "Let out!"

"You both are going to leave," Nakamura explained, in her sweet motherly voice. "You didn't think we'd just leave a body in there, did you? Only one of you leaves alive. You can't leave until only one of you is standing. Good luck!"

"Sucks this," Two said. He clenched his fists tightly, the fingernails cutting into the palms of his hands until they bled. His hands trembled at his sides.

Number Seven moved away from the larger boy. He cowered in fear as he leaned against the wall. Number Two sighed, and turned to number Seven, raising his fists. "I need out," he sobbed. "Come here! I can't do dis anymore!"

Number Two charged at Number Seven. Number Seven raised his arms over his head to protect himself from the much larger boy, who struck him with fists like rocks. He was kicked in the side; his face was slammed into the wall. Two grabbed Seven by the hair and repeatedly knocked his face into the wall. He tripped Seven and started stamping his feet on his face until he stopped moving. He took his free foot and kicked the head into the ground, hoping for certain that Seven was dead.

Number Two cried as he walked back to the door. He went to open it, and there was no click. He looked back to the mirror. "Momma! Open up. He dead, just like you wanted. He dead. Let me out!" he sobbed, moving his fists to his sides. "LET ME OUT!"

"I said, only one of you leaves alive."

"I already told you! He dead!" he cried out. He cried into the camera monitoring the room, pointing with open hands where he thought Seven was laying.

"N—no. I not," said Seven. His face was bruised and swollen. He put his hands up, in defense position. "I do dis arr day. I can do dis arr day."

"Let me out!" Two cried as he swung at Seven.

There was a blue flash as the temperature dropped. Blue veins lit up Seven's arms, lighting up the room. The output of his mana veins was so intense that he was surrounded by blue crackling light, burning parts of his own flesh. Seven punched Two repeatedly with lightning-fast jabs. The impacts made a sound so violent that the mirror cracked. Seven grabbed hold of Two's throat with his hand. He clenched his teeth, baring them as he squeezed the air out of Two's lungs. The larger boy tried his hardest to rip himself free, but to no avail as the blue light burned at his throat, black smoke rising.

Crack!

Two's arms dropped down. Seven dropped him, as blood filled his mouth and his eyes seemed empty. Seven gasped as the mana veins receded into his body and his hands stood still. He slowly, mechanically moved his head to look at Two, dead on the floor. His eyes squinted as he let out a screamless cry.

The lock from the door came undone. The door creaked open. Seven looked up as Lieutenant Nakamura came in with a smile on her face and a plastic zippy bag. She walked over to him and kneeled, meeting him at eye level. She stroked the side of his face softly. "Good job, number Seven. You are my sweet little boy. Good job. For a job well done, here." His mother pulled out a black pill from the zippy bag and a bottle of water from one of her pockets, handing them both to him, "Eat."

Hungrily, Seven took the pill and washed it down with the water she provided.

"Good boy," she said, taking his hand in hers. "Come with me."

Seven followed her silently out of the oppressive white room. He walked with her down corridors where soldiers occasionally looked down on him with disgust.

His right hand started to tremble. Seven looked at his right hand, covered in Two's blood. He felt his heart beating in his chest, not from excitement, but guilt. He knew this wasn't a mere camping trip. No, Two would never see light again. He realized for certain, Two was dead, and *he* had killed him. Of course, who could blame him? After all, it was self-defense. But that didn't make it any easier. He'd still killed someone, his own brother. Breathing heavily, he tried to calm himself, but the vision of the room was just as vivid, and just as real, like he'd never truly left the room.

He let that sink in as he came to a large door. The gears and mechanisms in the door started to move, causing the metal to creak as it scraped against itself. Slowly it let in the welcoming moonlight, where he saw many of the other children outside in an area surrounded by chain linked fence. Nakamura brought Seven to the fence and opened the door. She ushered him in and locked the door behind him.

He stifled a cry as his heart grew very heavy, turning around to look Nakamura in the eye. She smiled back at him. "I'll play with you later, my sweet little boy. Good job tonight. I knew you had it in you, Seven."

He watched her walk backwards behind the vertical door as it closed in front of her. He looked up at the moon, and he could have sworn there were less stars in the sky. He looked down at the children in front of him. He counted them. One. Two. Three. Their faces were bruised, and he could have sworn the smaller red-headed girl had a black eye. Four. Five. Six. They were nursing broken limbs: arms, legs, fingers. Seven. Eight. Nine. These three were coughing up red blood. The larger black-haired boy, coughed up some baby teeth. He wheezed heavily. Ten. Eleven. Twelve. These three had blood, not their own, smeared over their faces. Thirteen. Fourteen. Fifteen. These three were huddled in a corner, staring and clawing at the fence. And Seven made sixteen. This morning, there had been thirty-two of them. Tonight, they were reduced by half.

He bit his bottom lip and clenched his fists at his sides. He started wailing, tears streaming down his face as the guilt of his first kill took hold of him. It felt like someone was inside his chest, punching his heart repeatedly. His knees buckled and he caught himself with his arms, kneeling on all fours like the dirty dog he was. His hands were covered in the sand, and his tears made mud in front of him. He looked at the rest of them. As if they had been waiting for someone to start, they all now wailed in the night air. Tears streamed down their faces.

Number Twenty-Seven, the thirteenth he counted, had her glasses tilted down on her face, with blood smeared over both lenses. She raised her gaze to the sky, her mouth open, blood drooling out of it.

Next to her was a crying girl, brown hair tied up in a ponytail, with bangs on either side of her face. Her face cringed and her teeth gritted against each other. She let out one squeal before she silenced herself, closing her mouth and letting her eyes scream with tears falling in a puddle. She was number Thirty-One.

Number Thirteen cried out loud, wiping his eyes with closed fists. His short dark hair was invisible in the darkness of the night. The blood got into his eyes as he collapsed to the ground, curling in the fetal position and holding his hands together in a tight ball, cutting off his own circulation in his hands. He brought that ball to his face.

Not one of them had names. These three would be part of Seven's personal squad in the future: Ticker, Butcher, and Slithers. All of them wept hard that night, leaving puddles of tears to reflect the coming sunrise.

CHAPTER 15

That is Enough

*~After it all, I'm falling apart and I don't want to be put
back together, but you're putting me back together anyway.*

JENNIFER WOKE UP IN the early morning, gasping for breath. She was sweating profusely. She mechanically turned her head to her alarm clock, which read 7:21 AM. She coughed, covering her mouth with her hand as she slowly rolled out of bed, striking the ground. She slowly pulled herself up, using her side table to support herself. Her joints trembled, filled with searing pain. Her bones felt as frail as thin glass. She pulled herself back onto her bed and leaned forward, taking deep breaths. She felt like her chest was caving in, the lungs bursting out at the seams of her ribs. She took numerous measured breaths.

She now felt at equilibrium. She leaned backwards, still breathing heavily with her hands resting on her chest. She looked up to the sky outside her window. The sun beamed down on her, glimmering as shadowy clouds slowly rolled in. She eased up on her breathing, and she felt her shortness of breath stabilize, but her bones still felt like glass. She pulled out her cell phone and opened her email. Her fingers trembled as she rapidly typed up an email to her work to let them know she was sick and couldn't come in today.

She went into her contacts. She scrolled down to Dr. Korowitz; her thumb trembled. She clicked the green call icon. She clicked speaker as the phone rang. She placed her phone on the side table. It rang and was answered quickly.

"Doctor Nicolai Korowitz's office. This is John, how may I help you?"

"Hi John. This is Jennifer Miller. I am one of Korowitz's patients. I woke up with a shortness of breath and I feel exhausted, and my joints are in searing pain. I woke up like this in the morning. It was sudden. Is there any way Doctor Korowitz can see me today?"

"Half a moment, Jennifer." Jennifer could hear him typing away rapidly. *"What is your date of birth?"*

"Eight. Second. Eighty-nine," she answered. *Click. Clack. Click. Clack.*

"He has an opening at nine o'clock."

"Please," she said.

"See you at nine o'clock."

Jennifer sat in the waiting room in the clinical office. The office was empty this morning, apart from a man sitting in the corner, waiting for his turn to get into the office. John, the receptionist was typing away on his computer, making notes and appointments for the doctors in the office. She waited patiently, still feeling weak in the legs. She crossed her arms over her lap as she stared ahead, concerned with whatever was going on with her body. It was all sudden. She had shortness of breath before, but not with this severity.

"Jennifer?"

Jennifer looked up and smiled at Dr. Korowitz. The doctor had a thick Russian accent and bright brown hair. He wore a full lab coat.

"Yes?"

"I will see you now."

Jennifer trembled as she stood up from the ground. Pain seared into her joints, and she put on a smile as she stood up. Korowitz frowned as he looked at her. He took her hand as she approached him and led her firmly to his patient room. She took a seat on the bed and he took a seat on a stool, logging into his computer.

"How are you feeling?" he asked in a soft voice.

"I'm in pain. This morning, I woke up with a shortness of breath. By itself, it isn't unusual; however, this wasn't usual. It was far worse, and it hurts my chest. I felt like my chest was going to collapse. I barely made it back to my bed after I fell off of it. My bones, particularly my legs, feel like glass." She grimaced, letting her tears stream down either side of her eyes. "I've never felt this way. At least, not with this severity."

He started to take her blood pressure. "Is this the first time you woke up like this?"

"Yes," was all she managed to say.

"Ease up on that arm," he instructed. His eyes angled at the machine, as if trying to piece together an age-old mystery. He wrote down the blood pressure. "Blood pressure is fine. Nothing to worry about there." He took a needle out and he drew her blood. "I'll be back." He placed a bandage on the spot where he'd drawn blood and left her inside the empty room.

She wiped her tears with her hand. She took deep breaths. She felt a vibration in her pocket. She took her phone out of her pocket. It was a text from Ted. *Tedward. I wonder how you're doing. That was a serious breakdown, or breakthrough, last night. I don't know what kind of pain you're going through, but it seems you and I will suffer together. Perhaps I'm being overdramatic. Yeah. That's it. I'm fine.*

She opened the text message.

Good morning, Jennifer. Words cannot express my feelings. Sometimes I don't understand them myself. Do you want to come and feed ducks with me by the Gardens?

She sniffled, smiling at the text. She returned it quickly. *I don't know yet, Tedward. I would certainly love to. Can you do me a favor and call me later? Whenever you get off work tonight. I'd really appreciate it.*

Immediately, he returned the text. *I'll call you after 6 pm.*

She smiled. He'd certainly been quick to return the text. A swift response, and a response with utmost certainty. She had no doubts within her heart that he would call her at that time. She wiped more tears from her face as she put her phone back into her pocket.

The door swung open. Korowitz took out a medical document and handed it to her. She looked over it. While much of it was a lot of medical jargon, there were some things she did recognize. These were the results of her blood test. Her CBC was alarming: three. Her eyes opened wide as the document trembled in her hand.

"We need to get you to the hospital. Did you drive here?"

"Yuh—yes," she stammered.

"We'll get the necessary call in place for a biopsy to be certain, but it's possible you may be developing leukemia." Korowitz took her hand. "Are you okay to walk right now?"

"Yes," was all she could say. *Leukemia?*

He took her hand. He led her out of the patient room and led her down the hall, leading her through the vestibule and down to a chair in the waiting room. He went into the front office, saying something to the receptionist inaudibly, who started typing away and sent something to the printer.

She sat down. Her hands trembled in front of her. She held back her tears, but her hands betrayed her feelings, for even the receptionist noticed the anxiety fueling her: Her eyes widened as the pupils trembled, streaming down reluctant tears as she began quivering uncontrollably. She leaned forward, frowning at her trembling hand.

She took another deep breath and buried her face in her hands. She spoke into her hands, muffling her words to God. "Lord. Forgive me. I don't think I've faltered. I don't think I have, but perhaps I've been caught up with Ted, and paid too much attention to him, and not enough to you. An innocent mistake by our standards down here below, but you are a perfect God, and our standards are not yours, and by yours I've made a fatal error. I'm sorry. I've escaped death before, twice. If it is your will, it would be a third time, but if not, I understand. I've had one too many second chances already. If it is your will, I accept. But please, let this not be my time. Just, please let me have a little while longer. Perhaps I haven't been as faithful as I think I have. Perhaps that is my fatal error. Lord, remove the callouses from my heart. Please. Please. *Please.*"

Jennifer woke up from the anesthesia to find herself sitting up in a white room. She looked out the window. The sun was setting. She looked around herself, seeing the nurses and physician assistants walking back and forth, attending to various patients. She looked around to see if she could find her own pants and her phone. She looked carefully, trying to find something to tell the time. She knew she wouldn't have the results from the biopsy for another seven to ten days. There was no use trying to worry about it.

She found her purse sitting by the side of her bed. She couldn't reach it. She looked back up and moved her braided ponytail off to her left shoulder. She looked for a free nurse and waved her down. The woman moved over to her swiftly and gave her a warm smile. Jennifer looked at the woman's name tag, catching only the last name: McCurdy.

"Hi. Miss. Could you tell me what time it is?"

McCurdy looked at her watch. "Five forty-seven," she answered.

"Oh, really? I guess I woke up just in time. Could you hand me my purse? I can't reach it, and I'm not sure if I should be moving around much yet, but I'm expecting an important call."

McCurdy handed Jennifer's purse to her.

"Thank you very much. Would you happen to know when I am to be discharged?"

"Let me find out for you. Do you have someone to pick you up?"

"Not yet."

The nurse walked away. Jennifer looked at her phone and saw no notifications just yet. It wasn't like she received texts very often, especially not on a Wednesday. She scrolled through her contacts. She went to Sam's number and texted: *Please pray for me. I woke up ill. I'm being tested. Pray that it's negative.*

There was silence except for the constant walking of nurses, the rolling of wheelchairs, and the constant stamping of crutches and walkers. Various machines filled with oxygen and other medical accessories rolled past. She waited as the time passed by, waiting for that call. She was still certain he would call, despite the constant efforts he'd kept making to put distance between them. She was certain that *he* really wanted to talk to her, even to discuss something mundane. Perhaps, he'd finally reveal something else, something not traumatic, about himself. She heard the imaginary clock ticking inside her head, like a little lost dwarf hammering away at her cranium.

She looked down at her phone, still waiting for any kind of response from Sam or Ted's call. Her notifications remained empty and silent as the sounds of the hospital drowned out the ticking of her internal clock. She looked back out the window, staring at the streetlights outside, illuminating the streets, which were still filled with pedestrians walking around with their phones to their ears or their faces bowed down and typing or reading away. Many others, children, seemed happy to be skipping along in the street with their parents. Many of those children were tugging on their parents' arms for attention. She couldn't help but smile.

She looked back at the end of the bed and examined her feet. She wanted to know and feel if her bones still felt like breaking glass as they had that morning. She sucked in the air through her teeth, anticipating pain as she lifted her left leg up on top of the covers. Her left leg trembled as it rose, but not so much from the pain, but rather with the anticipation of it. Her leg was growing defiant of her condition, however severe it might have been. She put left leg down and raised her right leg, which trembled as it rose. She smiled as she put her leg back down.

Buzz.

She looked down at her phone, smiling as Ted's name shone across the screen. She swiftly answered the call and brought it to her ear. "Tedward." Her tone was filled with excitement as her mouth rose from ear to ear.

"Jennifer," he spoke. His tone was not cheerful, nor did it seem grim or depressing. It was just there, empty.

"Tedward!" she exclaimed yet again. She smiled through the phone, not because of the empty monotone, but simply because his tone wasn't cheery. This time, he wasn't trying to hide anything. "Are you feeling okay? I mean, the other night, that was a lot. It couldn't have been easy."

"Well, I suppose I've seen worse," he replied. *"It is hard to say I've seen much better times in my life, but perhaps that was for the best. There's just only so much I can say."*

"I think we've all had our trials and faults. I think that it is not all you," she said, dropping her smile as she saw the nurse walking over to her. "I think part of it is on me, and Samantha. We did push hard on you when we had no right knowing anything, but we didn't want to see you alone. I recognize a fake smile, and while some fake smiles fade well into the crowd, yours stood out to me."

"I don't blame you. I don't. I find it difficult to express myself, even when you annoy me."

"Well, it was bound to happen. I annoy a lot of people. It is one of my quirks."

"You mean charms, don't you?" His tone was playful.

"You can be discharged if you have a way to get home," the nurse said to her.

Jennifer nodded. "I suppose it is one of my charms. You haven't ditched me yet, have you?"

"Discharged?" he said.

"I'm in the hospital for a biopsy. I'm about to go home, somehow," she explained. "Nothing serious." *I hope.*

"Did you drive?"

"No," she answered. "I was delivered here by ambulance. My car is still at the doctor's office."

"Are you okay?" he said. His voice was monotonous, and seemed uncaring, but he was trying. She knew; otherwise, he wouldn't have called.

"I'm sure I'll be fine. Hey, here's an idea. Why don't you pick me up and take me home? Sam's not getting back to me."

"Where are you?"

"The diseased manor," she answered.

There was silence on the other end of the line. And then he laughed. *"There is no hospital with that name."*

"We can make it one," she joked, smirking.

"Sure. So, where am I picking you up?"

"Jameson's Hospital. Thirty-two Broadway, Brookline. I'm on the fourth floor," she replied.

"Okay. I'll drive over. Give me about a half hour. I'm coming from Dedham."

"I'll see you soon!"

Click.

She looked back down at her phone, seeing a text message from Sam: *I will pray. Sorry for getting back so late. Work troubles. I hope you're doing well. Brunch on Saturday? Michael and Tim will be there. I don't want to invite Ted back just yet. I think he needs some time.*

She smiled down at the text, feeling accomplished. Not that she had Ted all to herself for the night, but the fact alone that he spoke to her without masking his emotions much. For tonight, maybe he would completely remove that mask. Perhaps finally, the iron heart *was* being softened, capable of being adjusted by a hard mallet.

She texted back: *I think I'll pass on brunch this week. I'll see you Sunday.*

Jennifer leaned back and looked up to the ceiling, placing both hands beneath herself. She let out a deep breath, sighing into the air as an indescribably heavy burden was violently lifted from her chest.

"Lord, be with me," she prayed. She closed her eyes and crossed her hands over her chest. "Lord, thank you for the gift of modern medicine, and thank you for Doctor Nicolai Korowitz and his insight in catching this. I am content. Thank you for pushing me through my limits, through my dreams and aspirations. Forgive me Father, even though I fall constantly, and fail to follow your laws. Please humble me when I am consumed by arrogance and pride." She opened her eyes. took a deep breath, and tried to move her legs again. This time, she could move both legs up and down, and she did so, taking turns, not grimacing with any discomfort, for it seemed to have subsided. She smiled. "Thank you for everything. Truly, I am grateful. I have more than enough, and more than I need. Thank you. Amen."

Ted walked through the doors into the hospital. He smiled as he walked in. No one here needed to know his *true* condition, or his *true* hatred. He noticed many people in wheelchairs, some amputees, many whose faces were void with sunken eyes. Long and skinny faces, devoid of all personality, just like they were completely dead inside, much like himself, only they'd stopped caring enough to hide it from anyone. He smiled at the thought of being dead inside. If only his heart would stop beating. He went to the receptionist, waiting in line, still scanning the busy hallways and the white floors, smeared with feces and urine, just waiting to be cleaned up. A staff member dressed in white and wearing gloves and a mask came by with a wet floor sign and a mop bucket and started mopping away.

"Sir. Sir. Hello! Is anybody home?" the annoyed receptionist called out. Her spectacles hung by her chest on a strand of grey beads.

Ted jerked his head toward her, catching a very unforgiving but friendly face out of the corner of his eyes. His fists clenched at his sides as he replaced his frown with a bright smile at the much older woman. "Sorry about that. My mind seemed to have slipped."

"Careful, or you'll end up slipping too. How can I help?"

"I'm sure. I'm actually here to pick up a patient. Jennifer Miller."

"What's your name?"

"Ted Anderson."

"I don't see your name here."

"Embarrassing." He chuckled nervously, as he was sure was the appropriate response. "I just got the call to pick her up. She does know me if you want to call her down. I'll take a seat somewhere. That is, of course, *if* she is a patient here."

The older woman motioned him to sit in a chair which was vacant.

"Thank you."

Ted went and took a seat on the chair, waiting, and scanned the room. He recognized a man he saw, an unforgivable man. The man still had that buzz cut, that sinister smile. Ted was sure his dog tags were hiding underneath his lab coat. The man looked like a seriously joyful man, smiling cutely at women who happened to walk by, as if encouraging niceties.

Dr. Adams. Are you really a medical doctor? It sickens me to think that you could actually care about people. I certainly never received such treatment from you. Not after you strapped me to that damn chair in leather straps, sending electrical currents all through my body until my pain receptors no longer worked. Adams, if I wasn't trying so damn hard to live a normal life, as normal as I can, despite my own psychological deficiencies that you caused, I wouldn't hesitate to kill you.

Doctor Adams disappeared as he continued to walk down the end of the hall. Ted knew who and what it was that he'd seen, and frankly, out of all the painful memories and people in his past, he was sure this was real, and that he wasn't merely having a psychotic episode at the end of the day.

Ted's hands relaxed as he pressed them against his pants, still scanning the hospital. He didn't feel safe here, not when there was a familiar face present—well, one that wasn't Jennifer's. For of all the things he knew, and it pained his heart, her smile, the least of all, was genuine. He took a deep breath as he stared down the vestibule and spotted a little nurse pushing a wheelchair. In that wheelchair was Jennifer, holding her purse on her lap. She smiled as she waved her arm at him. She had a light blue medical gown over her clothes.

He smiled at her, breathing deeply as he stood up from his chair. He forgot abruptly that he'd just had a faint encounter with someone from his past, however one sided, and turned his attention to Jennifer, walking to meet the nurse.

"Hi, Tedward!" Jennifer smiled that foxlike smile of hers. There was something suspicious, but beautiful about it. As always, her eyes were playfully half opened.

"Elizabeth." He gave a light smile.

"Well, is Mr. Darcy reading up on his Jane Austen for me? How romantic."

The nurse giggled behind her. "You got her?"

"I'll take her." Ted went to the back of the wheelchair to push her along.

"Onward! The chariot awaits!" She raised both her hands and kicked her feet out. "Weeee!"

"Well, I can't say I've had to be in a hospital before, but I don't think I would be in good spirits." Ted chuckled, pushing her out the door.

"Tedward." She leaned back in her seat and looked up at him from below. Ted noticed her watchful eyes watching him. He couldn't say he understood her true intentions, but he felt vulnerable, almost like when Slithers had broken him down after years of badgering to take her to go stargazing. "You need to learn to live a little. Life is too short to be miserable." She paused a moment. "I'm sorry. I know I can be overbearing at times." She sat back, all snugged in her little chair and hospital gown as Ted rolled her over the board walk and carefully into the parking lot.

He smiled awkwardly down at her. "I see. Well, I suppose I've lived long enough to know how short life can be. Some lives may be long; others tragically short." His tone dropped.

"Ted." She looked back at him as he rolled her to his car. "I'm sorry. This isn't my way of trying to pry anything out of you. I just want your company."

"I understand." He wheeled her to the side of his black car. He opened the car door.

"Of course, what kind of friend would I be if I didn't desire to know something else about you?" she said, sneering at him. She wobbled out of her seat and sat herself into the car. She smiled as she moved her feet into it.

"Is the chair yours, or do I need to put it back in the hospital?"

"It goes back into the hospital. There should be a little depot right by the front doors, if I remember right." She gestured back to the hospital. "It's okay. I'll be here waiting while you return it, Mr. Darcy."

"As you wish, Emma," he replied.

"Wrong Jane Austen novel! Emma was Mr. Knightly!" she snapped at him, pointing fingers at his chest. "Don't disrespect Jane!"

He snickered as he shut the door and rolled the wheelchair back to the hospital, leaving Jennifer alone as she stared out the windshield. She fastened her seatbelt as she adjusted the seat. The bones inside her fragile legs trembled as she applied pressure to the floor of the car to push her seat back. She grimaced as pain filled her joints again. She leaned her head against the window to her left as she scanned the skies, the dark clouds rolling in overhead.

"Ted. I hope you find it soon. The storm is coming." A shiver went up her spine as the temperature appeared to drastically drop; she felt it from within the car. She started rubbing her shoulders and gazed back out the window and saw a woman with crimson eyes, silver hair, and a youthful face skipping along the street. She seemed familiar somehow. Someone looking for adventure, or so Jenn thought.

The girl disappeared behind a crowd, gone like a wisp.

The door on the other side opened. Jennifer turned her head sharply as Ted got into the car, buckling his seatbelt. "Alright, Jennifer, let's get you home. Where did you leave your car?"

"It was at the doctor's office."

"I'll pick it up for you." He put his key into the ignition and started the engine.

Ted drove out of the parking lot into the street, through the heavily congested roads of Boston towards the Seaport District. Jennifer shifted in her seat, thinking about the tears Ted had shared that night, on the night she would remember, the Fourth of July. She was certain he had had every intention of wearing that mask, living in the façade of his own life, forgetting everything else that was important to him. This constant reminder of his condition she found most curious, and she was ashamed of her own compulsive obsessiveness over him, but she couldn't not think about it. *But does he really have anything important to him?* Then an image flashed through the back of her mind of walking in the darkness of the night, the quiet stillness of College Avenue when he'd broken down on all fours, weeping, crying, letting all of the pain leave his body. But truly, there wasn't an outlet big enough to let all that pain out at once.

The temperature had dropped drastically that night, and light had filled the air. An unnatural light that shouldn't have been. The light had come directly from his body. Maybe it was something small enough, small enough to pry that he would remove a brick from that wall he kept up.

"Ted?"

"Yes?" he replied, never taking his eyes off the road.

"That night, when you ran off," she began. She noticed him shift uncomfortably in his seat. "I'm not going to ask your feelings or what you are going through, I'm not going to pry, but perhaps you can explain something to me that I am having a hard time trying to understand. I saw those lights coming from your body. What was that?"

His smile faded, and he let out a deep sigh, keeping his eyes focused like a laser on the busy road. "I am the only person I know that has ever had them. I don't know what they are, but they are regrettably a part of me. I can't get rid of it. I've tried, but nothing works. I don't know what they are, nor do I truly understand what they do. All I know is that when I use this organ, the temperature drops. It's really hard to describe. I've never had to describe it before. It is like breathing, but it's something other than air. It goes into these veinlike things that protrude out of me. It appears to change colors depending on what I'm breathing in. I don't know how else to explain it; no medical doctors knew what these are either. I first noticed it was a part of me during an especially difficult time in my life that I don't care to discuss right now."

"That is enough, Ted," she replied.

"Hmm?" He turned to her slightly.

"That is enough." She smiled to him, twiddling the loose end of her braided ponytail with her right index finger. "Just to admit that is enough. You don't have to explain any more than that. The fact alone that you trust me enough with that is warming to my little frail heart. I want you to know that even while it may be unnatural, I do not judge you for it, nor will I condemn you. I just want you to know that."

"Thanks," he answered before turning his head back to the road with a sharp frown, like he'd made a fatal mistake.

The streetlights shone brightly on the sidewalks. He parked his car in the back of the Seaport, a short walk away from her apartment.

He turned the key off. "I don't think I asked, but maybe we can talk in your place. Do you need help getting up?"

"If you don't mind, Tedward." She smiled at him as she opened the door. "My legs are still a little weak."

"Hang on." He walked hastily around the front of the car to get to Jennifer on the other side. He took her hand and carefully helped her out of the car. She moved to the side, leaning against the side of the car for support. He closed the door and locked it.

He pulled her arm over his shoulders, pulling her closer to him. He held her close to him as they walked, using his strength so that she felt weightless, light, like a feather. He walked her across the street and into her big apartment building. He took her up the elevator and walked her down the hall. She breathed heavily with each breath, especially as she reached for her keys in her purse. The door creaked as she opened it. Ted walked her in and brought her to her couch.

"Thank you," she said, smiling up at him.

"You're welcome. I've been meaning to ask you, and I don't know why I waited this long: why were you in the hospital?"

She let out a sigh and patted the cushion next to her. "Take a seat." He looked suspiciously at the cushion before cautiously sitting down next to her. She looked up to the ceiling as if the answer to some unknown question was written on it. "Life, it is so fragile and ought to be protected. No matter how worthless it might seem, no matter how useless. All life has value, and I think sometimes I feel I take the life I have for granted. It became apparent to me today, when I woke up, gasping for breath like some devil was inside my chest. I am a survivor, Ted. I've survived a lot, and perhaps that is why I seem to be overbearing at times, so full of life—because I have already been on my deathbed."

Ted actively listened to her, the small details, how her tone changed from sentence to sentence. It was clear to him that she wasn't stalling to tell him the reason, but she still hadn't processed everything just yet. Death was something he was all too familiar with. There were times where he'd thought he would be on his death bed—that was, until he'd found out he apparently couldn't die by normal means. Those cursed veins prohibited it.

"I called the doctor's office and had a blood test, and my doctor seems to think I have a high chance of leukemia. I went to the hospital for a biopsy, and I did have some treatment to deal with the pain. I don't know if I have been confirmed for leukemia—that is what the biopsy is for, and if I have it, it will determine the type of leukemia I have."

"You seem to be in good spirits for someone who has potentially received her death sentence," he said grimly, turning his head away from her, not wanting to look into her eyes.

She took her hands and clasped them around his cheeks and turned them to her so she could smile that faithful smile, filled with cheer. Despite the cruelty of her uncertain condition, she was full of it. Of course, Slithers would never do this, but it was warming all the same. "This world can be a dark place. It is filled with despair and hopelessness. It is filled with tragedy and loneliness. It is filled with gloom; however, I know where I will go. If it is my time, I will gladly accept my deliverance from this world, and be all the gladder because of it. I don't know where your faith lies, or if you have any in the Lord, but I wholeheartedly believe, and He gives me peace in all of this. I may be cheery now, but like many others, I will cry—but not yet."

"I didn't grow up in a church. I've heard telltale mentions of a God who is loving and good," he replied. "However, I find it hard to justify a loving and just God created this world with so much tragedy."

"I thought the same thing once. Many years ago." She sighed. "But no point in dwelling on this now, if you don't want to. I'm hungry."

"You're not in any condition to cook," he said.

"I don't want to cook, silly." She giggled as she released her grip from his face. "What do you like to eat?"

"I can't taste anything. I can't taste anything. I haven't been able to taste anything in over eight years."

"Well, that's boring." She sighed as she leaned back in the cushion. "So then, the baklava?"

"I couldn't taste it. I tried it and tossed the rest."

"Ted." Her tone dropped. "I appreciate you being honest and showing me a part of you. It's like meeting a new person."

"You're welcome," he said flatly.

"I want Chinese food." She pointed to a brochure on her TV stand. "There is a menu right there. Can you grab that for me?"

"As you wish," he replied, getting up from his cushion to grab the menu. He brought it back to her. She looked at it. "Ted, I know you said you can't taste anything, but are you hungry?"

"I barely eat," he replied. "Only when necessary."

"I'll order you something." She dialed a number on her phone as she stared at the menu.

About an hour later, they sat at her dining room table with the brown crunchy paper bags and sturdy white boxes with aluminum handles sprawled around with some paper plates. They were filled with fried rice, chicken fingers, and teriyaki. It smelled delicious as the steam from the steamed vegetables assaulted their noses with their sweet and delicate fragrances. Ted ate sparingly.

"Ted?"

"Yes?"

"Last night, at Terri Nation, you came back there, and hid away on a Tuesday night around the time we would be there. Why did you come? I don't entirely understand why, if you were hellbent on avoiding us."

"I guess you could say I was running away. I quit my job. Fortunately, I can still do that with my computer and not have to worry." His voice trailed off as soon as he realized how stupid that was. "I don't worry for money; I have plenty of it. I'd be more worried about not having something to keep my mind occupied. I knew you all would be there. I wanted to say goodbye, to give that courtesy, but when the time came, I couldn't muster it up within myself to do it. So, I tried to leave, only, something else happened instead. Sam managed to find me there as I was finishing up some potatoes. Unfortunately, I am very good at hiding my own thoughts, my feelings."

"I know you don't wear your heart on your sleeve, but it came bursting out at the seams last night. Ted, forgive me, I know I said I wasn't going to pry, and I guess I won't, but I do want to know a little more about what happened to you. Would you be willing to share something?"

"I would be willing, but the question is what? A lot happened to me, and so much of it wasn't exactly legal." He let out a deep sigh as his eyes scanned the ceiling as if to study it. "You see, Jennifer, I was part of this group in the U.S Army, but the program itself was run by the CIA. They chose thirty-two men and women to be part of this program. I nearly didn't make the cut due to an earlier heart attack. We were all physically fit and battle-hardened by the time we started our series of deployments, lasting a total of four years. We barely slept. We barely ate at all during that time. For four years, we were up before the sun, and didn't sleep until the moon slept. One morning, we'd end up in Iraq, and fight a two-week fire fight. After we were done raising hell, we would go back to the Forward Operating Base to resupply. We wouldn't get a chance to go into our barracks. We had none; we didn't need them. We'd be on the next flight immediately to North Korea the following day. Repeat. Fly to Russia. Repeat. Fly to China. Repeat."

He stopped scanning the room, pausing briefly, waiting for Jennifer to respond. She chewed the food in her mouth slowly, peering into his eyes. She nodded her head, waiting for the rest of his story.

"The nations began to fear us, and rightly so. We learned their tactics and killed them in their sleep. Whenever there was a fight between America and any other opposing force, once it was known we were on the battlefield, the battle was already over. It didn't matter how many people they took with them; it was a matter of how fast they could arrange an organized retreat."

He paused again, biting his index finger, and looked down to the table, seeing a speck of dust. He took his free hand and brushed it off onto the floor. He returned his gaze back to Jennifer, who looked back at him, ignoring the fact that he'd just wiped dust on her floor.

"I too value life to the highest degree, but my actions tell a different story. You'd think that after killing so much I would become numb to it. I never did. I still see the blood on my hands, and I still see the light leave their eyes. I still see their faces and they never leave me, always staring at me like a murderer. Why shouldn't they look at me like that?" He choked up as he shed tears from both eyes. His heart was lying open on the table. But this time it wasn't something that needed to be pried open; he willingly gave her the key. "I didn't have a choice. I didn't have a choice." He wiped his eyes with two fists, twisting them about.

He felt warm hands cover his, and softly pull them away from his eyes, guiding them, palm upwards, to the table. Her fingers caressed his wrists, and he saw she never once looked away. "We always have a choice. At times there may not seem to be any good options, but there is always a choice."

Seeing Ted was hyper focused on their hands, she removed hers from atop his and laid them with palms facing upwards next to both of his. She noticed his hands tremble before they flipped, holding her hands firmly on the table, and with that, she saw his teeth clench. His watery eyes turned towards her, shimmering from the ceiling's light. She was thankful that another layer of his façade had come undone. *If only he could bring it upon himself to seek help; and yet, as if some cruel fate or curse was laid upon his birth, he is compelled to do nothing and carry the burden of guilt alone. Ted, you didn't tell me everything, and I don't mean you to.*

He took a deep breath, sucking the air through his teeth, then let the air out in a measured breath. "You're wrong," he spoke quietly. "And I can't tell you why."

"Can you tell me why you can't tell me?" she asked.

There was a silence. Jennifer gripped onto his wrist a little more tightly. Finally, Ted slowly shook his head. She slowly nodded, never once letting her gaze escape his as she finally clasped his hand with her second free hand. "What you've said already is enough. Like a shaken-up soda bottle, you need to release some of that built-up tension before you can open it properly without it getting messy and blowing up all over the place. You have told me what I have asked, and I will ask for nothing more tonight. And Tedward, I want you to know that what you've told me is not going to leave my mouth nor my lips tonight, tomorrow, or ever. I hope you believe me."

He nodded.

She scarfed down the rest of her food. "I could use a shower, but tonight has been a rough one. I think I'm going to turn in early."

"Good night."

She turned to get up, and her legs wobbled before she gained full composure of her legs. "Okay. It isn't that bad," she said to herself, hoping to use the placebo to stave off the pain. She started walking back towards the couch. "Ted, you are still in your house, right?"

"No. I sold it as soon as Sam started getting too close to me. I have an apartment in Waltham."

"Ted, I wouldn't normally do this," she said. *But I don't want to be alone.* "But I do have an extra blanket if you want to spend the night here. The couch isn't all that big, but it does pull out into a spare bed. I don't want you to be alone tonight."

"I'll stay."

She smiled and tilted her head down as her eyelids drooped halfway down. "Now, Ted, does this mean I'll see you in the morning, then?"

"Yes," he said slowly, his volume dropped to a whisper.

She smiled as she went into the other room. Ted watched her, carefully monitoring her every step. He watched as each leg shifted, and her feet turned with each passing step. They were disorganized.

Tonight, he felt an incredible weight lifted from upon him. It had been eight long years; at least, that was how he remembered it. Too bad. The memories wouldn't go away. The nightmares wouldn't stop.

She came back out of the room with a large blanket already folded up and placed it on the coffee table. She removed the cushions from the couch and moved them to the side as she pulled out the folded bed from the couch. She set the blanket on top of the bed and started to tuck in the sheets.

"There you go," she said.

"Thank you," he spoke softly.

"Good night, Ted."

He nodded to her as she slowly closed the door to her room.

Looking down at the soft futon, he let his arms drop to his sides. For once in his life, a bed was made for him, not one that he was forced to make and remake over and over again with a single wrinkle on the sides. This bed was made perfectly, no wrinkles, nothing drooping too far from one side to the other. His hand reached for the blanket. The hand trembled abruptly as it touched the blanket. Glaring, he found his hand pulled his nightmares again into his reality.

His hand, covered in crimson blood, lit by the burning flames. He saw iron and stone rubble in front of him, and the roar of the flames drowned everything else out. He covered his mouth as the awful scent of spilled petroleum assaulted his nose. His nightmare turned again into reality, and further smells assaulted his nostrils: burning flesh, and rotting corpses and other expiring fluids. The buzzing of flies filled his ears. He covered his nose as he reached for the futon that was no longer there.

Kicking the side of the futon, he tripped over it, feeling the burning coals against his palms. Head striking the pillow, he came back into the reality that was Jennifer's apartment, leaving the flames of regret behind him. He kicked off his shoes, taking numerous deep breaths. He stared at the blank empty ceiling as he rested his back against the futon, sprawling his limbs on the unnatural comfort of the bed.

"We trusted you, you know," came a voice out of the corner. Ted immediately sat up and scanned the room. Toward the corner of his eye, he found an all-too-familiar face, someone he'd forgotten. She had glasses on her face, and her black bangs framed it as the rest of her hair was tied back in a ponytail. She was wearing black pants and green fatigues. Her arms were crossed over each other.

"Roach," he said.

"Ghost," she said disapprovingly. "Why are you here?"

"The same could be said of you."

"You know why I'm here. Why are you here, trying to make a life for yourself? It was what you always wanted, wasn't it? To live as a normal man, with a wife, maybe have some kids, a job, get a house, and yet, here you are just as miserable as you were when you were with us." She dropped her hands and tilted her head as she took two steps forward to him. She sneered at him, showing him her blood-covered teeth. "You should be sacking Uncle Sam right now."

"You know how I feel about that."

"Ghost, don't give me that!" she snapped at him. "Everything we fought for was a lie. Everything we died for was nothing more than a sham. There is no point in lives like ours! If you don't sack Uncle Sam, then there is no point in a life like yours!"

"I don't want to." His eyes angled to hers, and he frowned, clenching his fists at his sides.

"You don't want to, but you need to, Ghost. Do you want to finally lay us to rest?" Her tone softened.

"More than anything."

"Then you need to sack Uncle Sam. You know what all of us sacrificed for that! Do you want your nightmares to go away? Do you want to stop seeing these vivid dreams? Do you want to end it all? I know you do, and if you do, you need to sack Uncle Sam!" She aggressively pointed a finger at him.

"There is no point." His voice was stern. "Roach, even if I did, I know that the nightmares will only get worse. There is no closure for a monster like me. It won't mean a damn thing." He gritted his teeth.

"Then you've given up."

"You don't understand, Roach. The difference between you and me is that your nightmare ended eight years ago. I wish mine ended that day. I go to sleep, and I see it all over again, and my nightmares refuse to end!"

"Ghost." She sighed as she took a step back and leaned against the back wall. "I know. I know. We all know that you don't have the damn guts to do it, and you're the only one of us who can." She sighed as she stared at the ceiling. "Well, I've got to go. This was useless. You're useless. Oh, and Ghost, don't blame yourself for what happened to us. It's not your fault. It's not your fault."

Ted's eyes glimmered, coated in tears again. He wept softly as he rolled his fists in his eyes.

"It's not your fault I died," Roach said coldly. Ted looked at her and he saw her as he'd left her. Her left arm was severed. Her right leg was completely torn off, and the stumps bled profusely on the floor. She removed her uniform with her one hand, revealing the cavity that was inside her chest; the bones were shattered inside. The right side of her face was completely burned. The oil on her face still burned and he could smell the roasting flesh. He could smell the soot of blowing gunpowder. "The fault was entirely mine for trusting my life in the hands of a wretch like you! I can't believe I trusted you to be able to protect me. You can't save anyone. How could you, when you can't even save yourself?"

He gasped as she shook her head in disappointment. The color in her body and blood began to slowly fade into transparency. The silence to him was deafening, but he knew it wasn't over. The demons and monsters were about to come out. He slowly went to lay back down as he started to choke on more tears. He grabbed one of the cushions and brought it closer to his head as his ears were filled with the unrelenting agonizing screams of men and women. It drowned out his thoughts completely as the room around him turned into a prison made from flesh and arms, walls tiled with dead and dying faces, their eyes seeking him out.

Servicemen and women surrounded him, aiming their weapons. The screams of agony outweighed the sudden bursts of gunfire. He felt the vibrations in the air as bullets passed over his head. He silently wept, his eyes filled with tears and terror as he tried to drown out the noise by squeezing his ears with the cushion to no avail. He could still hear them as plain as day. These men swore in the languages of all the people he'd killed: English, French, German, Chinese, Russian, Polish, Italian, and Korean. He saw every last detail in all their faces; the scars, the malformities, every last one of them.

Because of him, he thought, countless had been made widows and orphans. Because of him, there were families going without food. Because of him, there was going to be an emptiness in their lives, and those kids the parents had left behind were going to think ill of him, and should they know who he was, for certain, they would seek his head. And who could blame them? If only there was a way to achieve world peace without needless bloodshed, he could have found a purpose for his miserable existence. Roach was right. There really wasn't a point in a life like his.

Jennifer's eyes came open with a start as her ears rang with loud tormented screams. The temperature dropped drastically, and she pulled the covers off and hopped off of her bed. She opened the door into the other room, peering from behind it. The room was filled with rainbow light. *Tedward.* She investigated the bed where Ted should be, and she found the cushions ripped from the sofa, laying to the side, the blanket disheveled. *Ted.* She moved out of her room, dragging her blanket with her. She put her hand out in front of her to shield herself from the blinding light and found Ted in a corner, huddled up with his knees to his chest and multi-colored lights emitting from his body. These lights looked like human veins, and they covered his entire flesh from his fingertips to the top of his skull. The lights were beautiful, like a rotating rainbow.

She looked at him carefully. Tears streamed down his face, and he looked dead ahead at nothing in particular, as if he were in one of those horror movies and a monster had just killed everyone he was with and he was next. He looked terrified as his hands clasped both sides of his face, covering his ears.

Just like before. How vivid are your nightmares? She knew he needed help, and certainly a therapist, but she knew already he would never see one. All she could do was listen and offer a shoulder; any more would undo all the work she and Sam had accomplished with him. She walked toward him, maintaining eye contact with him, but his eyes didn't seem to react to her presence as the temperature continued to drop. Seeing the white mist of her breath, she took each step with care, knowing full well her condition. Her heart felt some strain on it, but not because of her condition, but merely because it hurt her inside to see anyone like this. *Ted, it is good you stayed. This was what worried me.*

She took another step closer and leaned against the wall beside him. She wrapped her arm around his shoulders and leaned into him. He jerked away as he stared into her eyes as if he didn't know her. She moved in front of him and placed her hands on his wrists ever so gently and removed them from his ears. She cried tears with him, and they streamed off of her face and into his lap as the strings of her heart were pulled. *I'm not a therapist! God, help me!*

"Ted, I can't hear what you hear. I can't see what you're seeing right now." She spoke softly and his hands dropped to her wrists. "I know you don't want to talk about it, and I'm not going to force you to. But at some point, you will need to talk about it, or you'll explode. I'm here."

She moved to the side of him and leaned into him again and wrapped the blanket around them. He started to take deep breaths as he wiped the tears from his eyes with his fists again.

"Why?" he breathed.

"'Why'?" she replied, turning her face to his.

"Why are you and Sam so focused on me? I am filled with regret and guilt. I try so hard to function in the real world, but I just can't. These nightmares and phantoms simply won't let me. My nightmares don't end when I wake up. Every night. Every night when I try to sleep, I wake up screaming because I see ghosts. These ghosts are people I've killed. I remember their faces, every single one of them. I see those who I fought with and fought for. They're all dead because of me. I couldn't save them. I can't save anyone. I couldn't save any of them, because I just couldn't muster the strength in me to kill anyone anymore. I couldn't save anyone. Perhaps they were all right, and there really isn't a point in a life like mine."

She nodded. "You may feel that way. It is human to believe in the sanctity of life, and while there are those that like to undermine it by defining life on their own terms, the truth remains the same: we all value life, and when we take it away, we feel guilt and regret. We are told to value life at a young age, or at least I'd like to think so, and taking that life is enough to break us. Ted, even when we are not the ones taking something away, we feel heartbroken by it. You remind me of my uncle. He came back from wartime, and he never expressed himself openly, like you, and he eventually took his own life. I don't want to see that happen to you."

She watched the light of the veins on his body shimmering on the ceiling and on her flesh. Despite the dropping temperature, the veins as they touched her were like a frying pan. *What is this? God, what happened to him that made him like this? Surely he wasn't born like this, was he?*

"Life can be hard, and like I said to you, life can be Hell. It's like that for everyone. We go through rough patches, and sometimes we feel like the light at the end of the tunnel is nothing more than where the last traveler fell, his lamp burning stationary in a dead end. And sometimes we get to dance in the meadows and see the fireworks."

The lights from the veins started fading and cooling down as the air around them warmed up. She didn't understand what was going on, or what exactly the veins were doing. Even Ted had admitted he didn't know what they were, but that he was the only one who'd ever had them. She felt his body cease trembling as he reached some level of homeostasis.

She continued, "It is no mistake to say I've become fond of you, even if I seem to know next to nothing about you. I know where you're from and that's about it. I know you served to protect our nation, and that whatever happened to you there is unforgiveable, whatever it was. It sounds like what you went through was nothing short of betrayal and regret."

She was right. She knew nothing about him, but was able to ascertain that much—that everything that had happened to him should never have happened to begin with. Could he trust her?

"Ted, do you trust me with your heart? I will never say anything to anyone that you don't want spoken aloud. But do you trust me?"

"No." He hesitated. "I don't trust you." He paused as he looked at her again. "But I am willing to try."

"That is enough."

CHAPTER 16

The Garden

JENNIFER WOKE UP WITH the sun beaming on her face. She stretched out over the back of her bed and yawned. She looked at the clock. 9:32. *A tad early. No matter.* She leapt out of bed and put the covers back on it. She looked at her phone; no text messages yet, but there was a voicemail. She saw that it had come from Doctor Korowitz's office. *Must be the test results.* She stared down at her phone and her hand trembled with anticipation. She'd felt much better these last few days, and even now, the pain in her bones had completely subsided. She took a deep breath as she opened her voicemail to listen:

Jennifer. This is Doctor Nicolai Korowitz calling. It is important that you call the office when you get a minute. Thanks.

She erased the voicemail and sat back down on her bed. She looked up at the sky, as if looking up to the Lord for her guidance. "Give me strength, Father. This is hard, but, not my will, but yours be done." She smiled with certainty. She scrolled through her phone to find the number for the Doctor's office. She dialed it.

"Korowitz's office. This is John, how may I help you?"

"Hi, John, this is Jennifer Miller. I'm returning a call from Doctor Korowitz," she replied.

"Sure thing. One moment."

She was immediately placed on hold and she danced to the annoying hold music with an obnoxiously loud saxophone. The music stopped, and Nicolai's thick Russian accent filled the silence. *"Jennifer, are you feeling okay?"*

"I'm doing fine. The meds are keeping the pain down. I can walk without wobbling, and I don't feel dizzy."

"That's good. So, your test results came back. When can you come in for an appointment?"

"Monday?" she asked.

"Let me see." Jennifer could hear him typing heavily on the computer on the other end of the line, his heavy fingers hammering the keys. *"2:30 PM work for you?"*

"Yes. I'll put it on my calendar."

"I'll see you then." Click.

She exhaled heavily. *It's not serious, not yet. No point in worrying about it right now.* She exhaled deeply, letting the air decompress her lungs. Her hands relaxed as she held her phone. She went back into her phone and scrolled through to Ted's phone number. She dialed it.

"Jennifer?" He immediately picked up. If Jennifer didn't know any better, she would have thought he'd been staring at the phone waiting for her to call him.

"Tedward." She smiled into the phone, filled with an overwhelming sense of felicity. "Hey, so I am feeling much better. Are you still up to go feeding the ducks today?"

"Yes." He smiled through the phone. *"Do you need me to pick you up?"*

"Ted, you're farther than me. Let's just meet outside the T at Park Street station. We can walk to the Gardens after and feed the ducks there."

"Sounds like a plan. What time?"

"I was thinking noonish."

"I'll be there."

"Do you play chess?"

"I used to play it frequently." His tone went low.

"I'll bring my mini chess board. I'll see you at noon!" *Click.*

Jennifer walked down the boardwalk, walking all the way from Seaport Boulevard with her purse hanging from her side. She had her hair held back with a green headband and wore a modest yellow sundress and white sneakers. She walked briskly over the bridge and crossed the sidewalk. She welcomed the warm gentle breeze caressing her hair as she made her way to the Boston Common. Of course, she could have just taken the T, but it was such a nice day outside with the bright sun shining down on her.

There were many people about at this hour; after all, tourist season was upon them, and there were many tourists, domestic and foreign, walking the Freedom Trail and exploring the many small local shops and antique bookstores. She walked up through Winter Street, ignoring the heavy traffic of pedestrians and street performers.

Winter Street was darkened by parallel skyscrapers. She welcomed the sunlight again as she walked across Tremont Street, admiring the lovely view of Park Street Church on the right. She walked towards the T stop, which was behind a woman exchanging cans of soda and bottles of water for cash at a concession stand.

She looked around her and found many people happily tossing frisbees or playing with their dogs on the grounds. She saw the gathering area filled with many round tables and folding chairs surrounding a big fountain. She saw the many birds of the air chirping around her, fluttering their little wings about.

She heard the doors behind the T stop open, and people came out in careless floods, excited to see the lovely Boston Common and all the things it had to offer. And out of that same crowd came a dark-haired man, modestly dressed in shorts and a plain t-shirt and holding a paper bag from which a large roll of bread protruded.

She giggled and hid her smile behind a hand. With her other hand she waved at him. "Oh, Tedward, that's a rather big roll you have there. I think that might be too much bread for our little ducks."

"One never knows." He smiled his warm smile.

She reached out with her free hand. "Come on. We have ducks to see!"

Ted took her hand in his and she led him away from the hustle and bustle of the gathering area and along a path leading upwards and closer to some more of the dogs and frisbees. She skipped enthusiastically down the path as they watched squirrels scurrying up the trees with their acorns.

"Tedward," she said to him, "You have shared a lot with me, and this week, I think it is time I tell you a little more." She smiled as he turned his head to look at her while they continued their little stroll. "You see, I got off the phone with my doctor this morning. I do have leukemia, but it isn't the aggressive kind. Of course, that little incident I had the other day may have just been an isolated incident, or perhaps it wasn't even related at all, but by God's grace, because of it, I was able to find out that I had something serious. Fortunately, I don't need to get treatment right away, but I will be starting more in-depth treatment as necessary. I just wanted you to know."

"Information can be a dangerous thing, and so is trust. This was something I regrettably learned the hard way. Thank you for sharing that with me," he said as he turned his face to something else that moved behind a tree, like eyes were watching him. "I'll try my best to not betray your trust in me."

Of course he'd say that. Information is a tool to him; that's how he's lived his entire life.

"A paradox, wouldn't you say?" Her eyelids dropped as they walked, finally reaching the end of the common and the entrance to the Boston Public Garden. The black gate was open, and the pathway on the other side of the street was pleasantly shaded by trees. "You can trust me, but you don't."

"And you can't trust me, but you do." His eyes continued to scan the pathway.

"I knew you'd say something like that, but if that was the case, you wouldn't have warned me of the potentially harmful nature of giving part of myself to you. Of course, I feel I know you much better after this week, and quite frankly, I don't think we've seen more of each other than this week at all. Seriously, Tedward, it is like pulling your teeth out to get you to hang out with me. Well, I must say, I am pleasantly surprised that you actually started this. Although, I did talk you into picking me up at the hospital."

"Yes, I am sorry. I'm trying to be better." He stared down at the ground.

"Don't try to be better, Tedward, try to be you. That's really all we can be."

"Right." His tone dropped.

"Tedward, I heard that," she snapped at him as the light changed and they proceeded to walk across the crosswalk.

"Hmm?" He turned his head towards her.

"Your tone dropped. What's wrong? You know what, Ted, I'm sorry. I shouldn't have asked. Eh. I take it back. I should be asking that question, but *please* don't feel pressured to answer."

He sighed as they entered through the gate. "No. You're right. I appreciate you asking. Just, that particular thing is something I struggle with, because I don't really know who I am. Part of my job was espionage. If you put me in Russia, Italy, or any other country, I could assume a different identity."

"You know, you seem to be very experienced for being so young. How old did you say you were?"

"Twenty-five," he replied softly.

"Sam thought you might be twenty-three." She squeezed his hand tighter.

"Sorry. The truth is, I don't know how old I am. It's complicated. I don't know when I was born, or where. That is really all I can say about it."

"I see," she said softly as she tightened her grip on his hand. "How is the sleep?"

"Still the same. Only thirty minutes," he replied as they continued to walk through the gardens, watching the trees and the beautiful lake with flocks of ducks paddling about in the waters. "I still see the nightmares, and they aren't going away. I don't expect them to."

"They will. They will," she assured him as she drew him closer to the lake.

She found a bench and pulled him down to it so they could be closer to the water. He ripped off a piece of the bread roll and handed it to her. She sniffed the bread and started pulling a little piece off and tossed it on the ground. A small flock of ducks started waddling out of the lake. Ted ripped off a piece and tossed it to the flock.

"Did you have friends? In the service, I mean." She ripped off a little piece and placed it in her hand and leaned down to some brown ducklings to feed off of.

"The only friends and family I had were those I immediately worked with. I didn't see much of anyone else. There were fifteen of us." Sighing, he ripped off another piece of bread and tossed it a little closer to the bench as more ducklings flocked towards them. "One of them I got real close with, and I proposed. She died. They all did."

"Did you ever have closure with them and their families?" She exhaled heavily as she tore off little pieces of bread and littered them over the ground.

"No. The only family any of us had was one another. I suppose you could say we were all picked up from the same cloth. We were never on speaking terms with our families, for good or ill." He kept picking and tossing more bread to the ducks. "In many ways, we were the only family we ever had."

"And are you on speaking terms with your family now?" She turned to him as she continued to rip bread up in little pieces.

"No." His tone dropped.

"I'm sorry for probing." She placed her free hand on his shoulder.

She took her pieces and tossed them in the air and let them fall down like snow to the ducks. The flocks of ducks became larger around them. There were white ducks, brown ducks, and mallards with green heads. They picked up the bread from the ground and quacked waiting for the next one.

"Why did you join?"

He sighed as he tossed aside his last piece of bread. "I suppose you could say I was forced into it. I was groomed to fight, you see, and pushed to pursue a career in the military. That's all I wish to say about that, but what I will say is why I continued to fight. I continued to, despite knowing full well what it was doing to me. Every life I took brought pain and regret, as if my heart was being torn to pieces inside my chest. But I kept fighting, because I was promised that if I kept doing it, the world would be safer once the foreign powers were left at bay. I killed, and I killed, and I killed. I killed without halting. I killed until at last, I stopped caring and became an empty hollow husk. And at last, my hope came true; there was peace for a time. Now, that doesn't seem to matter anymore, with NATO disbanding and all that. All my hard work was worthless."

Of course. All the wars stopped a decade ago, and you are responsible for that, but then you should be older. To be responsible for global peace, and now, after all this time, to watch it crumble must be a punch in the face.

"The world will be a darker place now because of it. That's certain," Jennifer replied. "But no one man should ever have to bear that burden alone. Not you, not anyone. No one should carry it by themselves. You should not have been held responsible for that; as you can see, that peace was very short-lived. Don't get me wrong, the peace was great while it lasted, and I think you might be closer to my age, if not older than me, Ted. My entire adult life I've lived in world peace, and it is now crumbling, but knowing what I know now, no one man should be forced to carry that burden alone."

"Yeah. You're right, but unfortunately that doesn't change the past." His voice became barely audible.

"No, but we can move forward, and you aren't serving anymore. It's not your problem, nor your responsibility." She tossed her last piece of bread on the ground and leaned into his shoulder. "Tedward, who am I to you?"

He leaned his head atop hers. "My friend."

CHAPTER 17

Ted Anderson

~No matter what good you accomplish, there is no point in helping others. In the end, you will find that humans are selfish conniving little dastardly creatures that aren't worth saving.

TED ANDERSON LOOKED UP into the sky, the red ashes floating up like snowfall in reverse. His left arm had a sharp piece of metal impaled in it, and his warm blood streamed down his arm and into the hot Nevada sand. He pulled the knife out and let it drop through his fingers onto the ground. He breathed deeply as he walked away from the carnage, fleeing the stench of dead bodies piled up high in the sand. His right arm dragged his AR15 along the sand, and his trigger finger rested on the side of his rifle, away from the trigger. His eyes drooped down, and his mouth was open wide as if to say something, but he couldn't muster up the courage to speak. He walked towards the forward operating base.

He smelled the burned-out oil and fuel; the rotting flesh assaulted his nose as flies buzzed around the dead. The Nevada sand was filled with blood after all that had happened. There were many other soldiers walking around with stretchers, trying to get the wounded out of the way before starting the long arduous process of identifying the dead. Gunpowder still filled the air, and he could still hear the loud revving of truck engines and the movement of the tanks as they were being driven away.

He looked at the desert sand. The sight would never leave his mind. Bodies littered the desert, so many, one wouldn't have thought there was a desert out there. Limbs strewn all over the place, the uniforms torn to shreds, and even helicopter parts were on fire, fallen from the sky. There were numerous failed parts from missiles that littered the flaming sands.

He stepped over the bodies, looking at the numerous dog tags on the necks of his fallen comrades, many of whose faces were unrecognizable. Many of them no longer had faces, and some missed their dog tags. Identifying this many was going to be damn near impossible without DNA testing for identity. And then, he found something most peculiar about many of them: not all of them had the American Flag on their emblem patches. Some wore the patches of Russia, Ukraine, France, Italy, and China.

What were they all doing here? he thought.

"Sergeant Anderson," said a soft but ragged voice. He turned swiftly and saw none other than Lieutenant Nakamura. "Go get some rest. You need it."

"Yes, Ma'am." He walked over the corpses of the unnamed soldiers.

He continued to cover his mouth as the flies were beginning to buzz around him like they thought him dead. He found an angry platoon dragging severed limbs and corpses into a pit. He watched them, and he was able to identify most of the bodies, man and woman alike. These were the corpses of Task Force 7. Every single one of them.

Two masked soldiers came from behind him holding large red plastic oil containers. They made it down to the pit with the bodies and dismembered limbs. Behind him was another man, a lieutenant: Lieutenant Malcom. He looked down angrily at the bodies as the two soldiers poured gasoline on them. The lieutenant took out a match and lit them aflame. There was one still alive. Her fair but dirty face began to scream in agony as it caught on fire. Her fists barely clenched. "I'll kill you! I'll kill you! I'll kill you! I'll kill all of you!"

"Sir?" One of the masked men pointed his pistol at her screaming head.

"Negative. She'll be dead soon enough. No use in wasting another round. We've already used enough of those as it is."

"What did they do?" Anderson heard someone ask. "They didn't deserve this."

"Evidence was found on Ghost that he was colluding with Germany to stage a coup. They are traitors," someone answered. "Now, don't get yourself in too deep in all of this. Much of this is need to know, and you don't need to know any more than you do now."

"Yes, sir," the private about-faced.

Anderson left it at that and continued dragging his weapon in the sand as bodies were being counted and collected and sent to the medics for identification. The amount was staggering. He continued walking to the base. *Didn't we just broker international peace? Ghost, why would you do this? At least I, at least I can finally go home.*

The entire firefight was completely endless and exhausting. Ted knew he had been sleepless for nearly two weeks, and he hadn't even been present for half of it. His legs were heavy, his arms were weak, and his spirit felt like it was being shackled inside his chest as he took heavy breaths, his lungs expanding. "It's over," he said under his breath. "I don't know what this was all about, and I don't care anymore. At least the world will be a little safer."

Sergeant Ted Anderson had never questioned any of the orders given to him over the last two weeks.

Six months later, Ted went on leave for a full week before returning back to active duty. No new wars had been declared; no recent terrorist activity in the Middle East, nor here in the United States. It looked like the military was about to do some downsizing and pushing people out of the service. There was now next to no need for an overabundant military force. The army was going to be cut first.

Ted was on base in Fort Bennington, Georgia. He was running his half marathon in the oppressive heat. He stopped towards the end, leaning against a military vehicle, sweating profusely, and inhaled the fresh scent of his own body odor. He went to the barracks and showered before heading back into his office to finish off some paperwork. He planned to resign today.

He was in his office on the computer and printing out some paperwork for his discharge. There was a knock on the door. He looked up; it was Private Hernandez. "Sergeant, you're wanted with Lieutenant Nakamura, immediately."

"Copy." He sighed as he got up from his chair. He followed the private down some lengthy halls through Georgia. He listened very closely to the conversations around the hallway, some small talk, others more political in nature. He didn't care. *Today's the day.*

He was ushered into Nakamura's office. She held a clipboard and pointed to a chair. "Have a seat."

Hernandez closed the door behind him as he took the seat in the black chair.

"Anderson, you're being reassigned," she said, looking him in the eye with a soft glare. "Effective immediately, you are being shipped out to Germany."

Fantastic.

"How are you holding up over that little incident?" She leaned back in her chair, crossing her arms over her chest.

"All things considered, could be worse," he said. *You crazy bitch.*

"It was Hell on all of us. We're not going to recover from that." She sighed. "Many good men and women died."

"It's behind us. Are we done?"

"Yes. If you're psychologically fit, you are flying out at 0600 tomorrow."

"Thanks." Ted got up from his chair and went to the door. His hand touched the doorknob. He turned to her as she filed the paperwork away. "Nakamura."

"Anderson." She looked back at him from her desk.

"I'd tell you to go to Hell, but I think they would spit you back out," he told her coldly as his eyes angled down his nose.

"Excuse me?!" She glared at him.

"Hell is too good a place for you." Ted scowled. "Why did we kill them?"

"Treason." She gritted her teeth, leaning back in her chair.

"Horse! Shit!" Ted shot back. "I want the real reason, Nakamura. If I killed them, I want to know why. Now tell me!"

"Wars stopped. They made that happen. There's no need for them anymore," she answered.

"You could have discharged them! What the hell, Nakamura?!" Ted was unsatisfied with the answer. He kept his voice down so as to not draw attention from outside her office.

"Really?" She frowned. "Really, Anderson? You know all the details; leave it alone. Knowing all the details as I do, I know there was no chance in Hell they could integrate back into civie life. Besides, too much confidential information was on the line should they have been released out in the world. You know the details. Now get out of my office!" She stood up, pointing violently at the door behind him.

Unsatisfied, he swiftly jumped over her desk and tackled her to the ground before she could scream. The various items from her desk slid off to the floor. His hands clasped around her neck and pulled her up from the ground. She struck him with her hand and tried to release his grip. "Hell is too good a place for you! What the hell were you thinking?! What's wrong with you? They were just kids, damnit! They were just kids! You know full well as I do, they did nothing to deserve any of it." *Crack!* Her arms immediately dropped down. He released her corpse to the floor as it tumbled.

He opened the door and briskly walked out of the room, closing it behind him. *Good riddance.*

The End

FROM THE AUTHOR

From the bottom of my decrepit heart and soul, I thank you, weary reader. It is no small task to finish a book that perhaps, seems to meander, but you've made it.

Writing this book has been a challenge, and a very long trek involving much loathing. I enjoyed it, and perhaps is one of my proudest books I've finished writing. Yes, it's not the only one, but this one I felt speak to me. All it started was one dreary day at the University and I wanted to write a revenge thriller, and this is what that turned into. While I stand by trying to identify this book in a specific genre would do it injustice, I do believe

If you liked it, it would mean the world to me if you left a review on your preferred retailers and book blogger sites, and maybe share it to your personal favorite book blogger. It makes a huge difference on my sanity.

My Newsletter: https://armanisarf.substack.com/

My catalogue: https://www.amazon.com/stores/Armanis-Ar-feinial/author/B086R9T1CS?sr=8-1&isDramIntegrated=true&shoppingPortalEnabled=true

Armanis Ar-feinial, in the gritty pits of despair, he comes from: Bridgeton, Maine, a terribly dreadful place. Currently residing in the Greater Boston Area with his family, he studied Criminal Justice, English, and currently dabbles in a little bit of Finance. His unfaltering passion for writing came from his first exposure from the Lord of the Rings, which he drew inspiration from in his first stories, but alas, as all good things come downward into the grimdark pits, adopting tones from Joe Abercrombie. He loves reading, playing games of all kinds, and he is what you call a practicing writaholic. He is personally known for his witty sarcastic unasked for remarks.